MY INNER CHILD ....
MURDER MINDFULLY

Karsten Dusse is a lawyer and has been writing for television for a number of years. He has won the German Television Award and the German Comedy Prize several times, with his work also earning him a nomination for the Grimme Award. He spent years working as a radio host in public service broadcasting and has also enjoyed success in front of the camera, appearing on comedy programmes and as a legal expert. He has previously published three non-fiction books and now writes successful crime novels.

MY INNER CHILD WANTS TO MURDER MINDFULLY

KARSTEN DUSSE

translated by Florian Duijsens

faber

First published in this edition in 2026
by Faber & Faber Ltd
The Bindery, 51 Hatton Garden
London EC1N 8HN

First published as *Das Kind in mir will achtsam morden* in 2020
by Wilhelm Heyne Verlag, Munich

Typeset by Typo•glyphix, Burton-on-Trent DE14 3HE
Printed and bound in the UK by CPI Group (UK) Ltd, Croydon CR0 4YY

A CIP record for this book
is available from the British Library

ISBN 978–0–571–38407–5

Printed and bound in the UK on FSC® certified paper in line with our continuing
commitment to ethical business practices, sustainability and the environment.
For further information see faber.co.uk/environmental-policy

Our authorised representative in the EU for product safety is
Easy Access System Europe, Mustamäe tee 50, 10621 Tallinn, Estonia
gpsr.requests@easproject.com

2 4 6 8 10 9 7 5 3 1

For Lina. And Rosa.

Prologue

It is never too late to have an unhappy childhood.
It is also never too late to have a happy childhood.
But above all, your childhood is always *in the past.*
Whether and how the past affects your present is up to you alone.

Joschka Breitner, *Parenting Your Inner Child*

As the massive Russian climbed into the boot of his own car, he looked almost like a scared little boy.

'And I'll see Dragan soon?' Boris asked me.

'You'll see Dragan soon,' I reassured him.

At peace with myself, I closed the boot lid with love and without judgement. Mindfully, even.

I got behind the wheel of Boris's car and started the engine. I felt content. Even though I'd lied: Boris would never see Dragan again, at least not in this life. Dragan had been dead for a week.

Boris, however, would not be killed. I was tired of killing. At some point, enough was enough. For Boris, Sasha and I had come up with a different solution.

With the Russian in the boot, I drove out of the lay-by. At half past four in the morning, there was hardly any traffic. For fifteen minutes, we simply zipped through the cosy darkness. Then I called Sasha.

'Is anyone following us?' I asked. The wiry Bulgarian had been driving some distance behind me to determine exactly that.

'Nobody. They've all gone ahead.'

'That's good.' I felt my shoulders relax.

'No more corpses?' Sasha asked.

'No more corpses.'

Sasha gave an audible sigh of relief.

I confirmed our plan. 'I'll see you at the preschool.'

'The cellar door is open,' Sasha said, signing off.

I hung up.

I

The Inner Child

Our soul is structured like a Russian doll. When something is rattling in the doll that is our adult soul, it is really the sound of the other, smaller doll inside it: our inner child's wounded soul.

Joschka Breitner, *Parenting Your Inner Child*

There were two things wrong with my childhood: my mum and my dad. But I only realised this forty years later, when, pressured to do so by my wife, I first considered my inner child.

If I hadn't already been sensitised to psychological issues through my very positive experiences with mindfulness, I probably would've thought the very notion of an inner child utter nonsense. Anything a gastroenterologist cannot discover during a thorough check-up simply isn't inside us. Or so I used to think.

A year ago, I would've thought a book about the inner child was targeted at people who were expecting. One of those books that might provide a man with a great deal of information about what was going on inside his partner biologically but was useless when it came to elucidating his own inner life.

By now, I know that the psychological concept of the inner child has nothing whatsoever to do with preparing for childbirth. It only becomes relevant after you've exited the birth canal. And that holds true for any sex. According to the notion of the inner child, we are emotionally constructed like a Russian doll. When something's rattling in the doll that is our adult soul, it's really the sound of the other, smaller doll inside it: our inner child's wounded soul.

It's not us who stand in the way of our own happiness, but our inner child. It's a part of us, along with all our childhood injuries. If we want the rattling to stop, we need to heal our inner child.

Taking my inner child into consideration turned out to be the ideal way for me to eliminate the *causes* of the problems whose consequences I had started to mitigate by practising mindfulness.

In my childhood, there was no Siri or Alexa. The people who turned lights on and off, operated the stereo and answered the stupidest questions incorrectly were called Mummy and Daddy. So, if anything got screwed up in my childhood, these two must be the culprits.

This explanation was reassuring in that it enabled me to comfortably blame my parents for my own marital problems, fear of the future and general irritability, as well as several murders.

The fact that I only conceived my inner child at the age of forty-three was partly down to an unprotected argument with my estranged wife. Katharina always had a very effective approach to problems: the person responsible for solving her problems was always the one without whom she wouldn't *have* them. This made me the one responsible for providing the protection when it came to conflicts in our dissolving marriage.

And that's exactly what I'd unfortunately messed up on our last summer holiday together. Against her express wishes, I had gotten into an altercation with a waiter at an alpine hut.

That alone was reason enough for her to demand that I seek therapeutic assistance for my constant mood swings. And this without her even knowing that, after a little retaliatory stunt on my part, the waiter had unfortunately died.

While still in the Alps, I made an appointment with my mindfulness coach for the week after we got back, like the good husband and father that I was. The fact that, if I hadn't, Katharina would've taken Emily and left was also fairly significant.

Completely independent of my wife's sensitivities, however, I had long since realised that I needed to work on myself. Something inside of me kept stopping me from enjoying life. If worries were a liquid, I felt like my mindfulness practice might've helped calm the waves inside the barrel of my soul, yet it was still filled to the brim with anxiety. And sometimes, when a new worry came along, something still splashed over the edge, making me freak out about things other people would consider minor.

So far, my freak-outs had been mere trifles:

One night, I threw ice cubes at drunks shouting in the park across the street.

I gave clients who annoyed me bad legal advice.

I brought the prisoner in my cellar his meal two hours late, just because.

Things basically anyone in the same situation would do if they were annoyed. And as long they didn't get caught.

The fact that I let a waiter plunge into a ravine, however, is of a slightly different order.

I didn't like this escalation.

And so, one rainy evening in early September, I found myself on Joschka Breitner's doorstep again. A week after my holiday. Almost half a year after my last mindfulness coaching session.

Before I pressed the doorbell, I stood outside his door and took stock of how I felt. Over the last six months, a great deal had changed.

Back then, it was spring. Summer was around the corner. Now it was autumn. Winter was on its way.

Back then, I had left Breitner's practice in the daylight, newly energised. With my new insights, I was positively surfing the flow of a mindful lifestyle into the world blossoming outside.

Now, I'd been washed back by the tides of life. It was already dark, and the first yellowed leaves rustled under my feet.

By now, my life should've been completely happy. In the last six months, with a lot of love and mindfulness, I had transformed my professional and personal environment the way I'd always dreamed of:

I'd exchanged a crippling permanent position at a large law firm for a financially sound freelance position as a solo practitioner.

Katharina and I had re-routed the dead end of our tired and stressed-out marriage into the parallel life paths of co-parenting individuals.

Our daughter, Emily, enjoyed her hard-won spot at preschool and was a cheerful, confident member of Little Fish's Nemo group.

I had not only my law office in the same beautiful old building as Little Fish, but my own apartment too. I managed the whole building for my main client – Dragan, the absent boss of a criminal syndicate.

All these changes had a lot to do with the fact that, half a year earlier, I'd killed Dragan. That no one knew about this was not entirely insignificant to my happiness. And to ensure no one would ever find out about it, I had no choice but to let his criminal consortium continue to operate under Dragan's name. And pretend to his gang that their boss was still alive.

As a lawyer, this shouldn't have been difficult. After all, I had hand-knitted the legal coverlets for Dragan's drug, sex and weapons trading, and, as a consultant, been its *de facto* CEO. This was the exact role I continued to play for everyone. Nothing more.

But a single clanger, one more ill-considered freak-out, a set of critical outside eyes trained too closely on my life – and this whole web of lies I'd woven would collapse.

I had to make sure anything I did stayed under the radar of both the police and any gangsters. This made my accidentally killing a waiter rather counterproductive. Not just for my spiritual life, but for my life full stop.

What was wrong with my life was that I couldn't put a foot wrong.

My present existence might be nicer than my past, but I was tremendously afraid of the future.

This was stressful. Mindfulness helped keep things under control. But it couldn't get rid of what was causing the stress. Mindfulness might've slowed my hamster wheel, but somehow I still couldn't get off. That's why I was here again, waiting outside Breitner's door. Organising my thoughts had brought a little clarity to the troubled particles of my soul. Still, I hesitated to ring the bell. For one, because I wasn't quite sure how much I could even tell Breitner about my problems.

I'd certainly be able to tell him about how Katharina's snippy remarks kept making it clear to me how fragile and unresolved our relationship actually was.

I could also tell him about my feelings of guilt towards Emily because Katharina and I had failed to save our marriage.

I wanted to talk about needing time for myself, outside of my family and my clients.

I could tell him about my little freak-outs, even if they were embarrassing.

I'd bring all those things up – and Breitner would be able to help me deal with all of it.

But I wouldn't be able to talk about what weighed on me most.

I wouldn't say a word about the murders I committed the previous spring.

I'd remain silent about the double life I'd led since.

And I certainly wouldn't talk about Boris.

Boris, the Russian gangster I was holding captive in the preschool's cellar. Boris, the only person who wanted (and already knew enough) to burst the bubble of my perfect world.

Boris, who I kidnapped six months earlier to save my life, and that of my daughter.

Boris, who I didn't want to kill because I was tired of killing. Who was my living proof that I could say no to murder. Yet who I could also neither hold captive forever, nor ever release. Boris, for whose future I hadn't yet been able to find a solution.

My prisoner would burden me as much dead as he now did alive.

I wouldn't be able to talk about him.

So I wouldn't tell Breitner everything. I'd pretend I was there for an entirely normal follow-up. As if, now that some time had passed, I just wanted us to take a look at what had transpired in my life since. Tighten a few screws. We'd have enough to talk about if I told him how my mind was turning mundane mini-mosquitoes into enormous emotional elephants. Which were now charging through the china shop of my otherwise untroubled soul. I'd openly admit that mindfulness exercises helped me to condense each and every one of these problems back to their core issue relatively quickly. But, after a brief spell of peace and satisfaction, the old familiar chill of anxiety and self-doubt would always set in.

I'd openly admit that, while I understood how mindfulness could help me get to grips with most of my problems, I had no idea why the same problems reared up again and again.

That was the part of the truth I needed to discuss. That's why I was standing outside Breitner's door. I rang the bell.

Inside, I could hear hinges squeak and wood slide over tiles. The hallway light went on, warmly illuminating the colourful frosted panes in the solid wooden door. Calm, unhurried footsteps came closer. Moments later, the door opened. In front of me stood Joschka Breitner, who greeted me as though I'd only walked out of this door two minutes ago.

'Mr Diemel! Nice to have you back. Do come in.'

'Thank you for making the time.'

We shook hands. He stepped aside and let me go on ahead. I walked down the long hallway into his practice. Nothing had changed at this end. Two armchairs, one table, a bookshelf and a side table with a glass teapot. Breitner was wearing the same casual clothes as always. Stonewashed jeans, plain cotton shirt, chunky wool cardigan. Felt slippers on his bare feet.

Yet he didn't give the impression that time had passed him by; it was more like he *was* time, that it was the world that'd passed him by.

While I took off my jacket, Breitner studied me with interest.

'You look like a changed man,' he remarked, without judgement.

I looked down at myself. Six months ago, I'd been wearing bespoke suits and expensive accessories. Now I was wearing jeans, a T-shirt, jumper and sneakers.

'Yes . . .' I shrugged with a smile. It was reassuring to be able to start with positive changes. 'I have less of a dress code now.'

But that wasn't the change Breitner had noticed.

'I mean your eyes. The last time we saw each other, they were beaming. Now you have circles under your eyes,' he noted, with a caring kind of candour.

Caring candour can be brutal. I hadn't even been in his office twenty seconds, but I already realised this wouldn't be some fluffy follow-up. Instead, it'd be an arduous confrontation with myself. Breitner had obviously already known this when I set up the appointment. After all, that was his job. He pointed to one of the comfortable tubular chrome chairs covered in corduroy. I hung my jacket over the backrest and sat down while Breitner poured me some green tea. My silence after his observation was confirmation enough.

'We have not seen each other in a long time,' he said. 'What has been going on?'

As I took a sip of the lukewarm tea, I considered my response. I had murdered four people, blackmailed my former employers, forced the former operators of the preschool to sell their shares so that my daughter could get a spot, and I'd kidnapped a Russian gangster. None of these were appropriate topics. And I could hardly share the fact that, while I was on holiday, a waiter had broken his neck because of me.

'I've taken a new career path. I quit the firm and am now a freelancer. My daughter is in preschool, and we went on holiday,' I stalled instead.

'First of all, I would like to congratulate you on your career decision.' Breitner knew how much the daily grind of a large law firm had got me down. 'That explains your new outfit. But why the sadness around your eyes?'

I said nothing. I wanted to but couldn't. Instead, I felt the sadness around my eyes liquefy. The question alone overwhelmed me. When was the last time someone noticed I was sad? Without also being the reason for my sadness? It took me two breaths to steady myself.

'I . . . It's . . .' I searched for words that, even if they weren't exactly the truth, at least didn't contradict it.

Breitner helped me out. 'Everything is all right. You are here. Just tell me why.'

'Well, my wife thinks that . . .'

'That wasn't what I asked,' he interjected gently.

'What?' I said, annoyed.

'I didn't ask what your wife thinks,' Breitner explained with a kind smile. 'If I wanted to know that, I would ask your wife, not you. I want to know why *you* are here.'

'Because . . . well . . . because . . .' I surrendered. Not to Breitner, but to myself. I wasn't the successful self-employed lawyer who had settled all his issues and only wanted a little mindfulness refresher. Neither of us would buy that. I was here because I was afraid that, in the not-too-distant future, my entire life was about to blow up. I caved as honestly as I could.

'Because I have no idea what to do with my life. . . with my marriage, with my . . . work . . . with what's to come. I have no time to myself in the present and I'm afraid of the future . . . And I haven't got a clue where to start.'

Breitner looked at me with an expression of reassurance. Not of pity.

'Do you know what? There must have been a trigger,

something that caused you to call me and set up this appointment, right?'

'Right.' The incident with the waiter.

And so I started talking about what had unintentionally led me to this appointment. Little did I know that this would be the beginning of a very intensive dialogue with my inner child, someone who very shortly would unselfconsciously pick right back up what I'd quit doing with such relief almost six months earlier: murdering mindfully.

2

Holiday

The purpose of holidays is to switch off. The more consistently you can switch off the stimuli negatively affecting you in everyday life, the more you will be able to relax. Switching off does not mean isolating yourself. Simply swap your smartphone's push notifications for conversations with fellow holidaymakers.

Joschka Breitner, *Slowing Down in the Fast Lane: Mindfulness for Managers*

Talking about my recent holiday was safe territory for me. There wasn't too much I needed to conceal. Sure, I'd have to creatively rewrite a few things. The waiter's death in which I was implicated, for example. But I should keep that the tip of the iceberg only I could see, the iceberg the ship that was my life was heading for full steam ahead. As a professional, Breitner would be sure to recognise my risk of collision even without that knowledge.

'We went down to the Bavarian Alps for a few days last week,' I started.

'Who is we?'

'My wife, Katharina, my daughter, Emily, and me.'

'You still live apart?' Half a year ago, Breitner had brought up the idea that we should live apart so as to more mindfully be able to deal with ourselves and our marital problems. And it had actually improved our relationship.

'Yes – and it's working out well.'

'So well that you went on holiday, despite your separation?'

'Well, we made a wonderful child together. And in our two separate lives we now co-parent that wonderful child. Each of us will forever love the part of the other person that's in Emily. On that basis, joint holidays can work perfectly well.'

'Are you and your wife having sex?' Breitner asked suddenly.

'I can't speak for my wife, but if you're asking me . . .'

'I mean with each other. You are married and going on holiday together. Do you have a joint sex life?'

I thought about how to answer that. We had a very imaginative sex life. In the sense that we only had sex in our imaginations, at least in mine. I would've slept with Katharina any time. We always got along well in bed. But despite the success of our spatial separation, a regrettable physical separation had set in as well. I put it this way: 'While on holiday, we shared a room. But sleeping together there just meant back-to-back.'

Breitner nodded sympathetically. 'I see. Not a position mentioned in the *Kama Sutra*. Have you ever spoken openly with your wife about your not having sex?'

'My wife uses an eye mask and earplugs when she's in bed next to me, which makes any conversation rather one-sided. But honestly, my sex life, or lack thereof, isn't why I'm here.'

'Two minutes ago, you could not even formulate the reason you are here. That is why I suggested we first talk about the occasion of your call. We are still a way away from the reasons you are here,' Breitner explained. 'But I do not want to interrupt you any longer. You were saying you went on a family holiday. Please continue.'

'We picked the timing intentionally. On the first of October, Katharina will go back to her old position as a department head at an insurance company. Emily has settled in well at preschool. By September, the school holidays are done, so the biggest tourist rush is over. It was the perfect time to go on one last holiday together.'

'And why the Alps?'

The fact that we hadn't felt like spending the first (and especially the last) day of a trip to Mallorca with a three-year-old at an airport full of drunken package holidaymakers sounded a bit crude to me.

'We were in the mood for some mountains.'

And when we'd decided on the Alps, that'd been true. The Allgäu tourist office had recommended a small family farm where we could have a relaxed holiday. And the recommendation proved to be spot on. Everything about the place was right. The farm was idyllically situated in a valley between two villages, in the middle of a promising dead zone. Here, digital detoxing wasn't trendy, but a centuries-old tradition. Diesel engines were still put to their intended use: to bridge distances between people – not to create them. For thousands of years, dairy farming had been considered a natural livelihood here – not a climate killer. At night, the only sound coming through the open window was the rustling of trees – not the roaring of drunks. Electric batteries were used to fence in cattle – not to power e-scooters.

In short: here, the world was still as it used to be, tickety-boo.

'And actually, the holiday was going perfectly. Until we took the cable car up and went on this hike.'

Sweaty, thirsty and hungry after a two-hour trek, Katharina, Emily and I had reached the terrace of a beautiful mountain hut. The hut was nestled on a small plateau above the treeline on the northern side of the Allgäu Prealps. It was almost noon, and the sun lit up the entire terrace, despite its north-facing location. On one side, the plateau descended steeply into a small ravine, where a freight cable car enabled the hut to get its supplies. Otherwise, alpine meadows were all around. The clang of the cowbells had the same effect as waves on a beach: their relaxing soundscape muffled the worries of everyday life. Exactly as I'd hoped.

Emily had been riding on my shoulders for an hour and a half. It had been a pleasure to rediscover the joy of spotting a mountain peak, a cable car or a pasture through my daughter's eyes. And Katharina hadn't been as even-keeled as this in a long time. No more bitter sniping. The hike's exercise and natural beauty actually seemed to be giving her some peace. It wasn't quite noon yet, and almost all the rustic benches were free, inviting us to enjoy this alpine Arcadia. Only two of the ten long wooden tables had other hikers enjoying refreshments in quiet contentment. The weather was fantastic, and every single spot offered almost a hundred kilometres of picturesque views across the Allgäu.

'When I had taken Emily off my shoulders and put down my backpack, the only things that could make the day more perfect were a steaming plate of icing-sugar-dusted Kaiserschmarrn pancakes, an ice-cold bottle of fizzy Almdudler and a semi-dried Landjäger sausage polished to a high gloss. And a toilet.'

'Why?' Breitner asked.

'I needed a wee.'

'No, I mean, why this particular meal? "Steaming plate." "Icing-sugar-dusted Kaiserschmarrn." "Ice-cold Almdudler." "Landjäger polished to a high gloss." These are all very specific, vivid descriptions.'

'They're images from my childhood. Experiences I wanted to pass on to Emily. Having Kaiserschmarrn with my daughter, tired, hungry and happy after a great hike in the mountains. That's what I had planned for the day.'

'Did you often go to the Alps as a child?'

I considered his question. My parents had actually only taken me to the Alps once.

'No . . . not that often.'

'But you always had Kaiserschmarrn, Almdudler and Landjäger when you did visit these mountain huts?'

As I considered his question, I sensed how the topic, even here with Breitner, made me uncomfortable all of a sudden. 'Is that important?'

'Maybe. But go on.'

Breitner's query briefly irritated me. But I continued.

'Anyway – Katharina sat down in the sun, Emily ran up to the closest cow in the pasture and I headed to the toilet.'

On my way to the facilities inside, I met Nils. He stood next to the door of the hut drinking a bottle of Almdudler and scrolling some social media on his phone. The hand-held POS device hanging from his belt told me he was the waiter on duty. As did his name tag.

I politely asked Nils if I should order inside, or if we could do so at the table. Without looking up from his phone, all he hissed to me was an annoyed, 'Yeah, yeah. Be right there.' This was neither an answer to my question nor the helpful disposition I expected at an alpine hut.

'I was just politely asking whether . . .' I started, trying to harmonise the small part of my holiday I had to spend at this hut with him.

'I'm on break.' Nils turned away from me, obviously only serving his phone screen. So much for 'be right there'.

I took a closer look at the back he'd turned to me.

Although Nils was in his late twenties at most, he looked like someone who'd been bored to death for at least four decades. His guests wore hiking shoes, softshell trousers, sweaty tops and healthy tans. Nils was pale as a corpse, wearing purple suede sneakers, black skinny jeans and an oversized dark-green V-neck with glitter sequins in camo colours. The sequins spelled out the beautiful slogan 'SAVE THE PLANET'. He could've passed for a hipster barista in Berlin's Prenzlauer Berg. In the Alps, however, he looked like Heidi had got lost at Berghain.

At around five-foot-nine, he seemed almost two feet too tall for his weight. His hairstyle was the only thing that fitted the setting: it was basically one big cowlick. His wispy moustache, on the other hand, fitted neither the Alps nor his face. Nils was the exact type of person one hopes to avoid when escaping to the Alps for a week.

Before I went to the toilet, I provided him with all the information he'd need to find us and prevent his 'be right there' from falling at the first logistical hurdle: 'Well, we're at the third table from the entrance. But you'll see that yourself after your break. It's not that crowded yet anyway.'

'Yeah, yeah,' Nils replied, again without looking up.

It would've been better for everyone involved if Nils and I had never met.

3

Other People

Mindfulness removes the stress you put on yourself because of other people.

It does not remove the other people.

But above all, mindfulness does not remove what causes you to keep being triggered by other people.

Those causes are inside you. Only you can uncover and eliminate them.

Joschka Breitner, *Parenting Your Inner Child*

Tired after that beautiful hike, I really should've taken some quiet time. But for some reason, I couldn't get that waiter and his dismissive behaviour out of my head. It was just the opposite atmosphere I'd imagined for our lunch break on this hike. But, as a mindful person, I had mastered the tools to face such petty annoyances with composure. I did a little standing meditation in the toilet cubicle: I was on holiday, I was in the mountains with my wife and daughter, and the weather was great. All I needed to complete this perfect day were that ice-cold bottle of Almdudler, the Kaiserschmarrn, and a pair of Landjäger sausages.

On the terrace, I sat back down with Katharina and Emily, whose interest in cows had given way to an interest in cuddling up to her parents. The terrace gradually filled with other hikers who apparently also had an interest in nourishment. Only one person didn't seem to care about this growing interest: Nils, who remained markedly absent for the next ten minutes. Katharina and Emily, meanwhile, used the majestic panorama as the largest possible arena for a game of I Spy. As they played, Emily was enjoying her favourite snack: a squeezy fruit pouch I'd carried up the mountain by the sweat of my brow. My hunger and thirst and I sat beside her and looked around the terrace.

All but one table was now filled with customers. Katharina asked me if I wanted to join their game. But I was too antsy. My little eye couldn't simultaneously be on the lookout for an inattentive waiter and something beginning with 'I' – I might have weaned myself off multi-tasking through mindfulness, but I was annoyed that the waiter didn't show.

'I don't spy with my little eye someone working as a waiter,' I remarked drily. For the first time that day, Katharina, who often didn't share my sense of humour, gave me a disapproving frown.

Emily loved my take on the game, however, and enthu-siastically piled on. 'I don't spy with my little eye something that looks like a unicorn!' Since my daughter had never had Kaiserschmarrn, this waiter's absence was obviously not as disappointing to her as it was proving to me.

The last free table was taken by a group of five soldiers who may have been wearing civilian clothes, but whose camo-coloured backpacks revealed their Bundeswehr affiliation. I tried not to get upset about the fact that we were now one table among many, my Kaiserschmarrn order getting further and further away from me. Instead, I tried to enjoy the moment mindfully. But somehow I preferred that moment ten minutes earlier: when we were the only new customers. And full of hope for quick service.

I had noticed the Bundeswehr's 'We. Serve. Germany.' slogan on a bus down at the cable car's base station that morning. I'd have appreciated it if the hut followed their lead.

'Björn, will you please order us a Kaiserschmarrn with apple sauce? We're just heading to the little girls' room.' And with that, Katharina tore me out of my gloomy thoughts and disappeared inside with Emily. Our daughter left her empty squeezy pouch on the table.

And then, finally, Nils appeared, a stack of menus under his arm. He distributed them randomly at the various tables, without any discernible system. I saw my chance to take quick advantage of his apparent lack of knowledge about which party had arrived first.

'I don't need a menu, I'm ready to order. I would like some Kaiserschmarrn, Almdudler and . . . do you have Landjäger?'

'Are those the meat thingies?' was his slightly disgusted response. 'I personally believe you should only have vegan food at mountain huts. But sure. One sec . . .'

Nils tried to balance his hand-held on the remaining menus in his hand. Without success. I tried to understand what led people who'd completely voluntarily decided to take a paid job serving other people to start trying to *teach* those people instead. Also without any success.

I braved another attempt. 'Surely you don't need that computer. I'd just like to order three very simple . . .'

'One sec, I have to hand out these menus first,' Nils interrupted, disappearing with the menus to another table, his 'SAVE THE PLANET' sequins glittering where his service decidedly wasn't. I thought saving the entire planet was a bit of a tall order for someone who couldn't even get a handle on 70 square metres of rustic seating. Nils left me speechless, simmering with anger.

That's when Katharina and Emily returned. Emily happily climbed into my lap, but Katharina sat down opposite me, took in the still-empty table with irritation and censoriously asked: 'You still haven't ordered yet?'

Barely five minutes earlier, I'd been deemed a grouch for complaining about the waiter. Now she was somehow chiding me for the behaviour of the waiter on duty. Two and a half hours of alpine relaxation vanished in an instant. I started to get worked up, especially about the fact that I was getting worked up. Also: was that Kaiserschmarrn I smelled?

'I would've liked to, but even that unicorn Emily didn't spy is a little more organised than that waiter. He hasn't even been to our table yet.'

'No need to get so worked up. We're on holiday!'

'*We* are, yes. That waiter isn't.'

When Nils passed our table again, he had already forgotten not only what I wanted to order, but also that I wanted to order at all. What he did notice, however, was Emily's empty squeezy pouch. He picked it up with pointed fingers. Instead of asking what I'd like, he expressed his own desire for a perfect world:

'Did you know that producing a single pouch like that releases a hundred grams of CO_2? If it were up to me, the Alps would be a plastic-free zone.'

I'm a fan of making environmentally conscious choices. And I'm happy about every new bit of knowledge someone shares with me. But at that moment I was hungry and thoroughly fed up with servers dishing me out unsolicited opinions on an empty stomach.

'Your father was obviously plastic-free down there when you were conceived. Probably wasn't such a great idea either.'

Had I said that out loud? Horrified, Katharina put her hand on my arm before I could pull the waiter towards me. I was a little surprised I'd been able to spontaneously combine two completely unrelated facts into one targeted insult. That wasn't usually my style. Fortunately, the Bundeswehr chose this moment to stage a de-escalatory intervention, calling loudly for libations. Without another word, Nils fled to the louder table.

'Where did that man's daddy have a plastic-free zone?' Emily wanted to know, sparing me an immediate reprimand from Katharina.

'Daddy was only joking, sweetie,' Katharina clarified, throwing me a look that revealed she absolutely wasn't in a joking mood. We'd made it a rule never to argue in front of Emily.

'Daddy – I'm hungry,' Emily nudged me as I was ducking Katharina's stink eye. That was the point when waiting any longer stopped being an option for me. I didn't care whether someone trampled all over me and my gastronomic childhood fantasies, but not over my daughter's very real childhood need for sustenance.

Nils was just about to randomly walk past our table towards some other waiting customers when I took action: I grabbed the hem of his glittery T-shirt and pulled him back to our table. Once again, I was a little surprised I did this. I detested physical confrontation. Katharina looked mortified.

'Hold up! It's our turn now.'

'I . . . want to . . .' the waiter stammered.

'The polite thing to say is "I would like" not "I want". And *I* would like to order now. Right now!' I said in a lowered but very determined voice.

Once Nils understood that my grip on the hem of his T-shirt would only loosen if he brought out his hand-held, we could finally place our order: two Kaiserschmarrns, one ice-cold bottle of Almdudler and a Landjäger to take away.

'That was unacceptably rude,' Katharina scolded me, once Nils had feebly fled our table.

'Would you have come up with a gentler approach?' I asked in response.

'No, it's just that you've been so well balanced the past few weeks. Mindfulness also works in the mountains, you know!'

'I would happily have ordered mindfully. But that would require an attentive waiter, not a wanker like that.'

'Please don't ruin this beautiful day with your bad mood. Our food will come soon enough.'

It's never the problem that destroys a beautiful day, but the one who points out the problem – that was Katharina's attitude to life.

Our food would come. However, neither soon nor to us. The first two Kaiserschmarrn were served at a table that had ordered long after us. My ice-cold bottle of Almdudler was given to one of the soldiers, who gulped it down between the two Hefeweizen beers he'd already received, because Nils obviously no longer knew which order went with which table. Under the warm sun, Katharina and I used the time to refresh ourselves with some icy silence. After twenty minutes, we finally got our Kaiserschmarrn. And a lukewarm bottle of Almdudler. By the time our plates were long empty, however, my Landjäger still hadn't left the kitchen. But Emily had left our table for the trough in front of the terrace, where she was cheerfully and exuberantly playing with its ice-cold, crystal-clear running water, which I could have drunk immediately and for free.

And what was I doing? I was boiling with rage. Katharina could tell. She tried a conciliatory approach.

'The Kaiserschmarrn were delicious!' she said with a content and reassuring smile.

I said nothing.

'What's wrong?' she asked, more reproachful now.

'That idiot forgot my Landjäger,' I noted.

'Then go check on it, don't take your temper out on me.'

'That's not the issue though, is it?' I almost shouted. 'All year round I get things done. And then, on holiday, I'm supposed to just submit to idiots who don't have a clue what they're doing?'

'But you can't let some missing sausage . . .'

'This isn't about the sausage! This is about . . .' I realised that I honestly had no idea why this missing sausage was making me so incredibly angry, or what this was really about for me. But deep down, one thing was incredibly clear to me: I'd been treated incredibly unfairly. Sitting down to a steaming plate of Kaiserschmarrn, an ice-cold bottle of Almdudler, a Landjäger polished to a high gloss – these were three self-evidently small things. That's all I wanted. I hadn't got any of that. Inside me, a small voice, loud and almost inaudibly high, was crying out against this injustice. Katharina could only see the missing sausage. To me, it felt like the waiter's cluelessness had made my chock-full barrel of worries overflow.

'This is about me for once! Is it too much to ask to have one single thing on this holiday go the way I'd like it to?'

'Oh, so it's all about you again? Do you even know what a selfish bastard you are?'

'You usually don't seem to care as long as I selfishly pay for everything.'

Four tables away, Nils ignored all of my signals that I wanted to pay. I was about to get up and walk over when Katharina stopped me.

'Just leave it. It's no use you . . .'

Was my wife really holding me back like I was a child? Not a chance. I got up, walked over to Nils, stood next to him.

'The bill.'

'One sec, I . . .'

'Now. At that table.'

I stomped back. The people at the other tables looked over sympathetically. In retrospect, however, I can see that they were mostly sympathetic to Katharina. Not to me.

'I'll pay,' Katharina decided. 'Please go stretch your legs a little and calm down first.'

I was about to hand Katharina my wallet, but she waved me off. Bitchily.

'Ever since my husband has been living his own life, I've learned to carry cash myself.'

Aha, so I was financially redundant too. Thank you, Nils, for pushing our marriage right back onto thin ice, especially since we're on holiday.

'Fuck this fucking hut,' I said.

I know where he can stick that Landjäger, I thought.

'Thanks for your support!' I stomped away angrily, leaving behind my now equally angry wife.

'Why do you even bother with all that mindfulness stuff?' I heard her bleat after me.

Why indeed? I didn't recognise myself. I'd never had a temper, quite the opposite. I used to bottle up my anger. Until I discovered mindfulness, thanks to which I had functioned wonderfully over the past few months. And now one missing sausage sent me out of whack? But maybe that was it. Maybe I was tired of all those months working on myself with iron discipline, while any passing waiter was allowed to run roughshod all over my needs. And my wife treated me like a child. I was furious. But Katharina was right about one thing. Instead of having another scene, I needed to get out of this impasse. That's why I got up and went looking for a place where I could calm down. I decided to walk around the building.

I had half-rounded the hut when I found myself on the loading dock of the transport cable car. All alone. You couldn't see the dock from the terrace. There I stood, amid stacked crates of empty Almdudler bottles apparently waiting to be transported back down. It looked like the alley behind a pub, which it basically was. The shade cast by the hut ensured that it was pleasantly cool. Here, all was quiet, and the air was fresh.

'In order to cool down my mind, I positioned myself feet shoulder-width apart, arms loosely on the railing, looked down into the valley and felt my breath.' This part of the story I could even proudly share with Breitner. 'As you taught me, I calmed down very quickly. Nothing felt nearly as bad. There and then, I was satisfied. I was no longer thirsty. My daughter was enjoying the trip. I was on holiday, and we could look forward to a nice cable car ride back down to the valley.'

'You got agitated. That is something that happens to most people. Then you de-agitated yourself. This is something that few people can do. So, what is the problem?' Breitner wanted to know.

'The problem is that that same inner voice came back, the one that'd got so outraged by the injustice, shooting my heart rate up to 180.'

I told Breitner the rest of the story: after I'd calmed down, the childlike, almost inaudible voice that had been shrieking so loudly and shrilly earlier now indignantly stated that surely this couldn't be the end? Nils had ruined the day in the Alps I'd been dreaming of for so long. At the very least I should ruin his day a bit too. And wherever that voice inside me was coming from, I felt like it was right. A little revenge would do me good.

As I glanced over the small area behind the hut, an idea came to me. The barrier to the freight cable car consisted of a small, double-bolted gate. The Almdudler crates stood next to the gate. What if someone were to push the Almdudler crates in front of the gate, then tilt them slightly and undo the two bolts? Then the next crate of empties some goofy waiter put on top would make the tower of crates tip. The crates would fall against the gate. The gate would open, and crates with a few dozen bottles of empties would plunge into the ravine. Knowing that this was sure to get Nils in trouble was satisfaction enough for me.

I pulled a stack of three crates one metre to the left, in front of the gate to the freight cable car. I tilted the small tower towards the gate and stuck a flat rock under the bottom crate. The tower was now leaning towards the valley, but not falling over. Only the next crate would topple it. I unbolted the gate. Something inside me giggled with glee. I went back to the terrace in childlike anticipation of my little prank's certain success.

Katharina had just paid. And calmed down as well. As a sign of reconciliation, I wordlessly put a hand on her shoulder. She shook it off with a suffering look that said: *I'm very disappointed in you right now, so I need some time to process your behaviour.* Reproachful silence felt even more degrading than outspoken accusations. I had broken off my obligatory yearly birthday call to my mother over sighs that were much less reproachful.

I shouldered the backpack and followed Emily, who was already running in the direction of the cable car, Katharina silently trudging twenty metres behind us.

We only saw the helicopter of the alpine rescue team thirty minutes later, when we were in the cable car back down.

4

Blaming Yourself

Blaming yourself is pointless. It does not solve anything. All it does is copy a problem from the real world into your mind, where it then grows to a size it would never actually reach out there.

Joschka Breitner, *Slowing Down in the Fast Lane: Mindfulness for Managers*

The helicopter didn't land on the meadow in front of the Alpine Association hut but was hovering above the mountain station of the freight cable car. Probably that's where one of the mountain rescuers would abseil down with a rescue basket. I had a bad feeling that this might have a little something to do with a few shaky crates and an improperly bolted gate. When we arrived in the valley, I asked the cashier in my best concerned-tourist voice what kind of rescue operation was going on up there. The man, a volunteer mountain rescuer himself, like all employees of the cable car company, was being kept abreast of the operation over radio.

'Quite a nasty thing. A waiter fell off the terrace.'

Holy. Fucking. Shit. My prank had overshot the mark. I suddenly felt ice cold.

'Did he . . . Is it bad?'

'No idea. Doesn't seem to be able to climb up on his own, at any rate. My colleagues are on their way over.'

So he'd broken a leg at least. Fuck. I hadn't wanted that to happen. Getting him into trouble, sure. But this was too much, and I felt horribly sorry. However, since I wanted neither my wife to treat me like a child, nor to do so myself, I had to face the facts like an adult: I'd screwed up big time.

By blaming myself, however, Nils wouldn't be any better off. And self-pity wouldn't help much either.

'That poor lad,' the cashier muttered to himself.

Katharina, who, unlike me, really didn't care about the waiter, wanted to head off, but something in me needed to find out more.

'Do you know the waiter?'

'No, but my brother does. He runs the mountain hut. The waiter is a city kid from up north. Wanted to do some kind of "sustainability" internship in the hospitality industry. No idea what that might be. But it's probably over now.'

'And how did he fall into the ravine?' Katharina chimed in.

'Apparently, he sat down on a crate when he went on break and then somehow crashed down into the valley. Probably forgot to close the barrier gate.'

The next tourists arrived at the counter, and the cashier turned his attention to them. Mountain accidents were a normal part of his life.

We left the station and headed to the car.

'That poor waiter,' Katharina said to me quietly. 'And to think you got so childishly upset with him.'

I had no valid arguments to defend myself. Quite the opposite. Fortunately, Katharina had no idea about the most childish part of it – my revenge prank. To provide some kind of response, I started fumbling for words. Which didn't improve matters.

'Yeah . . . sure . . . But he was also acting like a complete idiot. I mean – who does a "sustainability" internsh—' I didn't get any further.

'I only noticed one person acting like a complete idiot up there, and that was you. I'm fed up with your incessant mood swings. Promise me you'll get a handle on this.'

'How do you imagine I do that?'

'Mindfulness training worked, didn't it? I want you to call that Breitner tonight and make an appointment to work on yourself . . .'

'Otherwise?'

'Otherwise, this holiday is over.'

'And then I called you,' I concluded my story.

'And, how is the waiter doing?' Breitner asked.

'Broke his leg.' Which wasn't a complete lie. He'd also broken his leg.

In addition to his neck.

As I learned online that evening after calling Breitner.

Fortunately, Emily and Katharina were already in bed by then. The latter with her eye mask and earplugs. Neither of them witnessed my collapse.

I hadn't wanted this to happen. Six months earlier, I had killed four people. Intentionally. Mindfully. To protect me and my family. I hadn't enjoyed doing it, but I got rid of the associated stress through mindfulness. I didn't want any more violence in my life. Yet now a young man had lost his life because I got agitated about mere trifles. Something up there had triggered me to act entirely out of character. And spurred me to pull a prank that'd spiralled out of control. Nils was dead. That was a fact. Which was horrible. And irreversible. I needed to come to terms with that.

As I sat there trembling on the couch of the holiday

apartment, paralysed, ashen-faced and cold, staring at the news on the local newspaper's website, it was my mindfulness practice that helped me restore myself. Specifically, it was the serenity prayer.

There, in our farm rental, I prayed for the courage to change the things I could. The serenity to accept the things I couldn't change. And the wisdom to know the difference.

The fact that Nils was dead could not be changed. Now, I no longer needed courage, only serenity. Which was hard enough, as wisdom helped me realise.

But looking at it mindfully, I recognised that, at this point, blaming myself wouldn't help.

Nils wouldn't be any better off if I felt bad about it. And as much as confessing would relieve my soul in the short term, that short-term relief would make my life catastrophically worse in the long term. If I surrendered to the authorities, my mindfully balanced double life would plunge into the abyss faster than Nils had.

Only I could incriminate myself. No one had seen me. We hadn't left any digital traces at the analogue hut. Katharina had paid in cash. I even bought the tickets for the cable car with cash. After the discount we'd gotten through the 'guest card' the tourist office had given us, the price had been negligible anyway.

I wouldn't realise until weeks later that I was still identifiable via witnesses at the hut, the cable car's surveillance camera and the guest card's digital record.

Emotionally, it was what it was: I'd overreacted. The past couldn't be changed, so all I could change was my behaviour in the future. I could work on myself and never again listen to a voice inside telling me to stack drink crates next to a ravine and unbolt a gate.

And that was why I was at Breitner's.

'A broken leg,' Breitner remarked, matter-of-factly and without reproach. 'How does that make you feel?' He *was* my mindfulness coach after all, not Nils's orthopaedist. I briefly deliberated how to answer that question.

'I'm sorry about what happened. I didn't want it to happen. I feel guilty, but I also cannot change anything about it now.'

Above all, I wanted to dissuade Breitner as quickly as possible from further enquiring into the waiter's state of health.

'Though my wife doesn't know I unbolted that safety gate, she was already of the opinion that I should work on myself a little more because of the argument we'd gotten into.'

'But you didn't call me just because your wife wanted you to, did you?' Breitner looked at me as if I'd told him that I had traded my penis for a nose ring by which my wife could lead me around the domestic arena like some biddable bull.

'No, I . . .'

'So let me repeat the question I asked earlier: why did you call me?'

I considered his question. Only briefly. Because the reason had become clear to me.

'Because I have no idea why I reacted so emotionally at the hut. Because it doesn't do me any good. Because it doesn't do other people any good. And because I want to know why I deliberately do things that make me feel guilty afterwards. That's why I'm here.'

The fact that I'd even told Breitner about the waiter's injury constituted considerably more candour than I had planned for. But that level of candour was probably necessary if I wanted to get to the root of my behaviour. What I didn't talk about, however, was my well-founded fear that this or any future freak-out might draw unnecessary attention to the balancing act that was my double life. I was already plenty afraid of the future as it was.

5

Childhood Photos

The images you have of your childhood are a bit like the pictures you drew when you were small: highly imaginative, with hardly any basis in reality.

Joschka Breitner, *Parenting Your Inner Child*

During my story, Breitner had finished his tea. He seemed to be far less shocked than my wife that I'd gotten so upset over excruciatingly slow service. He refilled his cup. Not mine.

'Now, if I do not immediately fill your cup to the brim, will a voice inside you tell you to freak out?' he asked, without a hint of irony.

'What? No! Why would I? I'm not here for *tea*.'

'Now see, that is exactly what this is about. What were you at the hut for?'

'I told you: I wanted to pass on a beautiful childhood memory to my daughter. And this idiot waiter made that impossible.'

'And that is precisely where I am not so sure,' Breitner said, clearly doubtful of my statement.

'What do you mean?'

'You are a criminal defence lawyer, right? So you know that a fictitious statement is clear, striking, whereas a true statement is rich in detail, but fuzzier. After all, the truth is more intricate.'

'Am I on trial here?'

'No, so I want you to avoid issuing a wrong judgement in your own case. What I am getting at is this: you described your childhood memories of this lunch order in very striking terms: "Steaming", "ice-cold", "polished to a high gloss". Anyone who has ever seen Kaiserschmarrn, a bottle of Almdudler or a Landjäger could say that. You remember the mindfulness exercise we did with the apple?'

I nodded. Six months ago, we had each eaten a slice of apple and paid attention to how it sharpened every individual sense. Afterwards, I could not only describe how bright red the apple looked, but also go into great detail: how the peel quietly snapped when sliced, how the juice seeping from the fresh pulp smelled, how the cold piece of apple felt in my mouth, how my chewing sounded, how the fruit tasted on my tongue.

'If you actually had a true memory of these Kaiserschmarrn, you might have described the delightful smell of melted butter, sweet icing sugar and fresh apple sauce. How much you had been longing for the fluffy feeling when your tongue presses a piece of pancake against the roof of your mouth and it gives like a pillow. You would have internalised the feeling of raisin skins bursting in a true flavour explosion. You would have mentioned the warmth moving from your mouth through your oesophagus into your stomach.'

I was getting hungry – and stroppy.

'Listen, can't you just show me some exercise to help me get a handle on my next freak-out before I hurt any more people?'

'I would love to teach you how to completely avoid any freak-outs in the future. But to do that we both need one last piece of information.'

'And what is that?' I asked, defiant.

'How many times did your parents really take you for Kaiserschmarrn?'

Now I was really annoyed. 'Sorry, but I really don't feel like going on any sentimental journeys.'

Breitner's gentle tone didn't waver. 'It doesn't have to be a long journey, as long as you stop resisting. Why not turn your childhood holiday into a short slide show: close your eyes, then I'll give you three words, and you simply look at whatever images your memory projects onto the inside of your eyelids. OK?'

I wanted to get the navel-gazing over with, so I lowered my defences. I closed my eyes. 'Fine by me.'

'Parents. Holiday. Pasture.'

The first slide in my memory carousel immediately clicked into place. Lost in thought, a small blond boy in lederhosen – me, obviously – walks towards the terrace of a mountain hut. Followed by his serious-looking father carrying a backpack. His mother silently trudging twenty metres behind him. At the tables are families: parents smiling, children eating Kaiserschmarrn. Next slide. I ask my father if we can get Kaiserschmarrn too. My father, already looking past the hut, says we don't need that kind of nonsense, and points to the spring-water trough we're going to sit at instead. Next slide. My father has opened his old backpack. My mother takes out the sandwiches she prepared for us. While all the other children are drinking Almdudler, I have to cup fresh water from the trough with my hands. Next slide. My father eats a supermarket

Landjäger. My parents are silent while I sit at the trough, staring at the other children and passionately wanting to find out what Kaiserschmarrn taste like.

An empty slide snaps into place. The slide show was over.

I was overcome by a deep sadness. But all this was only about the food – or was it?

Breitner could see I was sad, and his soft voice brought me back to the present. 'Eating Kaiserschmarrn on an alpine meadow with a pair of happy parents after a long hike was never a childhood memory of yours. It was a childhood wish that has gone unfulfilled to this day, wasn't it?'

'Well, if you look at it like that . . .'

'So what you really wanted to do was make this childhood wish come true with your daughter, not pass on an actual lived memory.'

I was taken aback. 'What difference does that make?'

'A big difference. With the waiter, it was not about how long it took him to bring you something to eat. It was about someone once again not giving you what you most wanted as a child. Even a complete stranger. That is why you responded so strongly.'

'That's why I freaked out so much?'

'It was not you who freaked out up there.'

'Then who?'

'It was your inner child.'

That was the very first time I ever heard about my inner child. It would change my life.

6

Childhood Memories

The most beautiful thing about childhood is the fact that you have repressed most of what was not beautiful about it.

Joschka Breitner, *Parenting Your Inner Child*

I admit, I was curious. 'And who might this inner child be?'

Breitner responded with a metaphor. 'If you have a bruise on your thigh, does that restrict how you move through life?'

'No.'

'And if someone were to pummel that bruise?'

'It would hurt like hell.'

'You see, the same happens with your inner child. Only your inner child bears the bruises on your soul.'

The number of question marks now swirling around my head far exceeded the number of bruises I'd ever gotten.

'I have no idea what you're talking about.'

Breitner put down his cup. 'In depth psychology, the inner child is a concept that helps explain certain processes. Your inner child is the part of your subconscious that stores emotional injuries from your earliest childhood. Imagine that these psychological injuries left bruises. In your everyday life, you never glimpse or feel these old injuries. You have no idea that this injured child inside you even exists. But if someone even grazes those bruises, your inner child is the one that feels the awful pain. Since you are not aware of your inner child, however, all you hear is someone crying.'

'What does that have to do with my freak-out in the Alps?'

'That waiter happened to touch a bruise your parents inflicted on your inner child decades ago.'

'What bruise?'

'As a child, your parents apparently made it very clear to you that your needs or wishes did not count. All the other children were allowed to enjoy Kaiserschmarrn and Almdudler, but you were expected to make do with water and home-made sandwiches. Your need to experience the same pleasures as the other children was ignored. As a result, your parents also taught you that pleasure is somehow inessential. "Fun and games are stuff and nonsense" and "your needs don't count" are so-called core beliefs. And your parents probably inculcated these beliefs in you not only up in the Alps, but throughout your childhood.'

'But how can something someone says cause a bruise?'

'Let us go back to that metaphor from before. Imagine your parents' core beliefs were printed on pin badges. One badge says, "FUN AND GAMES ARE STUFF AND NONSENSE!", the other, "YOUR NEEDS DON'T COUNT!" And whenever you expressed a need, these two sentences were pinned into your soul. That leaves bruises, believe me. These beliefs were literally drilled into you.'

'That might be the case, but this was years ago,' I objected sceptically. 'And surely not getting any Kaiserschmarrn at some alpine establishment isn't as bad as breaking a leg.'

'Your waiter might agree,' Breitner relativised. 'And it is entirely understandable why you cannot see how deep this goes. Since you were a child, you have repressed many of these parental injuries from your consciousness – repressed, not addressed! – yet your inner child is not part of your consciousness but your *sub*consciousness. That is where all your injuries and core beliefs have been stored to this day. The bruise caused by the core belief that "your needs don't count" is still there too. On that terrace, your child's subconsciousness reminded you of a very painful experience your adult consciousness had long repressed.'

'Which specifically means what?'

'You subconsciously wanted to teach your daughter something very different from what your parents always taught you. You wanted to reward both your daughter and yourself. And you also wanted to meet a childhood need of your own. Unlike your childhood self, your daughter should learn that pleasure is a beautiful thing. But once again, just like your parents did almost forty years ago, someone dashed your dreams. The waiter ignored your needs. Kaiserschmarrn and Almdudler? Nope. To the contrary. Completely unprompted, he also tells you that, if it were up to him, Landjäger and squeezy pouches would be banned. That was a kick against the bruise on your soul. It made your inner child cry out. Earlier, you described it very clearly as a small, high voice inside you. That voice – that was your inner child.'

'But why did that aggravate me so much?'

'It aggravated your consciousness. Your subconsciousness knew exactly why your inner child was freaking out, your consciousness did not. After all, your consciousness repressed these connections years ago, hence your conscious irritation over behaviour that subconsciously was entirely valid.'

61

I needed to let that sink in for a bit. It sounded very logical, yet equally absurd. It took me a few seconds to think it all through. 'So the child in me got stressed over an old incident and then passed the stress from my subconsciousness on to me?'

'That is perhaps oversimplifying things, but yes.'

'But I was able to get rid of the stress my inner child passed on to me through my mindfulness practice, right?'

'You got rid of your *conscious* stress through mindfulness. Your inner child and its subconscious stress are both still there.'

'And . . . even though I calmed myself down, my inner child insisted on playing this childish prank, which then led to the waiter . . . well, breaking something?'

'Not a childish prank, a child*like* prank,' Breitner corrected me.

'What's the difference?'

'"Childish" is when an adult displays non-age-appropriate behaviour, thus degrading themselves. "Childlike" is the completely understandable behaviour of a child, thus explaining their motivation. From a childlike point of view, what happened behind the hut is completely logical. Children live in the moment. They revel in their pride and petulance to the point of excess. Children indulge in the present. Your inner child told you: this guy has been ruining my day, so I will ruin his too. A child does not stop to consider the possible consequences.'

This session with Breitner had already achieved one of my goals. Thanks to the discovery of my inner child, I could start channelling my feelings of guilt over Nils's death and guide them far away from me. That alpine argument hadn't escalated between me and the waiter; the waiter had picked a fight with my inner child. Mentally, that was something I could work with. Essentially, Nils hadn't fallen into that ravine because of me. He'd fallen into that ravine because my inner child had fought back after he'd poked its bruises. My inner child couldn't be blamed for that. For one, it couldn't be charged as an adult. Plus, Nils had almost forced my inner child's hand. And apparently my parents were not completely innocent either. After all, they had been the ones who'd given my inner child the bruises the waiter had poked. But my parents could no longer be held accountable. They were already dead. Not because of anything my inner child did, but because of prostate cancer and heart failure – years ago, at this point.

7

Basic Trust

The apple does not fall far from the tree. If no one gives it the confidence it needs to germinate its seeds or have a bird carry them to a new home, the apple is left worrying that it will rot right there in the shade of the tree.

Joschka Breitner, *Parenting Your Inner Child*

I wanted to learn more. I wanted to find out what my inner child was like. Why I was only meeting it now. But above all: how I could get a handle on it before another careless act drew more attention and put me in serious danger.

'So in the future, how do I ensure no one else ends up in a ravine just because they remind my inner child of its past injuries?'

'First of all, it is great that you are already thinking positively about the future, and that you are aware it has not only problems in store for you, but solutions too.'

I only gave him an annoyed look.

'Do you remember? Not half an hour ago, you mentioned your "fear of the future", as you called it. That is also what you experienced up at the hut.'

The first part was right. Since Breitner had told me about my inner child, I hadn't thought about my fear of the future once. I hadn't thought about Boris either. I hadn't thought about any of the things I didn't want to tell Breitner. But what that hut should have to do with my fear of the future was unclear to me.

'Up there at the hut I wasn't afraid of the future, I was hungry!'

'Up there with your family, you didn't even trust the next twenty minutes of your future. Every minute that the waiter didn't show gave rise to a darker vision of the immediate future. If that is not a very concrete fear of the future, what is?'

'And what does that have to do with my inner child?'

'For years, your parents taught you that your needs do not matter. How likely does that make it that you can confidently assume those unimportant needs will be met in the future?'

'So my parents are also to blame for my fear of the future?'

'Your parents certainly did not provide the child who now lives inside you with sufficient basic trust.'

'Basic trust?'

'A fundamental confidence that everything is going to be all right. That nothing bad will happen to you. That someone is there to protect you. That your needs are acknowledged and met the way they deserve. People with basic trust have a positive relationship with the future.'

I was completely taken aback. 'There are people who *aren't* worried about the future?'

The existence of such optimists was almost more astonishing to me than the fact that I clearly wasn't one of them. Breitner answered my question with an optimistic smile.

'But how do I get that basic trust back?'

Breitner calmly took another sip of his tea. As if it didn't matter that valuable future seconds were dissipating into the present.

'We can look at which of your parents' specific core beliefs took that basic trust away from your inner child. We can then try to heal those injuries. This will show your inner child that you are there for it now. As an adult, you are in a position to ensure that nothing happens to you or your inner child. Then, in the future, you can protect each other.'

That last image looked good to me. Too good. 'It's *that* easy?'

'It is not easy. This is an arduous path. But I can accompany you along the way.'

My next question served as my first step on this path. 'And what would that look like?'

'We will journey into your childhood to see what injuries your inner child has suffered. Which core-belief badges were painfully pinned to your inner child's soul. Which of these beliefs it has resigned itself to, which it rebels against and when.'

That already sounded very curious. But it got even curiouser.

'You will reach out to your inner child and offer your help as an adult. Then, we will use various exercises to try and heal your inner child's injuries. In the end, you should have an inner child without any bruises. An inner child who no longer plays tricks on you from your own subconsciousness.'

If I hadn't such great confidence in Breitner's abilities, this would've been the point I burst into incredulous laughter. But I didn't, I just kept listening.

'At the end of our journey, you will have an inner child who can be relied upon as a partner. Someone who no longer stands in the way of your happiness but may even boost it. How does that sound?'

Breitner was always open with me. I wanted to be open with him too.

'*Honestly* honestly? That all sounds positively idiotic to me.'

Breitner was not at all offended I'd answered his question honestly. Still, he countered my scepticism with one very simple argument:

'Your relationship problems, your issues with your job, your fear of the future – what if childhood injuries were behind *all* of it? The result of your inner child appearing from your subconsciousness and forcing you to behave in ways you cannot consciously explain? How much more idiotic would it be *not* to start on this journey? What do you have to lose, other than your problems?'

What if my inner child had something to do with me keeping Boris trapped in the cellar, with me killing Dragan and now lying to two criminal syndicates, with me living a very fraught double life? This was starting to make sense to me, or at least it was too tempting to ignore. I decided to take Breitner up on his offer to introduce me to my inner child. I immediately scheduled six closely timed follow-up sessions.

8

Reality

We feel afraid *before* something happens, not in the
actual moment we are so afraid of. We are afraid
of uncertainty – not of reality. And that is good.
Feeling afraid means that at least there is a chance
that what you are afraid of will not actually happen.

Joschka Breitner, *Slowing Down in the
Fast Lane: Mindfulness for Managers*

Breitner hadn't been exaggerating – the path *was* arduous. Over the next few weeks, I learned that substantially engaging with my inner child was anything but idiotic. It was upsetting. It was heartbreaking. It was illuminating. It was healing.

As I lugged a lot of junk out from my soul's cellar, I discovered my inner child behind it. When Breitner and I travelled back to various moments in my childhood, I found that not everything had been as 'normal' and 'happy' as I remembered. At the same time, I realised that, as a child, I'd had no choice but to see my childhood as 'normal'. That my parents weren't the best parents in the world, just the only ones I had.

I saw which of my parents' core beliefs had hurt my inner child and unmoored it.

I learned to understand the offensive and defensive strategies my inner child had been using to protect itself.

I visualised my inner child. I gave it a body, a place in my world.

I reached out to my inner child. I wrote it letters. I talked to it. I spent time with it, the two of us on a time island all our own. I built trust. My inner child became my adviser.

After six intensive sessions spread out over three weeks, this couples therapy with me and my inner child was over.

I had theoretically understood everything Breitner had taught me. Practically, however, my new-found abilities still needed to prove themselves.

That last Friday afternoon, Breitner dismissed me with a few final words.

'Now that you have the tools, please apply them very consciously. Respond to your inner child's needs. You don't have to meet every single one, but each is an indication that something is missing from your life. Close these gaps lovingly and mindfully.'

That all made sense. The same went for the assignment he gave me.

'This next week, try to really take your inner child seriously. Consider these seven days a week of partnership between you and your inner child. Try to sense what the child needs – it might be little things. Sometimes you will be equal partners, other times you will need to provide clear guidance. Remember everything we worked on. If you can consistently integrate your inner child into your everyday life for a week, you can also do it for a month, a year, a lifetime. I wish you the best of luck.'

None of us had any idea how intense this week was going to be. Neither Breitner nor I, not to mention my inner child.

By the end of my sessions, the cost of healing my inner child amounted to the kind of money other people would've invested in the assisted conception of a real child. It did, however, also include a signed copy of Breitner's handbook *Parenting Your Inner Child*, summarising his findings and exercises. This way, I could look anything up at any time and remind myself of what we had worked on. In short, the book was an instruction manual for the child living inside my soul.

Breitner had also packaged it very stylishly – in a small tote made from old newsprint. To this day, I don't know whether it was a coincidence or a deliberate joke on Breitner's part, but on the outside was an article with the headline: 'WHERE IS THE GOLDEN CHILD?' It was a report from the previous year about the spectacular theft of a golden Jesus statue from the roof of a monastery church in the Hessian hinterland. This article, it turned out, would affect my future at least as much as the book inside.

With the book about my inner child in its newsprint tote, I said a grateful goodbye to Breitner. Newly empowered and partnered with my inner child, I now felt like I was in the best possible position to solve or mitigate my old problems, plus dodge any new ones, in the days and years to come.

Only three days later, reality would throw a bucket of cold water all over me and my inner child.

It was Monday, 5.41 in the morning. I was asleep in bed when my phone ruthlessly tore me out of my REM sleep. The screen read 'SASHA'. Sasha was Dragan's former driver. A native Bulgarian, he'd studied environmental engineering back home and come to Germany in his late twenties full of hope. It probably would've been easier for him to pose as a minor without identification and pass the authorities' age assessment than to have his engineering diploma in environmental technology recognised here. So, Sasha didn't start working as an engineer, but as a driver for a mob boss – and in order not to let the job dumb him down, he completed an apprenticeship as an early-years educator on the side.

Sasha was the only person who suspected that Dragan might be dead and knew that I kept Boris prisoner in my cellar. After Dragan's disappearance six months ago, he'd helped me deal with both Boris's threats and the hostility of Dragan's crew. In return, Sasha became the managing director of the preschool I'd brutally usurped in Dragan's name – for my daughter. Sasha quickly transformed from Dragan's right-hand man into a friend. Together we'd exercised quite a lot of violence, and together we'd now renounced violence as well.

Sasha didn't just work in the same building as me, he lived there too. Above the preschool. All day long, he looked after the preschoolers' needs with love and incredible tranquillity. He got the necessary energy from his daily exercise. Every morning before work, he ran his 10K. Sasha was an early bird, but him calling at half past five in the morning, before his run, wasn't a good sign. Hardly had I sleepily greeted him before he burst out:

'He's gone.'

Only two words. But those two words were enough to send an ice-cold panic from my kidneys along my spine up to my neck. My greatest fear of the future turned into a very present panic.

'He's gone' could only mean one thing. Boris had disappeared from his cellar prison. I closed my eyes. Automatically, the inner slide projector Breitner had introduced me to clicked on and projected terrifying images

76

onto the back of my eyelids. A rapid-fire sequence of sepia-toned images.

I saw Boris and Dragan as teenagers. Best friends selling their first drugs together.

Boris and Dragan as young men. Two muscle-bound lads pimping out their first girls together and ascending to red-light greatness.

Then there was Dragan, fucking Boris's wife.

The next image showed Boris decapitating his wife in response. Click. In the next image, Boris nails her torso to Dragan's door. There's a rupture between the two. From then on, each leads his own gang.

Click. Next slide. A lay-by with Boris's deputy in flames, Dragan beating the man to death with an iron bar.

Click. Me, tossing Dragan's sawn-up corpse into a wood chipper to eradicate any evidence.

Click. Boris threatening to kill me and my daughter if I don't take him to Dragan.

Click. Boris blowing up Dragan's number two in that same lay-by.

Click. Boris climbing into his own boot in front of his officers, expecting me to drive him to Dragan.

Click. Click. Click. In quick succession, I see a dazed Boris coming to his senses in the preschool's cellar. Boris raging and screaming in the cellar. I see the empty cellar. Without Boris.

One last, very loud click. A crystal-clear image, entirely without patina, is projected onto my eyelids. An image from the future. Boris smiling over the corpses of Katharina and Emily. And me.

I opened my eyes, shaking my head to chase away the images.

This slide show didn't serve me. I didn't want to see any of the violence I had renounced. And I certainly didn't want to see any of the violence I hoped to avoid in the future. But did I have a choice?

My head was spinning. Luckily, I was still in bed, so my knees couldn't buckle beneath me.

'Who's gone?' I asked, pro forma, just to say anything at all.

'Boris. He's gone. The cellar's empty.'

My worst nightmare had come true. It'd always been clear to me that putting Boris in the cellar was no long-term solution. The alternative would've been to kill Boris plain and simple. But Sasha and I had both hesitated. This killing business had to end. That's why we let Boris live. Even if it had been a mistake, as it now turned out.

He's gone.

Until those two words, our comparatively non-violent plan had worked brilliantly for over six months. I never thought it'd be so uncomplicated to keep a person in a lightly converted cellar. Uncomplicated for everyone except the guy in the cellar, that is; Boris did have to scale back a little. But in their blissful ignorance, Dragan's and Boris's criminal organisations readily accepted the solution. To them, making their bosses disappear even made me a hero. Everyone assumed I'd successfully ensured that both Dragan and Boris were safe from the police (and thus alive). Dragan after murdering one of Boris's employees. Boris after murdering one of Dragan's. I reinforced this impression to the best of my ability by crafting the bosses' memos to their officers and, as a lawyer, declaring those messages utterly official. All this time, I'd thus been running both criminal organisations.

Dragan didn't care at all. As he was dead, he adopted a decidedly tolerant view. But Boris didn't seem so keen on the arrangement. I'd actually hoped that, over time, he'd develop Stockholm syndrome and begin to see Sasha and me as not only his hostage-takers, but his friends too. Only he didn't. All that connected Boris to Stockholm was a certain resemblance to Greta Thunberg's demeanour: he showed no outward signs of joy and would've preferred us to panic at every opportunity. Now, he had succeeded. If Boris's crew found out I'd fooled them, this would also raise questions among Dragan's crew. Then there would be dead bodies, and the first ones would be Sasha and me.

But giving in to a panic attack wouldn't help. I tried to anchor myself in the present moment. I sat on the edge of the bed, my bare feet touching the floor to ground myself. I consciously took a deep breath in and out. I was afraid of what might happen. What was happening right now wasn't bad. What was happening right now was an empty cellar, nothing more.

'How did he get out?' I asked, once I could formulate meaningful questions again.

'The lock on his cell door was cracked, from the outside.'

So he hadn't escaped on his own; he'd had help. If Boris had been broken out by his own people, there was no time to lose.

'When did you find out?'

'Just now. I wanted to go for a run and saw that the downstairs door to the cellar was slightly ajar. I was sure I'd closed it yesterday, so I went down to check if everything was OK. It wasn't. The door to Boris's prison was open, the lock cracked in front of it. His cells are empty.'

Sasha and I living in the same building made for a very practical arrangement, especially if you were also looking after a prisoner together. But apparently it hadn't kept the prisoner imprisoned.

'And Boris was still in there yesterday evening?'

'Yes. The last time I was in the cellar was half past ten, when I brought him some new drinks.'

So Boris might already have been out for almost eight hours. That was an eternity. My brain went into crisis mode. Worst-case scenario: Boris wanted immediate revenge. Could Boris know where my family was?

He not only could – he actually did. He'd heard it from me. Over the last few months, I'd gotten used to delivering detailed monologues in front of him. This for the simple reason that, stuck in the cellar, Boris didn't have a lot of new experiences he could talk about. It was odd: while I'd completely ignored the inner child stuck in the cellar of my subconsciousness for decades, I'd been in close contact with the Russian stuck in the cellar of my building for months. I'd told him about my job, about what was new with his gang, and even about my personal life. I'd ultimately assumed that, down there alone in the cellar, Boris would be safely discreet.

But everything was different now, and I could think of only one move that made sense.

'All right. Please reach out to Walter immediately,' I told Sasha. In Dragan's gang, Walter was in charge of security. Officially, he managed a security company. Unofficially, he managed the very lucrative arms-trafficking branch of Dragan's former consortium. 'I want his people to provide a security team for Katharina and Emily, straight away, and one for you and me. And to secure the building.'

'And what should I tell him? If Walter learns that we've been keeping Boris in the cellar, that'll only create *more* problems.'

That was indisputably true. Only Sasha and I knew about Boris's actual living conditions. Walter, like everyone else, assumed that Boris and Dragan were living together on a farm somewhere. It was funny that the type of story children were told about their dead pets worked equally well on gangsters when they needed to be hoodwinked about their dead, or good-as-dead, bosses. Finding out that Boris's farm was really my cellar would certainly be rather alarming to Walter. I didn't have the slightest idea how to handle this. I needed to improvise.

'Pffff, I don't know . . . Just tell him . . . I *told* you to. You don't know why either. I'll call him myself after and explain the situation. If I can think of anything by then . . .'

'OK. I'll call Walter. And what do we do with the preschool?' Sasha asked.

I considered his question. The preschool was in the line of fire too. Plainly and simply because it was on the floor between Boris's cellar and Sasha's and my apartments. I couldn't hide behind the preschoolers when Boris started taking his revenge. So, we not only needed a reason we could tell Walter to protect ourselves, we also needed a plausible reason to temporarily close the preschool.

What might be a reason for a preschool to close overnight? Because something had happened overnight. But what?

'Please go and break a window in the preschool,' I told Sasha.

'Sorry?'

'We'll pretend someone tried to break into the preschool to steal something.' In the broadest possible sense, that was true. 'Then the preschool can stay closed today, the police will be in the building and the children won't be in any danger. The parents will buy that story.'

'Sounds good. I'll call Walter, fake the break-in and alert the police. The cops will probably think it was those lowlifes from the park across the street. I'll have the room leaders inform all the parents.'

'And I'll come up with an explanation to give Walter. As soon as I've talked to him, I'll head down to you.'

Only the day before, I'd been hoping to spend the week with my inner child, making some long-term positive changes. All so it wouldn't blow up my life with another freak-out in the medium term. The fact that Boris had disappeared could now end each of my two lives in the very short term. I was afraid I'd lose my fear of the future at the same time as any future at all.

9

Mental Walk-Through

If you want to stop your mental carousel from spinning out of control, send your thoughts on a walk-through. Start in the room where you find yourself. Close your eyes. What would you see if your eyes were open? How is the furniture arranged in the adjoining room? And what does the rest of the house look like? Mentally walk through all the rooms. Finally, return to the room you are in. Now open your eyes. You will find that, outside, the room will not have changed. But inside, things suddenly look rather different than they did just a few minutes ago.

Joschka Breitner, *Slowing Down in the Fast Lane: Mindfulness for Managers*

I hung up. My hands were shaking. Partly out of fear, and partly out of anger. In the terrified silence, I could feel my heart pounding cold and fast. A menacing static rang in my ears.

But there was another sound inside me. A small voice angrily shouting one word over and over: '*Tapsi!*'

Right – my inner child was still there too. The one I'd planned to spend an intensive partnership week with. But how did those safety instructions put it again, the ones on planes about to crash?

In the event of a sudden loss in cabin pressure, place the oxygen mask over your mouth and nose, and ensure it is fitted before assisting any children travelling with you.

In this case, my oxygen was mindfulness.

I knew that, very shortly, I'd need to give Walter some pretext for why we needed personal protection. Unfortunately, I hadn't the slightest idea how to do this without unravelling my web of lies. And in my panicked state, I wouldn't be able to think of anything plausible either. So, before I did anything else, I needed to get my fear under control. I could worry about my inner child later.

I put on my dressing gown and walked into the living room to get a grip on my emotions.

After I opened the sliding doors to the balcony, I moved to the middle of the living room, where I started a standing meditation to ground myself. I stood feet shoulder-width apart and felt the fresh air coming in from the outside. I felt the warm, rough wood of the floor under my bare feet. I noticed how the firmness of the ground I was standing on was passing through to me. I noticed the warm power of the wood running through my legs into my upper body. My head was invisibly pulled up and held by the sky. My spine straightened. My shoulders loosened, dropped and relaxed. I noticed a cleansing energy flowing into and throughout my entire body. With my eyes closed, I started swaying slightly back and forth, my feet automatically supporting me. I breathed in the fresh air and followed its path from the tip of my nose to the capillaries in my bronchi. And back again. What a wonderful feeling. After just five breaths, my body felt substantially calmer.

To focus my thoughts on all that was good around me, I practised a mindfulness exercise Breitner had taught me: the mental walk-through. With my eyes closed, I mentally walked through my apartment as if I were seeing these rooms for the first time.

I'd been living here for six months. The room I was standing in was 5 × 6 metres and over 3.5 metres high. On the ceiling, an elegant stucco medallion encircled a modern chandelier. Towards the street, two large sliding doors led to a small balcony. On the opposite side, double doors opened to the kitchen.

I had furnished the room in minimalist yet comfortable fashion. In the corner by the balcony, a shaggy rug covered the polished, century-old floorboards. On the rug stood a comfy oversized sofa, perfect for naps. In front of the sofa, an old steamer trunk from the early 1900s served as a coffee table. A large TV hung on the wall opposite, below it an old stereo system with a record player. Next to it, a shelf for records and CDs. Between the sofa and the kitchen stood an old wooden table and three chairs. That was all.

My mental walk-through continued. After passing through the galley kitchen, I looked left into the small cloakroom, which only had a toilet, a basin and a mirror. Further down the hallway was Emily's room: a small bed with pink princessy sheets, a colourful play rug, a small pastel-pink wardrobe and some shelves with boxes of toys. Framed on the walls were some of her first drawings.

The last room at the end of the hall was my bedroom. A box-spring bed, a wardrobe. A door to its en suite bathroom. Opposite the bed was a 1.5 × 2-metre Ikea print of a long rope bridge in a misty jungle.

I mentally walked back into the living room.

High above the streets of the city, this apartment was a refuge. The only drawback – and one that really bothered me – was the noise from the playground in the park opposite. Not the clamour of the children, but the shouting of drunks who violated all the playground regulations only to leave the place strewn with shards at some point in the early hours of the morning. Since I'd moved in, there'd been three armed muggings in the park, and one 'little free library' had been smashed and torched. With the exception of these gentlemen responsible, no one dared enter the park after dark. Not even the community safety officers. And it was precisely this law-enforcement-resistant crowd whose sounds now acoustically penetrated my mindfully managed peace and quiet.

'Gentlemen' was definitely the wrong word for these lowlifes. Although these men were adults, if they were to undergo an admissions interview at Emily's preschool, their mental immaturity meant they'd certainly be held back a year or two.

My deep revulsion of their behaviour could get me so worked up I'd be unable to sleep. And that wasn't quite the point of the exercise I was doing. I wanted to calm down. So, why was I getting this worked up?

Thanks to Breitner, I had figured out that my alpine incident hadn't been my first inner-child-related freak-out. Desperately angry one night, before our holiday in the mountains, I'd thrown an ice cube from the balcony into the darkness of the park. Into a darkness brightened only by a burning rubbish bin and soundtracked by booming speakers punctuated by the men's drunken roaring. Judging by the pitiful howl that rang out three seconds after my lucky toss, I probably hit one of the park's paragons in the head. Which had given me some satisfaction, but ultimately didn't change anything about the situation.

By now, I'd learned that the anger I felt despite my mindfulness practice was really my inner child's anger. Its need to sleep in peace was blatantly being ignored.

But now that Boris had escaped, this was all suddenly irrelevant. I felt my relaxation exercise slipping away from me. I had to focus. I continued my mental walk-through, leaving my apartment and strolling through the rest of the building.

Below my apartment was the office of my law firm.

I'd signed lucrative consulting contracts with Dragan and Boris – with the former after his death, with the latter after three days of food deprivation. This turned my law office into the cover I needed to manage two underworld operations. As further camouflage, I still took on additional cases, whose triviality annoyed me no end.

In the first place, I hated other people's quarrels. I really didn't like arguing. Finding this out ten years after my admission to the bar might've been a little late. After all, a lawyer's *raison d'être* primarily lies in other people's quarrels. But it's never too late to adapt one's profession to one's outlook on life.

All the clients I took on were 'pretend': the clients pretended to be the most important people in the world, and I pretended to care.

At more than one of my appointments, I found myself wanting to rudely interrupt my client and ask whether they'd gone completely barmy. Why the hell do you drive at 180 kilometres per hour when you can clearly see the large, round, red-rimmed sign with a black 80 painted on it? What is wrong with a person that they want to spend 120 euros on a lawyer's letter to complain about a 36-euro difference on a utility bill for an apartment that costs 2,200 euros a month?

But these little freak-outs were completely silent. I simply let the cases wreck themselves and told my clients they should consider themselves lucky. My cheeky inaction might cost the client their driving licence, but I could very plausibly explain that I'd negotiated the unavoidable minimum penalty – without me, they'd have lost their licence for much longer. That wasn't true. But such arguments sound sufficiently convincing to people who couldn't even parse the simple gist of a road sign with only two digits on it.

That, too, had a lot to do with my inner child. Its simple need to live in peace was ignored by every single client and their need for quarrelling.

But at that moment, I'd have offered to relitigate these cases I had so childishly wrecked pro bono if it meant Boris was back in his cell. I walked on.

On the floor between my office and the preschool was where Sasha lived. I mentally went on down to the preschool's door.

Despite my annoying cases in recent months, it'd been immensely fulfilling to leave my apartment and only have to walk down one storey to my own law firm every morning. And if I felt like it, I could go down two more sets of stairs to my daughter's preschool whenever I wanted. And now that would all be over?

Taking over the preschool had been one of the first and best decisions I'd made for Dragan's crew after his death. Not only because I needed a preschool spot for my daughter. Preschool spots were also an unbeatable way to develop crucial dependencies. The preschool's allocation of spots was therefore based on one very objective criterion: the best interests.

If the child's parents could benefit my interests, the child would get a spot.

If the child's parents could harm my interests, they were given a priority spot.

If the child's parents *wanted* to harm my interests, the child would unfortunately lose their spot. But so far that hadn't happened once.

Taking over the preschool with some gangsters and running it was one thing. It was something else to be a preschooler's father. And I was very happy in that role. I loved watching my little girl take ever bigger steps into a wonderful world within the preschool's safe space. In order to support her as much as possible, I'd stood for election to the parents' committee of the Nemo group two weeks earlier. Together with a very attractive representative, Laura, Max's mum. To underline my paternal commitment, I'd even invited all the groups' parent reps to my apartment for an initial meeting tonight.

Tonight, of all nights. But tonight was a lifetime away. My thoughts slipped back into the negative. I tried to concentrate on my positive mental walk-through, but I'd almost reached the end of it anyway.

One floor below the preschool were the extensive cellar spaces, a few of which had recently become vacant.

Everything I'd just mentally walked through would suddenly crumble when Boris revealed to his crew that I'd been keeping him imprisoned for months. If I hadn't renounced violence, I could've slapped myself for not being a more violent person, for not killing Boris immediately.

At that moment, I heard a clinking through my open balcony doors. It wasn't quite as loud as the sound of the drunks in the park throwing bottles at the stone slabs lining the sandpit. Instead, it was slightly muffled, like when someone is being deliberately quiet and wraps a stone in a woollen blanket before they smash the window of a preschool office.

I opened my eyes. My mindfulness practice had achieved one thing: my fear was gone. Now I was just angry. And a little voice inside me screamed, '*Tapsi!*'

10

Creativity

Your inner child is an inexhaustible natural source of creativity. When you were a child, you could use your imagination without cares or limits. At some stage on your way to adulthood, you have ousted your creative potential from your consciousness. But all that talent is still present in your inner child. Use it!

Joschka Breitner, *Parenting Your Inner Child*

Tapsi was a small cat that I'd secretly fed for a few weeks when I was six years old. She was a year old at most, and had pitch-black fur with some white spots on her paws. She'd showed up one day in the garden behind our apartment building, and we became friends. I started feeding her and set up a little nook for her in the cellar. For weeks, we played together every day. Until my father found out and scared her away. According to the building's rules, no cats were allowed. My father removed the little food bowls and took the cellar key away from me. I heard Tapsi meowing a few more nights, then she was gone. 'Your needs don't count' – the core belief my parents had painfully taught me over and over again. It was therefore quite clear to me what my inner child was trying to tell me by calling for Tapsi. It was angry because someone had poked that bruise on its soul again. Against our will, this someone had driven out a creature we were secretly keeping in our cellar.

Boris's disappearance had frightened me, but it had infuriated my inner child.

This was only day three of our first real week of partnership. But one thing was certain: my inner child and I would tackle the Boris problem together.

Over the last few weeks, I had learned to take my inner child's needs seriously. I had learned to enter into a dialogue – and I do mean that literally.

Breitner had advised me to choose a symbolic, external representation of my inner child. I'd chosen a small stuffed animal, a pink parrot toy I'd bought for my daughter a few months earlier. Thanks to its internal audio recorder, this stuffed animal could repeat anything you told it in an absurdly high voice. It comfortably fitted any jacket pocket. As the voice recorder had broken soon after I bought it, however, I'd never actually given it to Emily. But I liked it and kept it in a box of miscellaneous stuff. By now, the battery was flat. In search of an avatar for my inner child, I'd brought it out again.

Now I took it everywhere, securely secreted in one of my pockets. Whenever I was alone with my inner child, I'd take out the bird and talk to it. When I was on the go, just touching the bird in my pocket already helped boost the connection to my inner child. Now, too, I took the defective parrot out of my jacket pocket, sat down on the sofa and placed it on the steamer trunk in front of me. I collected myself, despite the threatening atmosphere, so I'd be able to hear my inner child's concerns openly, lovingly and thoughtfully. Breitner had provided clear guidelines:

Communicating with your inner child can be easy. Ask how it is doing. Concentrate on listening. Don't judge what you hear. Often you and your inner child will already feel better once you openly express your needs and concerns to each other. With a little trust, you can work together and meet many of your seemingly divergent needs.

By now, I'd been convinced of the usefulness of these conversations, and my inner child and I had formed the smallest possible support group.

I took a deep breath. Felt my breath inside me. Breathed out. And started talking to my inner child.

'How are you?'

Immediately, a clear, bright, innocent voice rang out. I'd gotten to know this voice very well in recent weeks, but it had never sounded this upset.

'I'm angry! No one has the right to take something from us that we want to keep.'

'Us' and 'we'. That was good, especially during this partnership week. And I definitely preferred the raging anger of my inner child over the crippling fear that I'd managed to contain for the time being. Over the past few weeks, I'd come to realise that I wanted to respond to my inner child's needs in the way I'd always wished my own parents had. Meaning completely differently.

My parents would have told my inner child, *'Keeping living creatures in the cellar is nonsense. As if we didn't have enough on our plate already. What you want, what you need doesn't matter. What is more, it's also expressly prohibited by our landlord.'*

This hadn't been effective when I was small, nor would it be now. So, I responded to my inner child very differently than my parents would've done:

'I promise we'll find out who freed Boris. We'll get Boris back. And we'll hold whoever took him from us accountable.'

How, I didn't know. And I was afraid, not entirely unfoundedly, that I'd be made to pay for Boris's imprisonment very shortly. But mentioning that to an already emotional inner child would certainly be counterproductive. I preferred focusing on my inner child's needs.

'What else is bothering you?'

'*Please make sure the guy who took Boris doesn't hurt us.*'

How about that? My inner child was a little scared too. In this respect, we needed the same thing. We could work together to carry it off.

'I'll do everything I can to make sure nothing happens to us. How about the two of us make up a story to tell Walter so he can protect us?'

'*Why do we have to make it up? Why don't we tell it like it is?*'

To have lying be the first thing you teach your inner child isn't exactly educationally sound. But sometimes real-world circumstances take precedence over pedagogical standards. I could at least try to package our need to lie more appealingly.

'We have to make up a story, because . . . because Boris is a bit like Tapsi. And Walter is an adult, just like my father. If Walter finds out we kept Boris in the cellar, I'll get into trouble with Walter – just like we did with my father over Tapsi.'

That made sense.

'*So if we can't tell Walter about Boris's disappearance, what reason do we give him?*'

Now I could be frank.

'I have no idea.'

'*Then let me help.*'

I had an inner child. And it wanted to help. Both things I'd have considered unthinkable six weeks earlier. And so my inner child and I faced our first task as a team, as Breitner had asked me to do.

First of all, we needed a creative story we could tell Walter. Breitner and I had talked in great detail about the inner child as a wellspring of creativity. I went to look for my copy of *Parenting Your Inner Child.* It was still in the newsprint tote I'd left on the dining table. I pulled out the book and flipped to the relevant chapter. I soon found the section I had in mind.

When you were a child, your creativity was boundless. You were able to turn a bed into a pirate ship, speak the language of elephants through an empty toilet-roll tube or invent the silliest justification for why a shoe on the rug was making it impossible for you to fall asleep. All you needed was a bed, a cardboard tube, or a shoe. At some point, adults – usually your parents – explained that beds are not ships, 'Elephant' is not a language and shoes are no obstacle to sleep. As you grew up, you unlearned how to create an entire universe around a single object. But your inner child still has this ability. It only needs to be reawakened.

Breitner had shown me some exercises I had worked through over the past few weeks, thus making a smooth transition from an adult sense of duty to a growing childlike sense of joy. At his instruction, I had engaged my inner child in creative games twice a week for at least half an hour at a time. The exercises were very simple. I would sit down on the floor in a random room in my apartment, the parrot toy placed symbolically beside me. My inner child and I were now tasked to use only objects within a 2-metre radius to immerse ourselves in a world of make-believe. My inner child and I had already visited a zoo made from socks – that time I happened to be sitting in front of the wardrobe. We'd gone on a safari through the cleaning cabinet and flown through space on interstellar saucepan-ships. It had all worked wonderfully, bringing my inner child and me closer, and rekindling my love for creative play. Why shouldn't it work in my current conundrum?

I put down the handbook and looked around.

Which object within a 2-metre radius could provide the basis for a plausible story I could tell Walter about why I needed personal protection?

My eyes didn't have to wander far. I immediately spotted the newsprint tote with the year-old headline: 'WHERE IS THE GOLDEN CHILD?'

I picked up the tote and read the article. It was about a statue of the most famous child in the world, Baby Jesus. The golden statue had topped the dome of a monastery church near Frankfurt along with one of his mother, Mary. Until one night they were ripped from the roof in a helicopter's cargo sling and ascended to the heavens. Twenty-four kilos of pure gold. The case had even garnered media attention abroad. The stolen helicopter was found a few days later, along with the DNA and fingerprints of convicted criminals that the police had on file. They were part of a convoluted clan that was rather the opposite of a traditional Scandinavian family unit. Despite that, one creative reporter had dubbed the members of this highly criminal brood 'the Holgerssons'. This had little basis in fact, but that lack of facts also prevented the reporter from putting himself in a vulnerable position. The extended family got its official nickname.

In and of themselves, the Holgerssons were very tolerant. At least tolerant enough to accept social-security benefits from the state as a gesture of goodwill, though they otherwise completely rejected its laws. This ensured that all four and a half thousand (give or take) members of the Holgersson family felt at home in pretty much every major city in Germany.

The article on the tote only dealt with the fingerprints and DNA evidence that individual Holgerssons had left behind in the helicopter with which they'd kidnapped the solid-gold Madonna and Child.

The Holgerssons that the police had on file were arrested soon enough, but they'd been silent ever since. There was no trace of the Baby Jesus.

What could my inner child and I make out of this? What fantastic tale could we spin that would explain why I desperately needed personal protection? I felt the creativity of my inner child take over. It elaborated on the newspaper story, first with a thin thread, which then became thicker and thicker. All of a sudden, it had braided a creative connection between the article and me being in mortal danger that looked both sound and sturdy. At least sturdy enough for a call to Walter. I thanked my inner child, put the parrot toy in my dressing-gown pocket and picked up my phone.

Walter answered after the second ring. Despite the early hour, he sounded wide awake.

'Björn. Sasha already told me that you're in danger. What happened?'

While my inner child specialised in making up creative stories, as a lawyer I specialised in selling lies. I'd pretty successfully briefed dozens of clients on how to tell the perfect lie. A lie should always be based on a verifiable truth. That truth was in the year-old newspaper.

'You remember the golden Jesus statue that was stolen off that church dome?'

'The Holgerssons? That helicopter job?'

'Exactly.'

'What does that have to do with you? That was over a year ago. The statue never resurfaced.'

Next, you awaken the other person's interest in learning a heretofore unknown part of the truth.

'Right. At least, nothing was ever found at any of the Holgerssons'. And since this morning, I know why.'

Walter's interest had been piqued. 'Go on.'

At this point, you can start lying to your heart's content. As the made-up part cannot be verified, the only yardstick left is the familiar truth. And the story that my inner child had made up was entirely unverifiable.

'Dragan just told me that Boris showed him a photo of the stolen statue last night.'

As a bonus, this created further confirmation that

Dragan and Boris were alive and well. Probably on a farm somewhere.

'What does Boris have to do with this? He's got no connection to the Holgerssons.'

Et voilà! Unverifiable fictitious elements usually aren't questioned but integrated into known facts instead. From this point on, my inner child and I could spin fairy tales.

'Now, hold tight. Boris had an agreement with the Holgerssons. Precisely because there is no connection between the two, Boris agreed to hide the statue for a year until the whole thing blew over. That term ended yesterday.'

This was the point where the other person either shook their head and walked away or bought into the story.

'And Boris isn't there to stick to the deal,' Walter yes-and-ed my improvisation. With that, he psychologically landed in the middle of my made-up story.

'Not only that,' I asserted. 'Boris told Dragan – rather drunkenly, at this point – that the golden statue was his nest egg. He never intended to return it to the Holgerssons. And in that respect, nothing has changed.'

A lie is like a wedding vow. It doesn't have to last forever. Only until one of the two parties dies. If Boris died first, it must've been his lie. If I died first, having lied would be the least of my problems.

The Holgerssons lie now had one very decisive advantage: Walter believed it.

'The Holgerssons must be rather angry,' Walter concluded.

'Indeed. It's no secret that Boris has disappeared and that I'm the lawyer minding his affairs. With Boris in hiding, the Holgerssons can't take their anger out on him – but I'm right here. And just fifteen minutes ago, there was a violent break-in at my building. Someone tried to get in through the preschool. Right in time for the deadline.'

'Holy. Fuckin'. Shite.'

To wrap up the well-packaged lie with a fancy bow, give the person you're lying to VIP status.

'Please keep this very much to yourself. Dragan found all this out yesterday. I have no idea which of Boris's people is involved. Only me, you and Dragan know about this incident. Plus Sasha, of course, and he's probably in mortal danger too. After all, he lives in the same building. This shouldn't go beyond that group of people.'

'Of course. You can rely on me. I've already sent out personal security teams. Also for Katharina and Emily.'

'Please keep theirs as discreet as possible. There's no need for Katharina and Emily to find out about all this.' Then I spontaneously had another thought. 'It might make sense to have Boris's people inconspicuously shadowed, to see if anyone approaches them.' Boris, for example.

'Sure. Will do.'

For a while, there wouldn't be any further questions. 'Thanks. Talk soon.'

There's a crucial difference between the stories children make up on idle afternoons and the lies adults tell. When the afternoon's playtime is up, a child's made-up story has no consequences. It's different with adults' lies. A good lie can get you anywhere. The question soon to arise for me and my inner child was: How do we come back from it?

II

Bad Bank

Economically speaking, your inner child is your soul's 'bad bank'. Because you store all your negative emotions in it, the rest of your mind ends up with a positive balance.

Joschka Breitner, *Parenting Your Inner Child*

I quickly showered, got dressed, put the parrot toy in my pocket and went downstairs. As I left my apartment, a text came in from Walter. The security teams were in position. That was a relief. Barely fifteen minutes had passed since Sasha's call. It was almost 6.30 a.m.

The ground-floor preschool didn't have a separate entrance and, like the other apartments, was connected to the main staircase. At the height of the building's front-door lock, the solid oak was chipped. Like someone had wedged a crowbar in there. I opened the door. Fresh morning air streamed into the stairwell. A patrol car was already parked outside. The police's quick response was certainly due to the fact that the toddler son of the local commissioner responsible for organised crime was in our preschool. He'd been given a priority 'best interests' spot.

I stepped outside. The window of the preschool's administrative office was on my left. Unlike the cellar windows below, this one wasn't barred. It *was* smashed. Both the window frame and the door were coated with fingerprint powder. So, forensics were already here too.

I went back in and entered the preschool. The entrance area was empty. To the right was Sasha's office, the one with the broken window. It looked ransacked. Paper all over the place. The rest of the preschool, however, looked undisturbed and peaceful as always. From the Nemo group's room, I heard the voices of two adults. One belonged to Sasha, the other was Peter Egmann's. Peter was a friend from my student days – and the commissioner who'd generously exchanged his investigation into Dragan's disappearance for a preschool spot.

'. . . don't think we'll be able to identify the perpetrators quickly,' he was just saying to Sasha.

'Well, the damage seems to be limited,' I said as I walked up to them.

'Hi Björn,' Sasha greeted me. 'Yeah, these guys only seem to have mucked up the office.'

Peter added: 'It looks like they first tried to prise open the outside door with a crowbar. That didn't work. So then the window was smashed and the office ransacked. Since the office door was locked from the outside, the perpetrator or perpetrators must've lost interest and left without entering the rest of the preschool.'

'Is anything missing?' I feigned interest.

Sasha already knew the answer: 'The petty cash box, of course. About fifty euros.'

'Who would *do* something like this?' I improv-ed like a pro.

'There are three options,' said Peter, the only one of us who didn't need to improvise. 'One, they were professional burglars. This is supported by the marks on the front door. But this theory is at odds with what happened in the preschool and the fact the break-in was aborted. The second possibility is that they were junkies. They often carry a crowbar and are usually stupid enough to forget to bring it in and then give up because they can't get through a thin locked door they could've kicked open. This is supported by the fact that only the petty cash is missing and the computer is still here. Yet this is at odds with the fact that the perps obviously wore gloves. The third option is vandalism. That one is at odds with their use of a crowbar and gloves.'

Interesting what scenarios an experienced policeman could derive from just a few traces. A fourth scenario, a faked break-in, obviously hadn't occurred to him.

But my inner child wanted to add a fifth scenario to the mix.

'*Maybe it was the drunks from the park.*'

I often needed to mindfully breathe away my anger over those drunks from the park. Except for that time with the ice cube, which had clearly been my inner child's doing. My inner child hated those drunks from the bottom of its heart. Permanently. And that was as understandable as it was justified. It was only a child anyway. In recent weeks, I'd realised that it wasn't me who always got triggered by these drunks' behaviour, but my inner child. In that light, my inner child didn't care that the drunks from the park couldn't have been behind the burglary, since Sasha and I had faked it. To steady my inner child, I stuck my hand in my pocket and stroked the parrot toy.

Because of our partnership week, however, I didn't want to ignore its needs either.

Since I had commissioned the fake burglary myself, I'd have found it morally reprehensible if, against my better knowledge, I accused someone else of the crime. So, I found another way.

'Sasha thought it might've been the guys from the park across the street,' I remarked. This was even true, insofar as Sasha had brought up this theory earlier, against his own better knowledge.

'There's no indication of that,' Peter explained to me. 'The mere fact that people get up to no good there doesn't justify suspecting them of burglary.'

'You don't want to follow up on this?'

'We have to conserve our resources.'

I was as dissatisfied with this answer as my inner child was. The fact that the police suffered from an acute staff shortage didn't justify ignoring a suspicion that wasn't completely unlikely.

'And do you think the preschool is in any danger?' I asked Peter.

'This matter is over. In all three possible scenarios, the perps won't try again. I think the preschool can open up again tomorrow, once the glazier and the cleaning crew have been in. Maybe consider barring the windows on the ground floor.'

Self-imprisonment, perhaps a sensible solution to Germany's crime rate. Of course, with the money you'd be paying to bar all the ground-floor windows in the country, you could hire enough cops to cover the same ground and *catch* the criminals.

'Thank you for that tip. And thank you for getting your people here so quickly,' I said to Peter, who was turning to leave.

'Don't mention it. After all, it's also about my son's safety.'

When Sasha and I were alone, I took in the office's entirely credible chaos.

'Well done,' I commended Sasha.

'Thank you very much. I guess I can clean this all up again now?'

'I'll help. And by the way – great that you also made it look like these guys tried to break down the front door first. Where'd you get the crowbar?'

'I didn't have a crowbar.'

I raised my eyebrows.

'The front door really was violently forced open.'

'So why does Peter think the burglars failed to?'

'Because the lock was put back in after.'

'By you?'

'No, by whoever freed Boris.'

I suddenly felt ice cold. Of course, I should've known that whoever had taken Boris out of the cellar must've been inside the building. But only now did I realise how close they'd gotten to me. And to Sasha too. After all, we only lived upstairs, the apartments' doors our sole protection. Why hadn't they simply exacted retribution and killed us last night? And why would anyone force open the front door, free Boris and then fix the door again? None of it made any sense.

Meanwhile, the first educators were arriving. Though Sasha had arranged for all parents to be informed via WhatsApp that the preschool would be closed for the day, he wanted an emergency staff on site just in case. He briefly explained the situation to the ladies and asked them to call a glazier and have the broken window replaced. In the meantime, I went back to my apartment and called Walter again.

'Thanks for sending the security teams,' I said. 'Really makes me feel safer.'

'Don't mention it.'

'Any news from Boris's crew?' I asked as casually as I could.

'We're currently shadowing four of his officers. Nothing stands out so far.'

'Which means?'

'Let me see, I always get my teams' status updates via WhatsApp . . . OK, so one of them is walking his dog. One of them locked up his club a few minutes ago and went straight home. One is fucking his neighbour's wife, and the fourth is on his way to a court date.'

This was as reassuring as it was surprising. If Boris had made contact with his crew, his management team wouldn't be quietly going about their day-to-day business. This gave Sasha and me at least a little time. I thanked Walter and hung up.

Just then, Katharina called. She'd also read the preschool's WhatsApp and got right to the point.

'Can you take Emily today?'

I suppressed my need for a wife who'd first ask how I was feeling about the fact that my building had been broken into. Not to mention the need for a wife I could've told that the burglary was only a front and that I was actually fearing for my life.

But I couldn't change my wife; I could only change my attitude towards my wife.

And the wife on the phone didn't care about either. She preferred to address her own needs first and foremost.

'Tomorrow is my first day back at work, and I'm meeting a colleague for lunch this afternoon. I'd hate to have to cancel because the preschool can't get its shit together.'

'Someone tried to break in. The police were here. We have to clean up a bit first, then . . .'

'I *know* it's been broken into. Otherwise, I wouldn't have this conflict with my appointment. So, can you pick up Emily?'

Of course I could – if I wasn't dead by then. But I couldn't tell Katharina that either. After all, this wasn't about my life for Katharina. She was all about power. Even if it was only about my schedule. I didn't want Emily to be mixed up in these little power plays. I'd pick her up. As long as Walter's people were guarding us, Emily was equally safe or unsafe with me as she'd be with Katharina. And if my life *was* about to end, then I wanted to spend as much of that time as possible with my beloved daughter. Maybe it'd even be good to surrender to the small problems of everyday life. If anyone should trample all over my life, better my wife than Boris.

'Yes. I'll push on here and call you when I'm done.'

'I have to leave here by noon at the latest.'

'Sure, I . . .'

Katharina had already hung up. My needs didn't count.

The doorbell rang. Through the peephole, I saw Sasha. I opened the door.

'Come on in. Coffee?'

'Yes, please.'

We went into the kitchen, and I made Sasha a Nespresso. I took the aluminium pod out of the cupboard, put it in the machine and tossed the old ones in the rubbish. Oh, to go back to the time when the ecological question of whether I should go back to filter coffee was my biggest quandary.

'Everyone seems to have bought the burglary, right?' I asked.

'It all went smoothly. A few parents had to make alternative arrangements. But they all preferred that over dropping their kids off at the scene of a crime.'

Katharina seemed to be the only parent who felt differently.

'I don't want to put a single child in danger over Boris,' Sasha emphasised. 'Not today, not ever.'

I nodded. 'If need be, we'll come up with another excuse tomorrow.'

'What did you end up telling Walter?'

I told Sasha my story about the Holgerssons. He found it creative enough to secure us at least a few days of protection without follow-up questions.

'How did you come up with *that*?'

'I've held on to my childlike creativity,' I said, which was as bland as it was true.

'Is Walter also shadowing Boris's people?' Sasha asked as I passed him his Nespresso.

'Yes. So far, none of his officers have displayed even the least unusual behaviour. If Boris had contacted them, they'd be fuming.'

Sasha raised his eyebrows. 'But how can that be? Why would Boris flee the cellar but not check in with his people?'

'That's exactly what's puzzling me. Just like the fact that they repaired the front door. Are you sure the lock on Boris's cell was cracked from the outside and not somehow ripped out of its bracket from inside?'

Sasha's eyes widened. 'You haven't been down yet?'

I stopped short. I'd simply not had the time. Sasha was right. The first thing I needed to do was examine the scene myself.

12

Minimalism

A fear of loss usually dissolves once you have nothing really left to lose. This can be a liberating experience. You will be amazed at how little a pure life actually requires.

Joschka Breitner, *Parenting Your Inner Child*

Our building had a vaulted cellar with many interconnected rooms. It was the type of place that, if tidied and renovated, could've been turned into a rustic wine bar. The foremost, largest room served as the preschool's storage space: wooden benches and tables, playground equipment and paddling pools. In one corner, a pink plastic playhouse now led a shadowy existence, a pedal car randomly propped up against its door.

Out of this front room, a corridor ran the full length of the building, offering access to individual brick storage compartments for each of the building's three apartments. The door at the end of the corridor led to the boiler room, which was non-standard. For one, because it also provided access to two rooms beyond. For another, it didn't look it.

In the 1980s, the building had belonged to a man stuck in the then-dominant doomsday triangle of nuclear war, ozone depletion and forest dieback. He was firmly convinced that neither international negotiations nor technological advances would solve these problems within ten years. Opting to act locally instead, he dug a survival bunker under his garden. Although the original purpose for these two additional spaces had so far proven premature, it had one decisive advantage for Sasha and me: these rooms weren't on any official blueprint.

Against all expectations, the world hadn't ended yet. But the bunker was still accessible via the boiler room. Which made it the perfect illegal digs for an unplanned guest. Yesterday's panic turned out to be today's prison.

The legal boiler room had long been home to a by-now-outdated oil heating system, a huge oil tank and an old Ikea cabinet. For environmental reasons, I would've liked to modernise the heating system. At Dragan's expense. The reason I hadn't yet was behind the Ikea cabinet. The cabinet covered the door to the unlicensed bunker rooms. Sasha, who was skilled at DIY, had provided the cabinet with invisible wheels and a hinge. The cabinet and its contents thus functioned as a false front. For a fifteen-minute bit of heater maintenance in our presence, this was camouflage enough. For a contractor renewing the entire system, it would've quickly become clear that something about this cellar was off.

But now, the cabinet was in ruins in front of the door it was supposed to cover up.

The opened door behind it had a story all its own. It came from a real prison, part of the first cell Dragan had ever stayed in overnight. It had a hatch through which you could pass food, have conversations or handcuff the occupant. That prison had closed a few years ago, its inventory auctioned off. Dragan had purchased the door for nostalgic reasons, storing it in the cellar of his old building. While planning Boris's prison, Sasha and I had chanced across it and decided that Dragan's first prison door should become Boris's last. Beautiful symbolism, though it had sadly lost its power now its massive padlock lay cracked on the ground.

Sasha had set up Boris's cells quite cosily. In the back room were the bathroom facilities, in the front a bed, a table and two chairs. (The second chair was there to remind Boris he'd never receive a visitor again.) In general, however, we had tried to make his stay as positive as possible. If not for Boris, then at least for the rest of the world. We fed him a largely vegan diet. Boris had two pairs of jeans and two T-shirts of organic cotton, all of which we'd deliberately bought from an eco-friendly shop – no Bangladeshi seamstresses had been exploited. Whereas Boris used to cover at least a hundred kilometres a day in an S-Class luxury sedan, for the past six months he'd been moving from one cellar room to another on foot, entirely carbon-neutral. He also didn't need plastic bags for his shopping. In other words: thanks to us, Boris had the ecological footprint of a one-legged toddler wearing a stiletto heel. Turning someone from a globalised spendthrift into someone who consumed only local and seasonal products wasn't really that hard. All you had to do was lock them in a cellar.

We were still standing at the prison door, and I couldn't think of anything cleverer than to state the obvious: 'The door really was cracked open from the outside.'

'Yes. That's one thing. But have a look inside.'

The table lay in pieces on the floor. One chair had tipped over. Boris's water flask, a reusable carafe made of shatter-proof enamel, was in a puddle on the ground.

'Either Boris smashed all this up himself, or there was a struggle.'

'Correct,' Sasha noted. 'But why would Boris fight who-ever freed him?'

That really was strange. And after thoroughly inspecting both rooms, I found no indication of what might've happened down here.

Sasha, meanwhile, had reassembled the disassembled Ikea cabinet as best he could. We shut the prison door and rolled the cabinet back in front of it. This was the clear advantage of flat-pack furniture: it looked practically the same torn apart as put back together.

On my way out, I noticed the pink playhouse and the pedal car again. For some reason, it annoyed me. Whoever leaned that pedal car there had made it looked messy. Without much thought, I went over to put the pedal car back on its four wheels.

But when I picked it up, I heard a rustle. The door of the pink playhouse, which the pedal car had previously been blocking, suddenly opened. A pair of men's legs in jeans and socks came poking out. There was a man inside the playhouse.

I put the pedal car down and called Sasha over. 'Check this out.'

Sasha saw the two feet and pulled out a gun.

'You carry a weapon?'

'Just for work.'

'You're managing director of a preschool.'

'And today, my most violent pupil went missing. I thought a gun appropriate.'

We came closer to the playhouse. Sasha gave one of the

legs a kick. They didn't move. We couldn't see into the playhouse. The windows were closed, the inside was pitch black. When I looked over at Sasha, he pointedly eyed the roof of the playhouse. It was loosely laid on top. Each of us grabbed one side and then carefully lifted it down. There actually was a man inside. Bound with zip ties.

The man was not dead.

The man was Boris.

13

Childlike and Childish

Childlike denotes the age-appropriate behaviour of a child. Childish denotes the non-age-appropriate behaviour of an adult.

Joschka Breitner, *Parenting Your Inner Child*

The sound of the weight dropping off my shoulders because Boris was obviously not at liberty was muffled by the sudden buzz of the oversized question mark hovering overhead. What was this tied-up mobster doing unconscious in a pink princessy playhouse? Squeezed into the far-too-small plastic play structure, he was obviously asleep. Wearing his jeans and T-shirt, both a little too cold for this unheated part of the cellar. The only new additions to his wardrobe were the zip ties on his hands and feet. But they didn't keep him warm, just still.

Only six months earlier, Boris had been a bear of a man. Large, muscular, hairy, with a deep sunbed tan. Spending so much time in a cellar prison without daylight can change a person. We were faced with a man who looked more like a polar bear starving on a lone ice floe. Boris had lost a massive amount of weight; he looked gaunt. Although his current location didn't allow him to unfold to his full size, he had already started looking more and more stooped in recent weeks. His once-full head of hair lacked bounce, and it'd turned almost completely grey. The fact that neither Sasha nor I had barber's skills, only a basic trimmer, didn't improve his look either. But I didn't feel guilty about that. If I hadn't trapped and captured Boris, my body would've looked even more transformed than his. Half a year ago, Boris would've killed me without hesitation. At least this way we were both alive. And Boris looked almost relaxed, lying there unconscious.

The profundity of his relaxation seemed to be related to something stuck in his left arm. An IV tube connected the crook of his elbow to a small box hooked to the playhouse's window frame. In the box was an IV bag. My confusion grew.

Almost mechanically I started stroking the parrot toy in my pocket to calm down the childlike voice inside me that wouldn't stop cheering '*Tapsi!*'

Sasha seemed as perplexed as I was. After we'd wordlessly gathered ourselves for a minute, he put his gun away. We got closer to Boris. I first checked his pulse: weak, but there. Sasha looked more closely at the box connected to the IV. It had a label.

'What's in there?' I asked.

'It says "Midazolam",' Sasha said.

'And what is that?'

'No idea. I studied environmental engineering.'

'Whatever it is, it seems to be responsible for Boris's condition. We should disconnect it.'

'Perhaps not in the part of the cellar everyone has access to, though.'

Sasha was right. We put the box on Boris's stomach, then I grabbed his legs and pulled him out of the playhouse. Sasha took his arms, and together we carried him back to his cell and laid him on the bed. Sasha cut the zip ties with a knife.

Boris didn't appear to have any external injuries. His breathing was stable and regular. The cannula in his left elbow was surrounded by four apparently failed attempts to tap a vein.

'Those jabs seem rather careless,' Sasha noted. 'Looks like Boris didn't have private insurance.'

'On the plus side, he got an appointment without even asking. Immediately, with whomever.'

We pulled the cannula out of Boris's arm.

I took a closer look at the IV bag inside the box. It was still half full. All my life I'd wondered what the point had been of taking Latin at school. This was the first time I was able to apply my arcane knowledge.

'In small print, the midazolam bag also says "DORMICUM".'

'Which means what?'

'*Dormire* means "to sleep". The stuff in there has to be a sedative, and the box seems to regulate the dosage. Apparently, someone wanted to time exactly how long Boris would sleep.'

'*Sweet dreams, Tapsi!*' I heard my inner child whisper contentedly.

For the time being, my inner child was no longer angry and I was no longer afraid. Boris was back in his cell. Along with quite a few question marks.

'Do we now have one less problem or one more?' Sasha asked.

I shrugged and tried to sum up the positives. 'Well, the good news is that we're probably not going to die today. Boris himself poses no danger to us.'

'But maybe whoever freed him does.'

'I have no idea. Whoever got Boris out of the cellar was obviously not a friend of his. Otherwise, they would've taken him along, not left him sedated in a princessy playhouse.'

Sasha folded his hands behind his head, probably to enhance his concentration. 'All right,' he said, 'let's approach this systematically. What do we know?'

'Someone obviously found out that we're keeping a prisoner here,' I replied.

Sasha nodded. 'They took him out of his cell. Yet they didn't free him. They also didn't notify the cops. They drugged him, zip-tied him and left him in a playhouse.'

'They didn't just leave him there. They *hid* him,' I added. 'They even repaired the front-door lock after cracking it.'

'Was that supposed to send a message?'

I considered his question. 'More like three messages,' I finally said. 'First, *I know your secret*. Second, *I'm toying with you*. And third, *for the time being, this is nobody's business but mine and yours*. That's why they fudged the burglary marks on the door.'

'Quite childlike, no? Playing with us like that?' Sasha noted.

'Childish,' I automatically corrected. 'Anyone who plays with organised criminals like this is obviously not averse to taking big risks.'

'Maybe they didn't know who he really is.' Sasha pointed to the sleeping Boris. A string of drool ran from the corner of his mouth. I felt it was absurd that someone would tie up and drug Boris without knowing who he was.

'You mean that someone happened to be carrying a sedative, a bolt cutter, zip ties and a crowbar,' I remarked, 'and then happened to find a trapped Russian in the cellar of the building that houses a gang lawyer, a former gang driver and a gang-operated kindergarten. And then dragged him to a pink playhouse . . . Maybe we should check all the kids to see if any of them are some kind of hobgoblin.'

Sasha made a sheepish face. 'Got it. Whatever, was just an idea.'

I tried to rationalise the situation.

'Let's say whoever drugged Boris knows who Boris is and how he's connected to us. If so, they obviously wanted us to think that Boris was missing. That we'd go looking for him. That we'd panic.'

'But they timed Boris's sedation.' Sasha started pacing up and down the small space. 'If Boris was sedated at some point last night, and the bag is only half empty now, then he certainly wouldn't have been expected to wake up until this evening. If we hadn't found Boris by then, he certainly would've started screaming – and by that time, only us two would be around to hear him.'

'Which in turn means that this guy knows who's in this building and when,' I continued Sasha's thought.

'That, too, is a message.'

'So – who out there doesn't care how long we panic because Boris is gone?' I put forward.

'Someone who knows us and doesn't care about our needs,' Sasha summed up.

'*Ouch,*' cried my inner child. There it was again. Prodded in its 'your needs don't count' bruise. I kept my own anger at bay through conscious breathing and lovingly patted the parrot.

'All right.' I summed up. 'The person who freed Boris and put him in the playhouse is a ruthless egomaniac who doesn't care about our needs. Does that narrow down the list of possible perpetrators?'

'Not in the slightest.'

He was right. From Katharina to my clients, the drunks in the playground and Nils the waiter – that description applied to pretty much every person in my life. And only the waiter had an alibi.

But whoever this person was, they'd entered my life at an extremely unfavourable time. For them. Never again would I allow anyone to trample all over my needs or those of my inner child with impunity. Not in our first week of partnership. Thanks to Breitner, I had made a pact with my inner child.

14

Time Travel

Returning to your childhood should be like an unannounced visit from the council inspectors. It has to be unexpected; otherwise, all you see is what has been tarted up.

Joschka Breitner, *Parenting Your Inner Child*

Working out why I reacted so violently to the message 'your needs don't count' took some painful work with Breitner. It had been the second of my inner-child sessions.

Sitting opposite me, he was completely relaxed, whereas I was tense.

'Today we are going to take a journey into your past. Back to your childhood. So we can take a closer look at your relationship with your parents.'

'Good thing my parents are dead. Surprise visits always sent them into a panic,' I replied truthfully.

'This journey is not about your parents. It is about you and your perception of your childhood. This needs to be a surprise visit. Surprising to *you*. This way, you will not have any time to mentally tidy up your childhood beforehand. We want to see it exactly as it was.'

I was anxious to know more.

'Last time, we noticed that, when you were small, your parents instilled in you the core beliefs that "fun and games are stuff and nonsense" and "your needs don't count". Today, we will try to journey back to the first time you became aware of these beliefs and the associated injuries.'

Breitner gave me a kind look to see whether I understood.

'How's this supposed to work?' I asked cautiously.

'We will build a bridge from the feelings that arose during your freak-out up in the Alps as an adult to the feelings that arose when your needs were ignored in the Alps as a child, and then extend that bridge further back into your childhood. And that is how we will trace back to the time your parents' core beliefs first began to shape you. OK?'

I nodded.

'Then please close your eyes and put yourself back in the situation that led you to unbolt that gate behind the hut.'

I closed my eyes.

'Can you picture how it felt when your needs were ignored or discounted?'

My anger at the waiter was still so present in me that I could summon it easily. I nodded.

'Now, please travel back to that childhood holiday in the mountains when your need for Kaiserschmarrn was ignored. Did that feel the same?'

I travelled back, took stock of how I felt, and nodded.

'Next, please go further back. Is there some earlier time when you felt the same way because your needs were ignored?'

I travelled on and ran into Tapsi. And my father chasing her out of the cellar. A very childlike sadness started mixing into my anger. I told Breitner about the cat. And about feeling lost because the person who was supposed to protect me had ignored my needs.

'Was this moment with Tapsi the first time you felt this lost, or had you felt it before?'

'I . . . was already familiar with it. That's why it made me so sad. Because this was not the first time my parents had trampled all over my needs.'

'We are approaching our goal, but we are not quite there yet. Please go even further back. What first triggered these feelings of anger and sadness?'

I couldn't think of a time. Although . . . there *was* one very fuzzy memory. But I couldn't put a name to it. It was like trying to come up with the name of some primary-school classmate, and only being able to summon up a vague image of his face. The vague image from my early childhood was a scooter. Very faint. And it was a pale red. Why this image? I gave my thoughts free rein. The scooter was getting redder and redder. Slowly a memory took shape. And suddenly I was right back in my childhood.

I was five years old. It was July. Flaxen hair covered my little head. I was wearing short lederhosen and had scratches on both my knees. It'd been hot and dry for days. Back then, beautiful weather was simply called summer. This one promised to be the best ever.

Because as I stood there in my lederhosen, I had received the best gift of my life: a bright-red scooter. Misha, an older boy from the neighbourhood, had given it to me. As simple as that. He liked me. He'd gotten a Raleigh Chopper for his tenth birthday and now felt too grown-up to be riding a scooter. It was great: with white tyres, a metallic red frame, white handles and a real bell. By pressing down on the rear fender, you could brake on the rear wheel. But what kid needed a brake? This scooter was the Porsche of children's transportation. My parents would've *never* bought me this scooter. And this boy had just given it to me.

Back then, it was completely normal, even for a five-year-old, to spend hours playing outside with neighbourhood kids without any adult supervision. Back then, our fathers didn't have projects, but professions. Our mothers didn't have air fryers, but cooking pots. Both were reason enough to dispense with the now-customary 24/7 parental surveillance.

My father had studied law and was a civil servant working for the postal service. Nowadays, none of the Romanian freelance delivery workers racking up eighteen-hour days would believe that postal workers used to be civil servants. But my father used to be the deputy head of the local post office's human resources department. With a pension. My mother, who'd previously worked as a secretary, had given up her job when I was born. I honestly don't remember what she did all day while I spent my mornings at kindergarten and my afternoons with the other kids from the neighbourhood.

Anyway, when I showed up with the scooter that evening, exhausted and happy, my parents reacted with stunned dismay. Despite my protestations, they didn't believe the scooter had been a gift. It was not up for discussion. My father immediately dragged me and the scooter to the neighbours to return it. Though the boy's parents didn't know anything about the gift, once their son confirmed my story, they fully supported his decision.

'It's Misha's scooter,' they said. 'If he wants to give it away, that's fine. Enjoy!'

My father apologised. Not to me, for his distrust, but to Misha's parents, for bothering them.

The next few days, whenever I wanted to take the scooter outside, my parents told me to be careful. *Scooters like that are expensive.* They measured its value in money, I in joy.

Within three days, I was already the world scootering champion. I could drive with one hand. I could drive it hands-free. I could even ride it hands- and legs-free by jumping off the scooter while I wasn't touching the handlebar. The scooter would continue straight on. Until it eventually fell over.

Unfortunately, during one of these manoeuvres, it didn't. Instead, it crashed into the side door of a sky-blue 1963 Opel Kadett A parked on our street. Though the handlebar of the scooter was padded at both ends, the bell tore an almost 6-centimetre scratch into the paintwork. The scooter slammed onto the pavement, its bell now warped.

The Opel belonged to a neighbour who we children only knew as the Grump. A self-righteous, arch-Catholic maths teacher who reprimanded children at every opportunity. Back in the early 1980s, that was not yet reason enough to file a criminal complaint. In short: I was afraid of him and how he'd react. Frightened, I immediately told my mother what had happened.

'Is it bad?' I asked her. No, that's not right. When a child asks if something is bad, they're not really *asking*. They want to be told it's not. But my mother didn't take away my fear. Instead, she took the scooter and called my father. He didn't take away my fear either. Instead, he took the afternoon off.

He came home and assessed the damage to the car. Not the damage to my scooter.

He then walked me over to the Grump and forced me to tell him what had happened. If it hadn't been for my father, of this I am still sure, the neighbour would've slapped me. If it hadn't been for my father, however, the neighbour would also never have learned who scratched his car at all. His car door already had plenty of dents and scratches. But my own father, who sold our cars after exactly 100,000 kilometres in order to avoid the supposedly expensive repairs, now told the Grump, whose car had certainly racked up more than 300,000 kilometres, to please have the paintwork touched up and send him the bill.

I got a week's house arrest. My father confiscated my scooter and placed an ad in the newspaper, selling it for five Deutschmarks the next Saturday. This monetary gain was entirely disproportionate to my loss of joy. My parents kept the money as my contribution to the scratch repair. The cost of respraying the Opel was reportedly 180 Deutschmarks. For years, my parents claimed that my foolish exploits had ruined them.

'Looking back on it now, this scooter thing was probably the first time I actually felt my needs didn't count.'

And it was this realisation that would open my eyes when it came to almost all of my problems.

15

Parents

Your parents were not the best parents in the world.
They were merely the only parents in your world.

Joschka Breitner, *Parenting Your Inner Child*

'Do you have any idea why this scooter story is only coming back to you now?' Breitner enquired. 'What it might mean?'

I considered his question.

'Until now, I think I'd always understood this whole story to mean something completely different. For decades, it was proof my parents were decent, respectable.'

'I see. Can you explain why?'

'Sure. When a child comes home with a neighbour's scooter, it's only natural for decent parents to follow up with the neighbours. And for decent parents to remind their children of the monetary value of toys. And for a decent mother to inform a decent father when their child has done something naughty. And for that decent father to survey the damage and take responsibility for it. And to take his child along, so it learns from its mistakes. It's natural for a five-year-old child to be slowly introduced to compensating for any damage it might've caused. This view was wrong, though – why did I never consider how it had made *me* feel?'

Breitner took a sip of his tea.

'It is not that your view was wrong. To the contrary. This very rational view conformed to a basic survival principle. Every child is existentially dependent on being able to trust their parents. That is why almost every child claims to have the best parents in the world. Yet they are only the only parents it has. Realising this *hurts*, even decades later.'

The thought had never occurred to me before. It really was painful.

'How would you interpret your parents' behaviour today?'

I felt a fury rising inside me.

'My parents trampled all over my basic emotional needs. My need for closeness? *We won't help you – quite the opposite: we'll turn you in!* My need for freedom? *House arrest!* Joy? *We'll sell the scooter!*'

I could physically feel how the pinpricks of the scooter incident had perforated the soul of my flaxen-haired inner child; grazed knees were a joke in comparison. 'Someone gave you a scooter? Here's a badge that says, "You're a liar." The neighbours confirm your story? Here's a badge that says, "Even if you are telling the truth, we have to apologise for you!" Are you afraid of the Grump? We are too, here's a badge that says, "Our fear is more important than yours." And for all of it, here's a big badge with a big pin and a scooter-red inscription that says, "Your needs don't count!"'

Breitner looked at me sympathetically, waiting for me to say more. No more words came, but I could feel tears coming to my eyes. Tears that reflected a little five-year-old. Tears that didn't quite start flowing yet.

'Are you surprised that your inner child does not have any basic trust? What with all these injuries, I am surprised that your child does not cry and rage *more*.'

I'd finally figured out what had hurt my inner child so profoundly. And for the first time I joined my inner child in unrestrained sobbing. It felt incredible.

After this session, I could easily apply the 'your needs don't count' theory to all my problems, not only Nils. The clients who annoyed me, the drunks from the park across the street, Katharina's withdrawal of affection – all this behaviour showed me that my needs didn't matter to them. That they couldn't give a toss about the little blond kid with the skinned knees inside me. No wonder my inner child kept crying out in pain, and that the only way I could get his suffering under control was through my mindfulness practice. These miserable core beliefs of my parents shaped my relationship with the people around me to this day.

I felt infinitely grateful to Breitner for this painful realisation.

Since he didn't know about it, Breitner couldn't confirm that even my murdering Dragan could be attributed to the fact that my needs hadn't mattered to him either.

And what about Boris? How could my core beliefs explain that Boris was still alive? I felt the need to not murder any more people. So, I didn't kill Boris because I didn't feel the need to. Boris was still alive because I wanted him to be. Was letting Boris live ultimately a kind of protest against my parents? Or was this thing with Boris not about letting him live at all? Wasn't it really about *keeping* him?

I had a living being in my cellar that I could take care of. Just like Tapsi when I was a little boy. In the broadest sense, I had a prized possession. Like my scooter back then. The little boy I used to be had to give up the cat and the scooter. As an adult, I could keep Boris. Because nobody knew about him except for Sasha and me. Until last night. And whoever had freed Boris and then sedated him, they'd shown me and my inner child that they held the same power over Boris as my parents had over my cat and my scooter. This stranger and my parents had one thing in common: they didn't care about my needs, or the needs of the little kid in lederhosen who I'd once been and who still lived inside me.

Recognising the reason behind my problems was one thing. Using it to develop a strategy to heal my inner child was something entirely different. And Breitner taught me this in our next sessions.

And for the person who'd messed with Boris, that was exactly what would prove fatal.

16

Core Beliefs

Core beliefs can be understood as simple sentences by which your parents taught you values. Like all sentences, they can be hurtful. Like all sentences, they can also be rewritten. By you.

Joschka Breitner, *Parenting Your Inner Child*

In the cellar, standing at sleeping Boris's bedside, Sasha and I contemplated our next move. The house was secure. No one could come in or out unseen. Walter's people were making sure of that. There wasn't any danger of immediate revenge from Boris or his crew. That had given way to a diffuse threat from an unknown entity. At least this had won us some time. Time I would've liked to use for some deep breaths. But I couldn't. Thanks to my wife.

I'd first have to fulfil Katharina's need for me to take care of Emily so she could go and have lunch or something. So that *she* had time to *herself* – instead of *me* to *myself*. But at least I'd have Emily.

On the way, I could pick up a new lock for Boris's cell. For now, an emergency solution would have to do. Sasha would check in on the cellar at short intervals. As soon as Boris's sedation subsided, someone needed to be by his side to hear his story.

We put the table and chairs back in their proper places in Boris's two-room flat, secured his cell door with an old bicycle lock and went back upstairs.

In the entrance to the preschool, we met the glazier, there to put in the new window. He was holding an A5 envelope. When he saw us, he asked, 'Do you live here?'

'We run the preschool with the broken window,' Sasha replied. 'Glad you could make it.'

'Then this letter must be for you.'

The glazier gave Sasha the envelope. A used, padded envelope. Affixed to the front was a printed address sticker that said: 'TO THE RESIDENTS'. In the upper-right corner was a shred of a foreign stamp – on the left-most edge, you could still make out 'EOS'.

'Where did you get this?' I demanded.

'It was on the pavement out front. I need to get a few more things,' said the glazier, and he went back outside.

Sasha and I looked at each other. An anonymous letter? That didn't bode well.

Without another word, we withdrew to the empty Nemo classroom. There, Sasha ripped open the envelope. He took out its contents and placed them on the craft table.

There were three Polaroids of Boris asleep in the pink playhouse and one sheet of printed paper, which read:

Nice that you're shutting down the whole preschool only because I tidied up a little in the cellar. You have until the end of the week to kill your house guest. On Friday morning, Boris's head better be in a cardboard box on the wall of the park across the street, or another set of Polaroids will be in the hands of the police come Friday evening.

Sasha and I slumped very awkwardly into the much-too-small chairs. My inner child was the first to find their voice again.

'*We're* not *killing Tapsi!*'

I automatically put my hand in my pocket and petted the parrot toy. This also helped me recapture the ability to speak.

'We're being blackmailed . . . by some idiot who doesn't even think we're worth a new envelope.'

'The fact that this guy would openly do that tells us a lot already,' Sasha countered.

'What do you mean?' I asked.

'Leaving aside that sick stuff about the head . . . this tells us a great deal.'

Sasha was right. We couldn't change the fact that we were being blackmailed. But we could at least approach the issue rationally.

'Let's gather our first impressions then. You start.'

'So,' Sasha started, 'the first thing that strikes me is that there's no salutation, no greeting. And the tone is rather informal. Ergo: no manners. Whoever wrote this is a real lout.'

'I agree. Also, this guy is watching us. Otherwise, he wouldn't know the preschool is closed today.'

Sasha nodded. 'Maybe he even has a kid who goes here. Then he'd have gotten that information via WhatsApp this morning and dropped off the letter after.'

I suddenly had a thought. 'But he couldn't have known whether we'd already found Boris. That's why he included the pictures of Boris in the playhouse. He wanted to make sure we found him.' And when Sasha stayed silent, lost in thought, I added: 'Thirdly: they have contacts in Spain.'

'Where do you get that from?'

'The letters "EOS" on that stamp fragment. "Correos" is the Spanish postal service. He must've been out of neutral envelopes and grabbed a used one.'

'So we're looking for a disorganised lout with contacts in Spain who's watching us,' Sasha summed up.

I nodded. 'Now for what the note says. He wants us to kill Boris and cut off his head. That gives me three pieces of information. First of all, he knows who Boris is.'

'Secondly,' Sasha took over again, 'we know that he's twisted. Cutting off Boris's head and putting it on a wall in a box makes no sense unless he's a nut job with a penchant for violence.'

I saw things differently. Before his time in the cellar, Boris had led a very violent life. And in this overground existence, beheadings had played a not-insignificant role.

'You know the story of Boris's ex-wife?' I asked Sasha.

'Annastasia? The one who had an affair with Dragan? Of course.'

Boris and Dragan had been childhood friends and started their criminal careers together. They'd been inseparable. Until the day Dragan fucked Boris's wife. An insanely attractive former sex worker from one of their brothels. Boris found out, killed her, sawed off her head and nailed the torso to Dragan's door. This was the beginning of their hostilities, which Sasha and I had painstakingly ended by disappearing both Dragan and Boris.

'If telling us to chop off Boris's head is a reference to his ex, there could very well be something personal at play,' I summed up.

'Then we're looking for a lout with a relationship to both the preschool and Boris,' Sasha concluded.

Aside from Sasha and me, I couldn't think of anyone connected to both Boris and the preschool. And neither of us was a lout. I hadn't freed Boris. Neither, I felt, had Sasha.

'And thirdly – we shouldn't forget this – he wants to see us suffer. Otherwise, he wouldn't be setting this whole thing up as a game. Freeing Boris only to hide him, timing his sedation, sending us photos of his hiding place – those touches are all horrendously playful. Perhaps they noticed we're basically too humane to kill Boris. Or maybe they think we have a reason not to kill him. In any case, they want us to kill Boris against our will.'

There it was again. Pressure on the bruise my parents had left on my inner child's soul.

'And if we just do it?' Sasha asked.

'What?'

'Well, kill him.'

'*Are you crazy? We. Won't. Kill. Tapsi!*' a childlike voice cried from my soul.

'You're not serious.'

'Only a thought experiment. What happens if we kill Boris and leave his boxed-up head on a wall?'

Then my inner child will feel pretty screwed over, was the answer that came to me.

'We wanted to put an end to the killing,' was the answer I gave Sasha. 'It's like quitting smoking after New Year's Eve. That kind of resolution should only be broken voluntarily, if at all. Not out of peer pressure, and certainly not forced by some stranger. In addition, if we gave in to this idiot, the murder would leave us exposed to blackmail the rest of our lives. We have until Friday morning to find out who's behind this. We should use that time well.'

'And if we don't find out who's behind this?'

'I'll worry about that when the time comes. I prefer to live in the moment.'

Although this didn't completely convince Sasha, it did stop him from conducting further thought experiments about Boris's death.

Sasha and I agreed to try narrowing down the list of possible perpetrators from two sides: he wanted to check all the preschool's patrons for possible connections to Boris; I would check all Boris's contacts for connections to the preschool.

In any case, we'd reopen the preschool the next day. There was no longer any immediate danger. And it's not like we could explain the situation to the parents.

For now, we wanted to maintain the security teams' surveillance for as long as Walter bought my story about the golden child. Who knows, maybe the lookouts would catch the blackmailer.

Four days, until Friday, was a lot of time to sort out a problem. In the recent past, I had very mindfully eliminated more problems in much less time.

Yet two things had been different then. I knew who was behind my problems. And I hadn't yet renounced all murder.

On the plus side, back then I hadn't yet made contact with my inner child.

17

Armour

Without your support, your inner child will act like
the German Wehrmacht used to: either it attacks its
enemies and demolishes everything in the process;
or it retreats from its enemies. And demolishes
everything in the process.

Instead, make sure that you and your inner
child act like NATO: Don't attack anyone. But
if one of you is attacked, that attacker makes an
enemy of the both of you.

Joschka Breitner, *Parenting Your Inner Child*

After saying goodbye to Sasha, I thought back to the session when I'd told Breitner about the scooter.

My tears had done me good. I felt like I'd been released, freed from an almost four-decade burden. I'd recognised the first time my parents had violated my basic trust. And now I had an actual image of my inner child: a small, flaxen innocent with scratched-up knees poking out of his little lederhosen. Yet I was curious to find out what I could *do* with this.

'All right – now I know my inner child has been hurt. That it's right to be wary. I completely understand why it's so sensitive. How do I stop that? How can I protect my inner child?'

Breitner put down his teacup.

'Not so fast. First of all, your inner child already uses two different protective strategies when it is confronted with the message that its needs don't count.'

'Two?' I asked.

'Depending on the situation, it can put on two different suits of armour, like a brave little knight. One is offensive, the other defensive. Both are intended to prevent anyone from being able to poke its bruises. If someone tries to anyway, your inner child either attacks or withdraws. Yet both suits of armour constrict your inner child considerably.'

'I'm afraid that's too abstract for me. Could you be more specific?'

'OK. Let's get specific: back in the Alps, why did you not chuck your wife down the ravine?'

I was thrown off guard. 'Because . . . Why would I?'

'Well, if I've understood you correctly, your wife does not care about your need for affection.'

'That's true. But I won't be able to change that, not in this life anyway.'

'See? This is your defensive armour at work. If your wife ignores your needs, you withdraw in resignation. As a result, your need for affection goes unfulfilled. But by putting your needs on hold, you do ensure you are not hurt again.'

That sounded logical enough.

'And what about my offensive armour?'

'You felt like you could have strangled that waiter who did not care about your needs, and then he fell into a ravine. That is because your inner child was wearing its offensive armour. Your inner child might not have fulfilled your need for an alpine family idyll, but it did satisfy its own need for revenge.'

This visual metaphor helped me understand the principle.

'OK, fine. Wearing the defensive armour, I don't get any sex. Wearing the offensive, I don't get any Kaiserschmarrn. But what kind of conclusions can I draw from this?'

'What do *you* think?'

'Actually, my inner child could just take that armour off.'

'Exactly.'

'But who would protect my inner child?'

'What would happen if *you* protected it?'

'But how?'

'Show it that meeting its needs does not depend on the people standing in the way of these needs. That you, as an adult, can meet these needs regardless of whoever's in the way.'

Breitner noticed my forehead furrow with incomprehension. He explained his idea a little more precisely.

'You want physical affection? Your wife is not the only woman in the world. You want Kaiserschmarrn? That waiter and that hut are not the only ones in the world.'

'You want me to cheat on my wife?'

'You should stop cheating *yourself*. You have spent long enough believing your needs do not matter, because that is what your parents taught you. Your parents are dead. But you should live! Go outside. Meet all your childhood needs. If not for yourself, then at least for your inner child.'

I should meet my childhood needs. If not for me, then at least for my inner child. That sounded like a good mantra.

'How does that sound to you?'

'That sounds . . . good.'

'So overwrite the negative core beliefs of your past. Create positive new experiences for yourself and for your inner child.'

'Gladly. And how do I do that?'

'To start, do one small, simple task within the next hour: start communicating with your inner child. See if it has some dream that it never got to live out in real life. But one

159

you can now realise as an adult. And then meet that unmet need from your childhood yourself.'

And that's why, by the next session, I was the proud owner of a Land Rover Defender.

18

Childhood Needs

Meet your childhood needs yourself. If not for yourself, then at least for your inner child.

Joschka Breitner, *Parenting Your Inner Child*

After discovering that Sasha and I were being blackmailed, I drove over to Katharina's in a relatively relaxed state. After all, neither Emily nor Katharina nor I were in any acute danger. Earlier that morning, I'd been under the impression that I might only have a day to wrap up my entire life. Less than four hours later, I assumed I had at least until Friday. While this didn't put me in the highest of spirits, it did mean I could postpone my fear of the future for a few days. I called Katharina and confirmed that I'd pick Emily up shortly before noon so she could make her lunch date. On the way, I wanted to stop by a home improvement store to get a massive iron lock. A lock that couldn't be quietly cracked with a bolt cutter but would require at least a loud angle grinder. I notified Walter that my team should follow me and that Katharina's team should remain discreetly close to her and Emily until I reached them.

Just in case.

I left our building and went to my car, which was parked a few metres down the road. I got in and pulled the door shut. With the click of the lock, my already raised spirits lifted substantially. It wasn't about getting far away from a problem; a simple car door in between would do. *My* car door, which was attached to *my* car. The childhood dream I'd fulfilled on Breitner's advice. A used Land Rover Defender. With its eleven litres of diesel per hundred kilometres and Euro 2 emission standard, it wasn't exactly a city car for low-emission zones. Yet it also didn't have an electric battery with a carbon footprint of 17 tonnes of CO_2.

It was the exact car that little boy in lederhosen had always wanted.

And as an adult, I loved it too. I'd retained the childlike enthusiasm with which I could recognise it as a technological marvel. This machine gave me a sense of freedom, of home. The freedom to affordably travel distances that would've seemed impossibly futuristic to my great-grandparents. And in a safe space that felt like home to me. Like in my childhood bedroom, I could close the door and leave the world outside – though my old room had been smaller than my Defender. On top of that, my adult self could now freely drive this oversized children's room across a continent without border checkpoints. What a brilliant invention.

At the home improvement store, I quickly found what I was looking for. I might even have arrived at Katharina's early. Taking the ring road, I could have covered the distance from the store to the house we used to share in ten minutes. Unfortunately, love got in my way. Other people's love. Halfway between the store and Emily, I ran into some people who wanted to share their joy over a lifelong bond with not only a wedding, but with a wedding car procession too. On the ring road. Which meant blocking the way for all other drivers, whose traffic jam now served as a backdrop for the wedding photo.

Somehow, my fellow citizens' behaviour calmed my conscience. Obviously, I wasn't the only one who had a very close relationship with my car. The S-Class Mercedes from a well-known car rental company that had been honking and swerving in front of me for five hundred metres now came to a complete stop in the middle of the road, together with about ten other luxury-class vehicles from equally familiar rental companies. I involuntarily got a front-row seat to the ritual celebrating family and marriage that followed.

Neither I nor my inner child minded getting stuck in this traffic jam; to the contrary. It wasn't *my* need for punctuality that was being ignored here, it was Katharina's. Together with my inner child, I got to enjoy a whimsical spectacle we would otherwise only know about from indignant newspaper reports: a motorway being blocked by a wedding convoy.

About twenty gentlemen got out of the rental vehicles in front of us. They were all wearing suits that were either too short, too tight, too shiny or all of the above – hopefully also rentals. The women who emerged from the vehicles looked like they might've been rentals too, but unlike the limousines from which they emerged, their paintwork had the kinds of cracks and dents that would've made returning them tricky.

It had never been quite clear to me whether showing off the wide array of what you could afford to rent was a sign of wealth or poverty. For this ring-road blockade, however, none of that mattered. The bride and groom climbed up on the bonnet of their rental. The bride wore a red sash around her hips. The rest of the wedding party took up perches on the other vehicles. After a group photo and dozens of group selfies had been taken, two little boys jumped off the car roofs and blocked the already halted convoy until the groom's driver handed them some cash. While police sirens slowly made their way through the traffic jammed behind us, the wedding party peacefully climbed into their vehicles to celebrate what is commonly referred to as the happiest day in a couple's lives. The road to my own wife was clear again.

Soon, Katharina would prove to me how much the spark between spouses fades the further they get from their wedding day. Due to the traffic delay, I arrived outside the door of our formerly shared house not at half past eleven, but at five minutes past half past eleven. Katharina opened the door stony-faced, refused a hug and instead greeted me thus: 'Now here I was thinking I could rely on you for *once* . . .'

For a lunch meeting with a colleague, Katharina had chosen a strikingly attractive outfit. High-heeled shoes, short skirt, tights that accentuated her gorgeous legs. The silk blouse perfectly matched the hue of her pearl earrings. Her perfume drifted around her like her blazer. In addition, she seemed strangely nervous. Which of course could be due to my slight delay. But I was tired of guessing at the reasons behind my wife's whims and letting them dictate my life. I was looking forward to spending time with Emily.

My enchanting daughter was unceremoniously handed over, and I was told Katharina would pick her up from mine around four o'clock. Peculiarly long for a lunch. But then I'd married a peculiar woman.

19

Overwriting

Your core beliefs were written by your parents at a time when you yourself did not yet know how to write. Now you are grown up. You know how to write. So, overwrite the core beliefs that no longer serve you.

Joschka Breitner, *Parenting Your Inner Child*

I drove Emily back to my apartment. When I texted Sasha to ask if Boris's condition had changed, he responded that Boris was still asleep.

Once we got home, I decided to take Emily and her balance bike to the park across the street. During the day, there weren't any drunks; the playground's population only changed after sunset. All that was left of them, scattered all around the playground's benches, was the broken glass from their vodka bottles – which they probably smashed for ritualistic reasons once emptied.

As a proud three-year-old, Emily zipped through the park like a world champion. Driving off, ringing her bell, braking – all with the utmost joy. I followed her at a light trot. Two months earlier, I had started jogging again. I wasn't a total gym rat, but at least I was now able to zigzag hunched behind my speeding daughter for sixty minutes.

Tired and happy after a good hour, we left the park again. On the pavement opposite our house, Emily started to swerve suspiciously. As she didn't slow down, her bike promptly slammed into the door of a parked car. I immediately ran over and checked to see if she was hurt. She was fine. Then I checked the bike: it had a flat front tyre. Probably from the drunks' broken glass.

'You've got to be kidding me!' I heard myself exclaim.

'Are you cross, Daddy?' Emily asked with a hint of a guilty conscience.

I didn't want my anger at the morons from the park to show in front of Emily. 'No, sweetie, why would I be angry?'

'Because of the car . . . I'm sorry.'

Emily pointed to where the bike had crashed into the BMW 3 Series. The bike's bell had made a scratch about six centimetres long.

'Is that bad?'

All of a sudden, I had an emotional flashback. I was five years old again. My scooter's bell had made the exact same scratch on the Grump's car.

'*Is that bad?*' I asked my mother. No, it wasn't. But at the time no one had told me that.

Here I was, standing at the same crossroads with my daughter as my parents had with me forty years earlier. I had no idea how or whether I'd ever forgive my parents. But I knew I could spare my daughter my parents' mistakes. I gave her a massive hug.

'No, darling. It's not bad at all. Only the tiniest scratch. But it's really great that you showed it to me. You'll never get into any trouble for anything you tell me, understand?'

Emily hugged me right back. 'Thank you, Daddy.'

'Now pick up your bike. We'll fix the front tyre at home. It has a flat.'

Emily looked at her tyre and then happily pushed the bike homewards without a care in the world.

A flaxen-haired child with skinned knees appeared in my

mind's eye. With a need that was almost forty years old, one that could metaphorically overwrite negative experiences from my past.

I listened to what my inner child needed, took my house key out of my pocket, placed its teeth on the six-centimetre scratch on the BMW and, in a single sweeping gesture, turned it into three twenty-centimetre-long deep scores in the paintwork.

'This one's for you, you fucking Grump,' me and my inner child said in unison.

That did us good.

20

Your Child's Inner Child

Once you know which core beliefs have harmed your inner child, you will also develop a sense of which core beliefs might harm your actual child. Use that. Intervene before negative core beliefs become entrenched in your child's inner child.

Joschka Breitner, *Parenting Your Inner Child*

We'd just arrived at the apartment with the defective bike when Sasha called.

'He's starting to wake up. Can you come down?'

'Not right now, sorry. I have Emily here with me.'

'When can you make it down?'

I looked at the clock: it'd gone half past three. 'In half an hour.'

'OK, I'll stay with him until then.'

'If need be, you can stick the IV with the sedative back in his arm again.'

Emily had already walked into the living room and was at the table, drawing. I brought her a bowl of nibbles and a squeezy pouch, her favourite snack. Normally, Emily would inhale a squeezy pouch. Not this time. Suddenly wriggling a little in annoyance, she stopped drawing and pushed the squeezy pouch aside.

'What's wrong?' I moved the pouch back towards her. She pushed it away again. This was very strange. 'What's wrong?'

'Promise you won't get cross if I say something?' Emily looked like she was afraid of the squeezy pouch.

'Sweetheart! You can tell me anything that's bothering you. You won't get into any trouble. Promise. What's up with the squeezy pouch?'

'I don't want the planet to die.'

I didn't understand what she meant. 'But . . . the planet won't die. And . . . what does that have to do with your snack?'

'Frauke said that the planet will die if we have squeezy pouches.'

Frauke was this year's placement student in the Nemo group. As I could never remember names, I always used nicknames. Most of the time, this meant I remembered the nickname rather than the real one. I had dubbed Frauke 'Gaia'. Because she seemed to mask her incessant cravings behind an 'Earth Mother' image. The fact that she couldn't even save her own figure didn't stop her from wanting to save the rest of the world. Still, I couldn't believe that she'd seriously told three-year-olds the planet was dying. And especially that she'd made them believe *they* were to blame. Because of squeezy pouches? Not even Gaia could be that naive. Emily, however, gave the impression that was exactly what had happened at preschool.

'I'm sorry,' Emily said guiltily.

'*Where is this Frauke?*' my inner child asked, reminding me that the last person who'd wanted to ban my daughter from enjoying her squeezy pouches had tragically plunged down a ravine.

As a father of two, it was my job to take seriously my daughter's feelings of guilt *and* my inner child's emerging anger, and then to alleviate both.

I took Emily onto my lap and promised my inner child I'd personally clarify all this with Frauke. Away from any mountains.

'Darling, our planet won't die. Frauke must've gotten it wrong. And above all, there's nothing *you* could do that would kill the planet, my darling. Even if the entire Nemo group mucked in.'

'But Frauke said so. She told us we couldn't have any squeezy pouches.'

Katharina and I had always kept any issues between us away from our daughter. Even back when I didn't know how fragile a child's basic trust is. We didn't keep Emily in a bubble, however, so we explained to her, in a child-friendly way, that animals and humans can die, that there are dangers in this world, and that Mummy and Daddy will protect her from these dangers. But we always tried to show her that life is beautiful. Simply because we were both convinced of the importance of at least pretending to children that life was beautiful. This despite all the issues Katharina and I had with each other and with ourselves, issues that were just a part of life. And despite all the dangers that simply come with life. Despite my own fear of the future, I wanted to conjure up the most beautiful version of the future I could for Emily. I had a very clear vision for my daughter: if I found out that an asteroid the size of Mykonos was set to crash into our preschool the next day at noon and end life as we know it, I'd still sharpen Emily's pencils so she could happily colour in unicorns in the morning.

And now some obese placement student came along and nullified all that by teaching my little one the dogmatic belief that squeezy pouches are killing the planet? And that it's all Emily's fault? I couldn't believe it. What kind of child-friendly explanation would take away my daughter's miserable worry that the world was about to end – and it was all her fault? I tried the truth.

'Darling . . . sometimes adults say stupid things.'

'But why?'

'Cos that's part of life. Sometimes it's hard to avoid saying stupid things.'

'So the planet isn't going to die?'

'The planet can't even die, because it's not a person. The planet will always be around.'

I didn't mention that, in approximately five to seven billion years, the sun would become a red giant and probably engulf our planet. Because even though she was forty years my junior, that would directly affect neither me nor my daughter.

'Does that mean I can have squeezy pouches again?'

'Please do!'

Emily gave me a hug. 'Thanks, Daddy!'

I kissed my little girl on the forehead and pushed the pouch over to her. She finished it greedily and then continued colouring. I inhaled and exhaled three times to calm the anger my inner child had passed on to me.

My outraged inner child, on the other hand, would've liked to march straight down to the preschool to hold Gaia to account. I explained why this wasn't possible: because I needed to watch my daughter; because Gaia wasn't there; because the preschool was closed today; because a gangster had disappeared from my cellar only to reappear, albeit asleep, and had now woken up again, if not in my presence, because I couldn't be there. Because my wife was at lunch.

Somehow it was all connected to everything else.

I promised my inner child it would get an opportunity for an in-depth conversation with Gaia before our partnership week was over.

Half an hour later, a cheerful Emily was picked up by a significantly more relaxed Katharina. When I told Katharina about the squeezy-pouch incident, she was as outraged as my inner child. I promised her, too, that I'd address the issue in a direct conversation.

'I have the parent representatives' meeting tonight anyway. I'll bring up the squeezy pouches.'

'You and the other five mums?' Katharina asked gleefully. She liked to stay out of the customary mums' functions. 'Enjoy! I'll take Emily to preschool on my way to work tomorrow and then pick her up from your place in the afternoon, OK?'

Totally OK.

After a peck on the cheek, Katharina was off. Emily got a kiss on her forehead. I was pleased. But when was the last time *I* got a kiss on the mouth?

21

Missing Information

How you react professionally to missing information is entirely up to you.

You can suspect someone is deliberately withholding that information, and thus weigh yourself down.

But you can also consider any missing information as a puzzle to be solved, and thus spur your childlike yen for adventure.

Joschka Breitner, *Slowing Down in the Fast Lane: Mindfulness for Managers*

Carrying the new lock I bought at the store, I went down to the cellar. Sasha was sitting on one of the chairs in the cell. Boris, looking gaunt, weak and exhausted, was on the bed, leaning back against the wall, almost catatonic.

'Has he said anything yet?' I asked Sasha.

'I haven't asked him anything. Wanted to wait until you got there.'

I took the second chair, turned it around and sat astride it. This allowed me to put my chin on the backrest and get on Boris's level.

'All right, Boris. Who got you out of here?' I asked.

The shadow of a man raised his head. He only seemed to register me now.

'Beats me,' he said, his tongue heavy. 'What do you mean "out"? I conked out in here and woke up here again too. Did I go somewhere else in between?'

'You must've seen the guy,' Sasha insisted.

'I didn't see nothing.' Boris was getting snappy again. A good sign, at least for the state of his circulation. 'The hatch in the door opened, but nothing else happened. So I went over to see what was up.'

'And?' asked Sasha. 'What did you see?'

'Nothing! That was what surprised me. I thought one of

you was playing some kind of trick on me again.'

'What kind of trick?' asked Sasha.

'And what do you mean, "again"?' I seconded.

'Well, like the other night, when you opened the hatch and pointed a torch at my face until I woke up.'

I raised my eyebrows at Sasha. He looked back, perplexed. Apparently, last night hadn't been the first time this stranger had been in the cellar.

'When was this torch business?' I asked him.

'No idea. Not that long ago, some time last week? Shortly after you played that joke with the annoying kiddie whistling.'

This time, Sasha raised his eyebrows.

'What kiddie whistling?' he asked.

'Well, it just kept going . . .'

Boris started whistling, awfully. But I recognised the melody. It was the theme tune to the children's cartoon *The Adventures of the Young Marco Polo*. I'd long ago gotten sick of hearing it, but my daughter loved the show. Since Boris had neither children nor cellar access to kids' TV, he had a bit of a blind spot. I had no intention of enlightening him.

'And what did you do after hearing that whistling?' I asked.

'Guys, I'm getting really tired of this. Who else could it have been but you? I yelled that if the fucking whistling didn't stop, I'd bite your lips off the first chance I got.'

'And then?'

'Then the awful whistling stopped, and I waited until it was dinner time. But you were *there*.'

'We weren't. And that's what seems to be the problem,'

Sasha concluded. 'So you've had at least two visits in the last few weeks. Once the stranger carried a torch, and once they whistled a tune.'

'So, last night the hatch opened again,' I said, echoing Boris's words in an attempt to get more detailed information out of him. 'You went to the door. Then what happened?'

'There was this disgusting smell.'

'Chloroform?'

'No, some repulsive fragrance. The chloroform came later. When I wanted to peek out of the hatch, one hand suddenly grabbed me by the hair, and another pressed a washcloth against my face. I think that one had chloroform on it. Otherwise, I don't remember anything. I collapsed and fell onto the table, I think. That's all I remember. So, what the fuck happened?'

'No idea. We don't know either,' I said, truthfully.

'But if your bum starts to hurt, you might want to worry,' Sasha interjected.

By now, I was sure Boris really didn't have a clue what had happened to him. No one could fake this level of cluelessness.

'Can you tell me what happened already?' Boris finally spat out.

'That's what we're trying to figure out, Boris,' I said. 'The fact is, someone drugged you yesterday. That same person cracked the lock on your cell door and dragged you into the main cellar. That's where we found you.'

'And for what fucking reason?'

'The reason seems to be escaping us, but that's why we're here now. To find out.'

'And the guy didn't leave anything? No note, no message?'

'Well, for one, freeing you and then leaving you here is already a message in itself,' Sasha explained. 'And that message is: he doesn't give a shit about you.'

'In addition, a letter showed up this morning,' I added.

'Show me,' Boris commanded.

'It was addressed to us.' Sasha briefly held up the envelope.

I gave Sasha a look. 'To be honest, it's addressed "TO THE RESIDENTS", which includes Boris.'

Sasha gave this a thought, then shrugged. Would keeping its contents from Boris serve any purpose? It would not. We gave him the envelope.

Boris scanned the letter and looked at the pictures.

'They put me in a fucking princess playhouse?'

'I'd have thought the beheading aspect would be more upsetting,' I mused.

'Come off it. You're not going to chop my head off. You could've done that six months ago. You don't have the balls. So this is first and foremost about finding this dumb fuck and taking him down. Right?'

'*Right!*' my inner child crowed.

'We're not quite completely sure about that yet,' I hedged, glancing at Sasha.

I thought I saw the slightest glimmer of uncertainty in Boris's eyes.

Sasha seemed to have noticed it too. 'We're not ISIS,' he said, reassuring our long-term guest. 'With the preschool's blunt little knives, we wouldn't be able to saw through your neck anyway. And before we invest a lot of money in new knives, we'll first invest some time in determining which idiot might've written this letter.'

'We are looking for someone who hates you, who knows you're here in this cellar, who's able to visit the preschool unnoticed and who's obviously several sandwiches short of a picnic. Can you think of anyone like that?'

'Except you two?'

'We don't hate you,' Sasha clarified. 'We just don't know what to do with you.'

'Well – I've got plenty of enemies. But apart from the two of you, I can't think of anyone who knows where I am. And now I think *Question Time* is over. Although – why do you think this guy is cuckoo?'

I pointed to the letter. 'Cutting off someone else's head is a clear sign your own head isn't exactly screwed on right.'

'Speaking from my own experience, it can be very liberating to saw someone's head off. I mean, it's a bloody fucking mess – but once you're actually holding the severed head of someone who has absolutely gutted you, they finally stop doing your head in.'

Ever since Boris had beheaded his wife out of substantiated jealousy, it was widely known he was utterly sick in the head. But what he said did confirm our theory about the blackmailer: they must hate Boris more than anything. The only question was: why?

After saying goodbye to Boris, who still sat slumped on the bed like a wet blanket, we went lightwards to the ground floor.

'Did you recognise the tune?' Sasha asked.

'Yeah, it's the *Marco Polo* theme song. Does that get us anywhere?'

'A children's song. But Boris can only hear anything from the other side of the door when the ventilation is on in his cell.'

Sasha was right. The ventilation of Boris's bunker was controlled electronically. With the ventilation flap closed, his dungeon was soundproof. Not when it was open. To ensure that Boris wouldn't use the ventilation shaft to scream for help, the air was only switched on when there were no more outsiders entering the building.

'During the day, the ventilation only turns on once the preschool closes,' Sasha thought aloud. 'And at night. But the whistling happened at the end of the day. Before dinner.'

I nodded. 'So before his pseudo-liberation, Boris was visited at least twice. Once in the late afternoon, with some whistling, and once at night, with a torch.

'By someone who whistles children's songs, hates Boris and wears a noxious scent.'

22

Hazards

Your inner child is usually sceptical. Use that. It reacts hastily and emotionally to any possible threats. It is up to you to identify them as either a danger or an opportunity.

Joschka Breitner, *Parenting Your Inner Child*

I'd only been elected chair of the Nemo group's parent representatives two weeks earlier. The position felt like both an honour and an obligation. I needed to represent the interests of all the kids in my daughter's group vis-à-vis the preschool.

Sure, as the lawyer for the childcare provider, I could already do this behind the scenes. But having been officially elected by the parents felt nice. Our violent takeover of the preschool six months earlier hadn't made me feel nearly as good.

I had won the election by convincing the other parents I was the best choice – and because, apart from my deputy, Laura, and me, no other parent had stood for election at the rather sparsely attended parents' evening. Laura got seven of the eight votes, with one abstention. I got eight out of eight. For the sake of fairness, maybe I should also have abstained from voting for myself. But that's how I was elected chair and Laura my deputy.

The chairs and deputies of the Flipper and Clownfish groups had been elected with similar turnouts.

Twice a year, there was a joint meeting with all the educators and parents' reps. The next was set for Thursday afternoon. At these meetings, parents could express their needs and concerns to the preschool. Needs were important to me. And thanks to Breitner, I now knew why. I therefore felt it would be useful for us parents' reps to take some time before the main meeting to reflect on what our children needed. That's why I had invited all the reps over to my apartment.

There's a lot of talk nowadays about 'helicopter parents', but I think 'helicopter' is the wrong word. A better one would be 'hand-grenade parents'. For this type of parents, children are simply the safety pin. If the pin is mistreated, the parents explode. To ensure these parents didn't explode the preschool, I wanted to use this opportunity to find out which of the parents' reps had which safety pins loose – not unimportant for Sasha to know before the meeting.

So, on my initiative, the six of us (five mums and me as the only father) met at my apartment that night.

Each of the five ladies brought something to drink to thank me for hosting. In a single evening, I thus came into possession of one bottle of Pinot Gris, one of Rioja and three six-packs of non-alcoholic shandies. I have no idea why women who lived off not-insignificant quantities of Aperol spritz before their first pregnancy would cart around non-alcoholic shandies after they became mums, but they tasted good. To me too. With increasing enthusiasm, four of the five ladies and one gentleman thus enjoyed the provided shandies. And within thirty minutes, the fifth lady had split the bottle of Pinot Gris – with herself.

My plan was to get an overview of the mums' moods and needs as quickly as possible. Within twenty minutes, I was up to date. Regretfully, however, I was up to date on topics about which I didn't really want to know anything. Topics that to me, as a man, almost felt exclusionary. I learned everything about the quality of our district's gynaecologists, for instance, or the need for better value for money when it came to pelvic-floor yoga and the problems with returning to work part-time. When the Pinot mum – by then she'd already reminded me to call her Steffi – started to discuss the scarring of her perineal tear, I left the living room and pretended to look for more drinks in the kitchen. I had just grabbed the Rioja and a corkscrew when I noticed Laura had followed me in.

'You have a lovely apartment,' she said.

'Thanks, I'm really happy here.' I held up the wine bottle. 'Fancy some Rioja?'

'I especially don't fancy any perineal scarring.'

I laughed. I liked Laura's sense of humour.

'But yes, I'd love a glass,' she added. 'It's my favourite.'

'What a coincidence.'

'I mean, that's why I brought it.'

So she had taste *and* manners. She'd already caught my interest at the representatives' election. She was attractive and in her mid-thirties. I was married. That was usually enough not to induce any further interest on my part. But this was the first time I realised a woman might also be interested in me. And I remembered Breitner's advice to finally *enjoy* life, if not for me, then at least for my inner child.

'I'm happy that bottle of wine didn't come by itself,' I said with a smile.

'*Forget it, she doesn't want to sleep with you anyway,*' my inner child chimed in.

'*Sorry, what?*' was my internal response. '*I'm allowed to flirt with an attractive woman.*'

'*One who won't think your needs are important either. Like all women. So quit it. Besides, you're married.*'

It was true: since marrying Katharina, I hadn't even flirted with another woman. At first, because I was happy with Katharina. In recent years, because it entirely sufficed to have one woman in my life who could hurt me. But at that moment I realised that this might've been due in no small part to my inner child putting on its defensive armour whenever flirting might be on the cards. Thanks to my sessions with Breitner, it had now removed this armour. I was the one protecting my inner child. And in our week of partnership, the time had come to clarify our position with regards to other women.

'*What are you afraid of when I flirt with Laura: hurting Katharina or getting hurt?*'

'*Getting hurt,*' it replied like a shot.

This was something I could work with.

'*I promise I'll protect you from getting hurt, OK? I'm just having a little chat with an attractive woman who might not find me unattractive either.*'

'*Promise?*'

'*You have my word.*'

My inner child acquiesced.

Maybe it'd do me good to flirt a bit. My wife had ignored my need to be seen as a man long enough. I wanted to try a different approach for once.

I allowed myself to look at Laura a little more freely, closely. She was exactly my type: a head shorter than me, slim and sporty. Not delicate, but gracefully athletic. A touch of Thai boxing and a lot of Zumba. And incredibly feminine at that. With a slight shadow of sadness in the little crinkles around her eyes – that immediately drew me to her. Her dark-blonde hair was in a ponytail, and she was simply but tastefully dressed: jeans, sneakers, T-shirt and a dark-blue blazer. A silver necklace with a single black pearl around her neck. Hardly any make-up, only a hint of dark lipstick. I poured us both a Rioja, and we clinked our glasses.

'So you're a single parent too?' Laura asked, once we had our first sip.

She must've noticed my puzzlement, and explained herself.

'I mean, this is a typical bachelor's apartment. Albeit with a children's room.'

'Ah, yes, that's right. As for the apartment, Katharina and I are currently separated. We each have our own time island, so to speak. But we're raising Emily together.'

'Great job! Tell her more about your wife,' my inner child commented. *'There's really no better form of defensive armour.'*

Not letting it distract me, I continued. 'I try to take in each moment with love and without judgement, and to enjoy every new encounter and experience.'

'Oh my God,' my inner child quietly muttered, but otherwise it stuck to our pact and kept shtum.

'Are you into mindfulness?' Laura asked.

Her question surprised me. 'Why do you ask?'

'Because of the time islands. Consciously creating space for yourself.'

Did she just wink at me?

'Right. And you . . . ?'

'I've got enough past experience and enough confidence in the future to enjoy the present.'

That was wonderfully put. But my tingling feeling could also be due to the fact that my inner child had thrown up its unarmoured hands in spontaneous despair.

'What's your apartment like?' I now asked Laura.

'A small bedroom for me, a big room for my son. You know – single mum. The communication between his father and me isn't going so well,' she added matter-of-factly. Apparently, she didn't want to get into detail.

I didn't insist. 'And who's watching Max now?' I asked instead.

'My brother. He's happy to step in whenever. Today, he even watched him all day, since the preschool was closed. And Wednesday is always a full favourite-uncle day.'

'Are you and your brother close?'

'We're OK. Kurt is my only family. Unfortunately, there aren't any grandparents I can fall back on.'

'Oh, my condolences,' I said sheepishly.

'Huh? Sorry, no! My parents are fine. They're not in heaven, just in Tenerife. Although – the way they describe it, heaven would certainly be a step backwards for them.'

'What kind of parents leave their children alone?' I asked with interest. And above all: what armour must *her* inner child be wearing, especially if her parents had also put their own needs above those of their daughter when she was small. The way Laura was acting, it must be the offensive kind.

'Parents who think it's enough if her brother is around.' She toasted me. 'Shall we go back in? We can talk more later.'

Another wink. That didn't look like defensive armour.

23

Time Capsule

Your inner child's emotions are pure. The formative experiences of your inner child are untouched by the passing of time, a time capsule, like a drill core from the permafrost – only an emotional one. Take advantage of that. If your inner voice thinks something is utter and eternal nonsense, it probably is.

Joschka Breitner, *Parenting Your Inner Child*

Back in the living room, I served a fresh six-pack while Laura brought her glass to the sofa. Steffi had obviously been able to wash away her perineal worries with the last bit of the Pinot Gris. At the moment, the women were speculating as to who had broken in last night. But Sasha had already answered all the main questions in his WhatsApp message and a small statement on the preschool's website: the police are investigating, the perpetrators are unknown, and the break-in ultimately failed due to the existing security measures, which would now be reinforced. The topic was soon exhausted. Tomorrow, the preschool would open again. The chat seamlessly shifted to the topic of the dads making paper lanterns with the kids for St Martin's Eve, which was just around the corner. I took a closer look at my other guests.

Perineal-scar Steffi seemed to be the only one of the women who made no secret of the fact that hopes and dreams had one thing in common with amniotic sacs: they all burst. Now that her son was a preschooler, Steffi had still only partially regained her old job at a bank. As she told it, her better half hadn't yet recovered from the pregnancy and primarily fulfilled his role as a father on Father's Day. In contrast to her husband, however, Steffi's household budget certainly noticed the hole her reduced salary left behind. Though Steffi was a good-hearted person, she processed her life's frustrations by over-committing to her son.

The other three women were called Tina, Beate and Claudia. All three with semi-detached homes in an upmarket residential area. Life-affirmingly upper-middle class. Grandparents in the city, dog in the garden, husband with a salaried position. They all wanted the best for their children. They were living the traditional family dream in glossy splendour. When I heard them talking, I felt torn between envy and relief. I'd also once dreamed of the security of a nuclear family. But I was glad that all the problems I could clearly hear a-rumbling under the surface with these three women had long since broken out into the open with Katharina and me. At least we no longer needed to pretend. Despite all the attendant melancholy, this granted us an honest kind of freedom.

I used a break in the conversation to toast with our new drinks and steer the conversation towards the parents' committee.

'Now that we've all warmed up a bit, I suggest we discuss the actual reason for our get-together. The first committee meeting is scheduled for this Thursday. And I thought it'd be nice for us parents to pool any needs and concerns that are important to us.'

Everyone nodded. I straightened my notebook and picked up my pen. I wanted to jot down everybody's needs with love and without judgement.

'So – any needs or concerns?'

No response. A good sign. Apparently, our preschool was leaving no one's needs unmet. But I knew it was impossible that these half a dozen parents were perfectly satisfied.

'Come on,' I insisted. 'Surely there's something you need the preschool to address. There's always something that could be improved, right?'

Tina, Beate and Claudia all took a sip of their non-alcoholic shandies. Laura lifted her Rioja to her mouth. Steffi stared into her empty wine glass. I took the opportunity and spoke up about my primary concern.

'I would like to talk about an issue that's very close to my heart. Have any of you heard that there's a ban on squeezy pouches in some groups? Emily said as much today.'

Four women looked bemused.

Laura spoke up and reported that her son, Max, had also told her that Frauke had issued a ban on the pouches.

'What did Max say was the reason?' I asked her.

'If I understood him correctly,' Laura explained, 'it had to do with the fact that the planet has a fever and is going to die.'

That sounded familiar. I was relieved that I could rely on Emily's report of events. I still felt it was a bizarre issue, so I responded with the appropriate level of sarcasm.

'Well, looks like we've finally found the culprits for the climate crisis. I think Max and Emily should make amends for all the damage they've caused. I suggest they should both be sent to bed without a squeezy pouch for about the next five thousand years – until the glaciers have grown back to their original size.'

Laura snorted with laughter. The rest of the living room was silent.

'I don't think that's very funny,' Beate finally objected, not from a child-psychological point of view, but from an ecological one. 'All this plastic waste is ultimately to blame for the fact that our children no longer have a future.'

The discussion sadly seemed to be veering in the exact opposite way I'd intended.

'What do you mean "no longer have a future"? And why should three-year-olds be to blame? Isn't that more a matter for . . .' I tried to express the absurdity of assigning guilt to preschoolers. But the mums' reproachful looks quickly silenced me.

'No one's too young to make the world a better place,' Beate informed me.

'Perhaps we should ban *all* plastic from the preschool,' Claudia suggested.

'Sorry, what?' I demanded, somewhat taken aback.

'Well, from the breakfast boxes to the plates and the Tupperware containers of sliced fruit – it's all plastic. We should set an example for our children's future.'

'I always thought the introduction of plastic tableware led to a significant decrease in cuts from broken plates,' I said naively.

Laura jumped in to support me. 'And airtight plastic packaging also led to a decrease in food-borne pathogen poisoning,' she said, macrobiotically informed. But to no avail.

'Well, climate action has to start somewhere. I'm also in favour of a plastic ban,' said Steffi in response to these apparently unwanted pieces of information. Not providing any detailed argument on what snack-break plastic had to do with the climate, but reaping approval nonetheless.

'*Going great,*' my inner child noted sarcastically. Not entirely without reason.

There was clearly no hope for any further pleas to acquit the squeezy pouch. Instead, it looked like my mention of climate change had opened Pandora's (lunch)box. I should've closed it at this point. The box, I mean. Unfortunately, I didn't. If I couldn't get the topic off the table, I wanted to at least push it to the other side.

'Of course, I am also in favour of environmental and climate protection. But maybe let's not start with the children, but with the adults,' I suggested timidly.

Tina took over with rapid-fire enthusiasm. 'Then what I'd really like is a low-emission zone.'

'What does the preschool have to do with—' I didn't get my next words out.

'Right in front of the preschool,' Tina interrupted.

Five pairs of surprised eyes looked at Tina.

'Why?' I said somewhat scathingly, even though what I'd meant to do was write everything down without any judgement.

'Because of the fine particulates, of course. Children are particularly vulnerable to that stuff. This is something concrete we can do for the future of our children. No more diesel outside the preschool!'

'*Are you really a lawyer?*' my inner child now enquired. '*Great negotiation skills.*'

'Good idea!' Beate agreed. 'When will diesel finally be banned? Since the week before last, there's even been one of those old Land Rovers parked there every day. Right out front!'

'I'd love to know what kind of person still drives such a horrible gas-guzzler,' Steffi demanded.

My inner child, I was about to answer. But I decided not to. Among other things because someone had started raging inside me.

'*Have they all gone mental or what? I've wanted a Land Rover since forever and I just got it! Back in the day, I was driven to kindergarten with five other children from the neighbourhood in a tiny VW Beetle. On ten litres of leaded petrol per hundred kilometres. Without a catalytic converter. The only reason we couldn't smell the giant exhaust cloud through the tilted triangular window was that the mum behind the wheel was chain-smoking. It wasn't only the very finest in fine particulates, it was completely normal. Didn't do me any harm either!*'

'*Nils the waiter might've disagreed with you there*,' I whispered back, '*if he hadn't died when you threw him into a ravine.*'

Aloud, I summed up: 'OK – I have noted the ban on plastic *inside* and a ban on diesel *outside* the preschool. Even if personally I'd rather fight the climate crisis at more macro levels.'

A line I really wish I'd swallowed. Since it led to more unwelcome ideas.

'How about,' Tina started riffing, 'our preschool becomes the city's first climate-neutral preschool? No plastic, no coal-fired power, no oil heating!'

'We have oil heating?' Beate was outraged.

Yes, and we're going to have to stick with it, I wanted to answer. *Because I'm keeping a Russian prisoner behind it.*

'That should be the first to go,' said Beate. 'Let's go take a look at that old monster!'

That was all I needed: for Boris to be discovered by climate warriors, all because I had stood up for my daughter's beloved squeezy pouches.

I needed to intervene, immediately.

'Well . . . the heating is for the entire building. The preschool is only one tenant. The owner probably wouldn't like it if half a dozen strangers went strolling through the boiler room one night. Plus, I don't even know where the key is. Maybe we should revisit the heating issue at some later date . . .'

'Then let's take a look at the heating on Thursday evening, together with the owner,' Claudia suggested. 'Surely the key will've turned up by then.'

I realised that I'd need to end this discussion before these women strode into the cellar to rip out the boiler with a crowbar and put it out on the street in a pioneering attempt to avert the apocalypse. It'd already be tricky enough to prevent the entire parents' committee from embarking on a field trip to Boris's hiding place on Thursday.

'All right, I've got it all written down: a climate-neutral preschool, a low-emission zone, a plastic ban, and no more oil heating.'

For now, I refrained from listing my own ideas – like a men's quota for the parents' committee. 'Anything else?'

Steffi wanted to talk about the upcoming photographer's visit.

'I think it's problematic that the management scheduled this visit without first discussing the contents of the shoot with us.'

I was taken aback. The last preschool photo day my inner child and I remembered was when I was a preschooler myself. Back then, photographic film was more sensitive to light. At least the less bright sparks among the kids had a hard time standing out. And the contents of a preschool's group photo were usually a group of preschoolers. But back then there weren't any model competition shows on telly yet, so nobody thought that striking a duck-face pose was a greater challenge than becoming a brain surgeon.

Even today, I felt like a preschool group photo was a success if twenty-two of the twenty-five children were looking at the camera when the photographer cried out, 'Look at the birdie!' The three children who happened to be looking down, up or behind them would surely find future happiness on some reality show. So, what was the problem with these group photos?

'Help me out,' I asked Steffi, 'what do you mean by "contents"?'

'Well, I mean with data protection and such. You can't just put our children online; they've got privacy rights.'

'Who's saying these group photos are going to be put online?' Laura wanted to know.

'Well, in my Facebook group. That's where we always share pictures of our kids.'

'OK . . . Maybe *don't* share the group photos,' was my suggested solution. 'Then there's also no data-protection issue.'

'I should be able to share pictures of my own child online if I want to!'

'In that case . . . it's clear that you personally don't have a data-protection problem.'

'But I don't want other parents posting pictures of my child online.'

Laura tried to summarise: 'You mean, the parents of the children whose group photos you're allowed to put online should not be allowed to share a group photo that includes your son even after *you* have already shared it online?'

'Right. Because of privacy rights.'

'*Can I please have my helmet and lance back?*' my inner child asked angrily, if politely.

'What if you don't let your son take part in the group photo?' I offered. 'Then no one has a photo of him either.'

'Do you *know* how important preschool photos are as a memory?' Steffi exclaimed.

'OK,' I concluded, 'this does seem to be an issue we should raise in the parents' committee,' jotting down Steffi's concern before her circular arguments made me even dizzier.

The group's initially high spirits had been significantly lowered by our children's impending climate death and the legal dangers posed by group photos. Laura tried to lighten the mood a little by voicing a sillier concern.

'And I would love it if someone finally caught the lippy monster lurking down in the cellar.'

Inside me, alarm bells started to ring.

'What lippy monster?' Steffi responded, asking the question that was on my lips too.

'Oh, Max claims there's a monster living in the preschool cellar that bites children's lips off if they whistle the theme song to *Marco Polo*.'

Five women burst into loud laughter. I burst into a cold sweat.

That was exactly what Boris had been telling me earlier, only from the other side of the cellar door. But it was the same song, the same threat. It'd clearly been Laura's son, Max, who whistled in the cellar and had been scolded by Boris.

'Where does your son come up with such silliness?' Claudia asked.

'No idea,' Laura laughed. 'Maybe because I told him that if he whistled that annoying song one more time, I'd sew his mouth shut.'

At the end of the evening, I had not achieved my desired rehabilitation of the squeezy pouch, but instead only jotted down a list of needs in my notebook intended to improve the world these other people were living in. In the world of my inner child, however, all they were was infuriating. And in my world, they seriously endangered the security of Boris's prison.

I would have to discuss these issues with Sasha before they were blithely brought up at the preschool's committee meeting on Thursday. And led to a disastrous field trip to the cellar. Not least because Sasha and I would need to cut Boris's head off after the meeting. And put it on the wall of the park opposite the preschool, in a box. To save our own heads. After that, however, the boiler room could safely be handed over to a heating company to install a carbon-neutral system.

Unless I could find out from Laura what exactly Max knew about the lippy monster and whom he had told about it.

24

Leadership

Your inner child needs direction. This is why you should treat your inner child like you would a real child: their needs should be acknowledged, discussed and appreciated. Whether all of them are met, however, is entirely up to you: the adult. Informed by love, care and respect.

Joschka Breitner, *Parenting Your Inner Child*

Finally, Claudia, Tina and Beate were ready to say their goodbyes. Tina offered to drive Steffi home. When the door shut behind them, the only ones left were Laura and me. And my inner child.

'I thought we could finish off that bottle of Rioja, what do you say?' Laura said, a teasing smile on her lips.

Right then, however, learning more about the lippy monster was more enticing to me than Laura's lips. 'Love to. Would you help me put these empty bottles away first?' I asked, trying to hide my interest. Laura grabbed some empty shandies to bring them to the kitchen.

'Where did your son *get* that thing about the lippy monster?' I asked, as if making conversation.

'Oh, he's always had a lively imagination.' Laura didn't seem to think the story warranted any further consideration.

'But isn't it strange that the monster lives under the preschool, of all places? When did he first start talking about this?'

'No idea really, maybe two weeks ago?'

'And . . . was there any particular occasion?'

'Not that I remember. But at least I no longer have to hear that *Marco Polo* song any more. Why do you ask? Are you afraid of the lippy monster too?'

'I mean, I do live in the building.'

My investigation seemed to have hit a dead end. Laura and I returned to the living room. I tried to relax and focus on the evening's more rousing aspects.

One thing that's great about being an adult is the fact that things you considered cheesy when you were younger can actually become more appealing. Power ballads, for example.

I put *Ultimate Power Ballads* on my record player, and the most beautiful songs of the good old 1980s filled the room. I was always touched by how expressive love songs could be when the singers were still emotionally compensating for the very real danger of nuclear war. Back then, our own insignificance was ironically evident. In comparison, dangers such as microplastics in toothpaste didn't seem a particularly viable stimulus for creativity.

We sat down on the sofa and settled comfortably into a conversation.

Laura and her five-year-old son, Max, had only been back in the city for half a year. She worked as an orthopaedic specialist at a clinic. After finishing secondary school here, she'd moved to Bavaria to study medicine. She also completed her speciality training there. For a few years, she'd had an affair with the head of orthopaedics. He turned out to know more about intervertebral discs than contraception, however, and after one fateful private pelvic-floor examination, Laura had fallen pregnant. The head of orthopaedics, who'd been married for twenty years and already had two children, didn't want to take on his additional responsibility as a father. Laura, meanwhile, didn't want to take up his professional offer of a free abortion. Laura got Max and lost her position at the clinic. Eventually, she moved back to her hometown, the city her retired parents had left for the Canary Islands.

Still, her brother lovingly took care of Max. Laura had settled in and was now single mum to a great preschooler. Plus, she was a doctor, and incredibly attractive. Even the way her lips moved, whatever the words they were forming. Every second word, there was a beautiful crinkle in one corner of her mouth. A wonderful woman. And single. And she hadn't stayed behind because of me, but because of her brother – as my inner child just informed me.

'*What did you say?*' I asked my inner child.

'*That she said she doesn't care about your needs. Try listening for once.*'

'Sorry, what did you say?' I asked Laura.

'That I actually stayed behind when the others left because of my brother. I wanted to ask you something.'

'Ah . . . that's . . . What do you need?'

'My brother has a legal issue with his company, and he would probably appreciate a lawyer's opinion . . .'

At that moment, I'd have liked to have put my inner child's defensive armour on myself. Motivated by Breitner, I had realised I needed an attractive woman to see me as a man again. At least, that had been the plan. And now that need seemed to have been disregarded once more. By Laura, this time. After barely ten minutes of conversation, I'd been reduced to the lawyer who could do someone a favour. Still, I tried to stay open and listen to what she was saying. I could intercept any pinpricks before they reached my inner child.

'. . . and since I see the sign for your law office every day when I bring Max in or pick him up, I promised my brother to ask if he can give you a call.'

The need for intimate touch that had arisen in me wasn't necessarily congruent with Laura's need to put me in touch with her brother.

'*Another person who doesn't care about our needs!*' the child in me protested, obviously offended. '*Tell her she can go drink her wine at home. Her brother should go find a lawyer with a healthy sex life and leave us alone.*'

No, I wouldn't do that. I tried to respond neither defensively nor offensively. Simply like a grown man who might have his needs, but also a law office.

'*Let's do her this one favour. She hasn't got anyone else,*' I argued.

'*And that sadness around her eyes makes her looks so helpless. And her parents aren't around . . .*' my inner child mimicked my internal voice. '*Why don't you check in the back of Breitner's handbook under H for "Helper syndrome". You'll find this is exactly the kind of bullshit we wanted to leave behind.*'

Indeed. Breitner's book described helper syndrome as another possible manifestation of the inner child's armour. If family life was disharmonious, the inner child tried to ward off the pinpricks of 'your need for harmony doesn't matter!' by *bringing about* that missing harmony. My parents had never openly argued in front of me. But that didn't mean it was all lovey-dovey Neil Diamond songs; I'd never seen my parents hold hands either. In my parents' house, harmony meant that dinner was served on time and that I did the dishes so my parents could watch the news in peace. Then I would be praised. Perhaps this lack of harmony growing up was the reason I always wanted to help other people. Why I kept accepting cases that didn't interest me in the slightest. And why I was so receptive to predicaments from the feminine realm, like Laura's. Though this one wasn't even hers, but her brother's.

On the other hand, Breitner had also impressed upon me that, however important it was to take the concerns of your inner child seriously, you shouldn't let it take the lead. Your inner child should be treated like a real one: their needs should be acknowledged, discussed and appreciated. Whether all of them are met, however, is entirely up to you: the adult. Informed by love, care and respect.

I tried to translate this into an inner dialogue.

'*You're afraid of being disappointed. I have a need for confirmation. I would really like to get to know Laura. If that means making one phone call to her brother, so be it. I also heard you when you warned me that this could be a pathological consequence of the lack of harmony in my childhood home. How about the following deal: I'm not playing with fire; I'm just looking for some warmth. If my fingers get burned in the process, they're* my *fingers. OK?*'

'*Pfft . . . Keep telling yourself that. You're the adult.*'

I had to admit: inner children sometimes sound uncannily precocious.

I turned my attention back to Laura and told her, against

the protestations of my inner child, 'Of course. I'll give you my mobile number. By all means pass it on to your brother.'

Laura put her hand on mine and briefly caressed it. 'That's sweet of you. You're a prince.'

'*Nice that they're your fingers. But I should remind you: I am no longer wearing any protective armour,*' my inner child complained inaudibly.

'*But it's working, isn't it? Look, she's already caressing me!*'

'*Caresses as compensation? You know what they call that, don't you? Toss her out.*'

'*Toss her out? I promised I'd protect you. That doesn't mean I have to hurt everyone you don't like.*'

'*It would be the most effective method. You'll see.*'

The stubbornness of my inner child was getting on my nerves. I just wanted to talk to Laura in peace.

'*OK, what do you need to finally leave me alone?*'

'*I want you to grant me one free wish.*'

'*What kind of wish?*'

'*I don't know yet,*' my inner child pouted. '*But I'll tell you when I do.*'

'*OK, I'll give you a free wish, and now you'll give me some peace and quiet.*'

My inner child gave me peace and quiet.

And I devoted myself back to Laura.

'What's your brother like?'

'He's actually kind of the exact opposite of me.'

'And I'm excited to find out who you are,' I flirted openly. 'But back to your brother.'

'He's fifteen years older than me – I wasn't exactly planned.'

Ah, that sounded like there was a pretty big 'you're unwanted' badge pinned to Laura's soul.

'Him being much older than you doesn't tell me very much about his character.'

'It significantly shaped him though. As I said, my parents hadn't been planning on having another baby. I didn't fit into their lives at all. That's why my brother was expected to take care of me from early on. Within nine months, the spoiled only child had become the second favourite. His classmates got mopeds; Kurt got a baby sister.'

So her brother had a big 'you can suffer for our mistakes' badge pinned to his inner child's soul. I was really enjoying how Breitner's teachings enabled me to psychologically analyse complete strangers.

'Since my parents moved to the Canary Islands, Kurt has been taking care of Max a lot. A bit like when I was small.'

'Would you call Kurt selfless?'

'Selfless? No. That would be the last word I'd use to describe him. But he is . . . incredibly committed.' Oh. My. God. Not one of those.

'To what?'

'Climate change, sustainability, carbon-neutral living . . .'

So, yes: one of those. A person who could be described in catchwords.

'I see. And you? Are you also . . . committed?'

'Like I said – I'm a mindful person. I like my life to be balanced. But if I tossed *all* my bad habits out the window, my disappointed high hopes would soon bring me back down to reality.'

What an intelligent woman. Entirely free of catchwords.

'And how does your brother handle that?'

'How he personally handles it, I don't know. But practically, he does without a car and gets a regional organic produce box delivered.'

Probably by the farmer's diesel truck. 'And he doesn't have any children of his own?'

'No. He has a hard time with women.'

'Are you trying to say he's gay?'

'No, no, he likes women. But many years ago, a passionate relationship got completely out of hand. A youthful indiscretion. He hasn't had a girlfriend since. And no children either. He doesn't really have any friends. And lives for his work. He even lives in an apartment above his company. But perhaps this lack of social contact is what makes him the best godfather in the world for Max.'

'What does he do for a living?'

'He runs a start-up for electric scooters.'

At the word 'scooter', countless pinprick scars on my inner child's soul started to itch.

'*I never ever want to have anything to do with scooters any more!*' echoed from the depths of my soul.

'Your brother has a scooter?'

'E-scooters, about five hundred of them. He's the biggest hire company in town.'

Aha. Laura's brother was one of those guys using the pavements my taxes paid for as his free business premises. These rentals littered the entire city. No one would even think to operate an electric drill rental company on a public footway without official permission. With electric scooters, for whatever reason, different standards applied.

When I was small, my scooter was taken away from me because it had accidentally defaced a single car. Laura's brother was defacing the entire city with his five hundred scooters, and he was allowed to keep them all. I should've listened to my inner child. This case already wasn't doing me any good. But I'd promised Laura. This helpless, attractive woman. I gave her my card.

'I've always wanted to meet someone who owns five hundred little scooters,' I lied, trying to put the subject to bed.

'Then you should meet Kurt's bank manager – as far as I know, the scooters were all bought on credit.'

So, Kurt was a poor little sod.

As Laura pocketed my card, she looked at the clock. 'Oh, it's already after eleven. I should go.'

'*Buh-bye!*' my inner child cried.

'Too bad,' I said. 'I had a lovely evening.'

'It doesn't have to be our last.' She winked at me as she got up. Then she pulled out her mobile and ordered a ride via an app.

'Can I use your toilet before I go?'

'Of course, the cloakroom's just past the kitchen, first door on the left.'

As Laura closed the cloakroom door behind her, I gathered the wine glasses and put them on top of the dishwasher. I'd rinse them tomorrow.

Had this been a date, or had I been used? I didn't know. The former felt unusual, the latter didn't.

Laura came back in.

'See you soon.' She gave me a quick kiss on the cheek and held my hands a little too long for two parents who had ostensibly only met to discuss their work on a parents' committee.

She left. The door fell in the lock, and the creak of the wooden stairs faded with every floor she descended.

A peek out of the balcony window showed me Laura's car was already waiting for her.

I went to the stereo and had Vanessa Williams sing 'Save the Best for Last' one last time before taking the needle off the record and opening the balcony doors for some fresh air – letting in the greatest possible climate change, at least when it came to my mood.

A roar of 'Twaaaaat' rang out from the park, accompanied by the shattering of a bottle.

Only a second earlier, I'd been remembering what it was like to be a teenager in love.

The next, I was an under-fucked husband again, an easily exploited lawyer who'd let himself be talked into another unwanted job, and a man whose actual erotic experience was currently limited to hearing vulgar terms for genitalia roared from across the street by uncultured scum. If Laura hadn't ordered a car, she'd have run right into those fuckers.

Through the sound of my rising pulse, I heard my inner child call out.

'*I'd like you to grant my wish now.*'

'*What wish?*' I didn't really have a choice.

'*Against my advice, you accepted a new client. In exchange, you gave me a free wish.*'

'Right, yeah. Of course. What do you need?'

'*I need you to make sure there's peace and quiet in the park. I want to sleep undisturbed.*'

'OK . . .' I was a little surprised. '*I'll call the community safety office, but I don't know if that'll do any good. The last few times . . .*'

'*They won't be any use at all. Call Walter.*'

'*You want me to do what?*'

'*Call Walter and have his guys quiet that scum.*'

I was astounded. What a brilliantly simple idea. I could've come up with it myself. If neither the police nor the community safety officers could safeguard this residential area, Walter's security team sure could.

My inner child seemed to have thought much harder about possible ways we could have a solid night's rest than I had. And with our story about being under threat by the Holgersson crime family, we could even provide Walter with a justification for cleaning up the park a little more effectively than with a single ice cube or a scared safety officer.

With its child's intuition, the little blond kid in lederhosen inside of me had found the simplest solution.

I called Walter. He answered immediately.

'Walter, it's me.'

'Did something happen?'

'I'm not sure. There are a few people hanging around in the park outside my apartment who aren't supposed to be there. Maybe your people could check to see if they're part of the Holgerssons' crew?'

'Will do. Is that everything?'

For me, it was. For my inner child, it wasn't.

'*Ask him if his team are carrying any duct tape and zip ties.*'

'*Why . . . ?*'

'*Ask him!*'

'Does your team have some duct tape and zip ties?'

'Of course.'

'Then here's what should happen . . .' My inner child told me in great detail how, in order to keep up our Holgerssons story, Walter's people should check the identity of these blokes – who might not be Holgerssons but had still been annoying me night after night – and then leave the poor yobs tied up and gagged in the park until they realised what they wanted most was to never come back there ever again.

The concrete details of this plan were a bit crude, I felt. Personally, I had renounced all violence. But I hadn't yet known about my inner child when I did so. Yet it was exactly the crudeness of my inner child's plan that made it so promising. Plus, I'd promised to grant one free wish. Given the choice between the physical integrity of the park's lowlifes and the emotional integrity of my inner child, the answer was obvious. I passed its wish on to Walter word for word. At that point, however, neither my inner child nor I knew that two of those blokes actually were Holgerssons. Another one of my inner child's tricks thus turned life-threatening.

25

Knowledge

Knowledge is power. Faced with an ignorant person who does not *know* that they do not know anything, however, a knowing person is powerless. You can only enrich others with your knowledge if they at least have an inkling of their own spiritual poverty.

Joschka Breitner, *Slowing Down in the Fast Lane: Mindfulness for Managers*

That night, I slept like a child. Like an inner child, I should probably say. Twenty minutes after my call to Walter, the park outside my doorstep was absolutely quiet. What a blessing.

I was grateful to my inner child for its creative solution.

My inner child was grateful I had fulfilled its wish. Both of us slept soundly, peacefully, restoratively.

Until the doorbell woke me in the morning. I looked at the clock: it was a quarter past eight. Normally I woke up by seven at the latest, even without an alarm.

I put on my dressing gown, shuffled to the front door and looked through the spyhole. It was Katharina. Though she had a key to my apartment like I had to our old house, we rang the bell if we weren't sure the other was home, to respect each other's privacy.

Katharina must've just dropped off Emily at preschool.

'Good morning!' I greeted her with an attempt at a kiss. She turned a cheek to me instead of her mouth.

'Glad that at least one of us could sleep in,' she said, glancing at my dressing gown.

Since the doorbell woke me up, I actually couldn't, thank you very much, I mentally muttered through my defensive armour.

'I could use a wee before I head to the office. Can I have an espresso?'

229

Rejection. Reproach. Demand. Her need for caffeine and the loo was more important than my need for harmony – or sleeping in. My inner child had woken up too, and it was in a bad mood. It wanted me to verbalise my need for adequate rest.

'*I'll take care of it when she comes back from the toilet,*' I tried to reassure my inner child. But I wouldn't get a chance to.

I had sleepily found an espresso capsule, put a cup under the Nespresso machine and pressed the button when first a scream and then a shattering clatter rang out from the cloakroom. Before I could go see what had happened, Katharina came storming out like a fury.

'Have your sluts be more discreet!' she sneered.

'What . . . ?'

Katharina pointed at the two wine glasses in the sink. She picked up the one that had a faint print of Laura's lipstick on it.

'And on my first day back at work after our daughter was born! You . . .'

She hurled the glass violently at the Nespresso machine. While the espresso's foamy crema was still running slowly, calmly down the kitchen wall, Katharina was already running hastily, frantically down the stairs.

I was speechless. To determine what had just happened, I went into the cloakroom. I never used it myself; my own bathroom was an en suite.

The ceramic soap dish was in shards on the wooden floorboards. The mirror above the sink had shattered but not fallen out of the frame. Despite the countless cracks,

I could still read what had been written on the mirror in lipstick: *Thanks for the wonderful evening! L.* With pinpoint accuracy, Katharina had lobbed the soap dish right at the word 'Thanks'.

At that moment, I felt convinced that a man's quality of life was inversely related to the literacy of the women around him. What had Laura been thinking to write such rubbish on the mirror? And what had Katharina been thinking? That I was seeing a woman who I trusted with my body but not my bathroom, so she'd scribbled all over the cloakroom mirror?

The woman who didn't want to have sex with me was upset because another woman had expressed her thanks for not having sex with me either. And *who* needed to see a coach to get a grip on their supposedly irrational behaviour? Right, me.

The sound of my ringtone drew me out of my mental confusion and back into the puzzling present. The unknown number on the display ended in 2211970. It didn't look like the disposable mobile numbers common in organised crime. It resembled a date of birth too much for that: 22 January 1970. It was usually uncreative corporate customers who requested numbers like that. I picked up.

'Hello?'

'Hi, it's Kurt.'

'Kurt . . . who?'

'Laura's brother.'

Right. The lady from last night had not only a disturbing graffiti habit, but an annoying brother too. A new client who presumed we were on a first-name basis, even though we'd never met. A nice violation of my need for respectful restraint. We were off to a smashing start. I could already feel a badge needling my inner child's soul.

'Ah . . . Mr Frieling.'

'Call me Kurt. When can we talk?'

'I'd have to check my diary . . .'

'You know what? I'll come pick you up later and treat you to lunch. Deal?'

That felt far too pushy and far too spontaneous. On the other hand, what I wanted was to put anything Laura-related behind me, close that chapter. The sooner I did, the sooner I could talk Katharina out of the palm tree she'd first imagined and then climbed into. One lunch, then I'd be done.

'Sure. Do you know where I live, Mr Frieling?'

'Kurt, call me Kurt.'

'Yes, well, Kurt. So . . . you know where I live?'

'Of course. Above the preschool. I pick my godchild up there all the time. I'll be there at twelve thirty. I'll buzz you.'

Since the phone was still in my hand, I tried Katharina. Maybe I could fix the mirror misunderstanding over the phone. Her phone was turned off. I knew this behaviour. It could be hours before she'd take my calls again. Fine then, I had enough to do. After this useless lunch with Kurt, I'd meet with Sasha to make a list of people who had a connection to both the preschool and Boris. I didn't expect too much from it, but we had to start somewhere. In addition, I had to tell Sasha that Laura's son had been telling stories about a lippy monster that lived down in the preschool's cellar and seemed to confirm what Boris had told us.

I provisionally cleared away the shards and then took a good long shower. As the water pelted down, I took the time for a little standing meditation. That made the world feel a lot brighter. My inner child had warned me about Laura and her brother. Had I listened to my inner child, Katharina wouldn't have freaked out. At least, not because of the mirror. But she probably would've because of something else, some other day. My inner child had been right. But when it came to my inner child, it wasn't about being right. It was about trust and leadership. I led; my inner child needed to trust my direction. I remembered an exercise Breitner had taught me.

26

Feelings

After decades alone in the cellar of your soul, your inner child must first learn to trust you and your feelings. To do so, you should become aware of your own feelings first. Write down how you feel and then honestly share those feelings with your inner child.

Joschka Breitner, *Parenting Your Inner Child*

Breitner had impressed upon me that getting to know my inner child wouldn't be a walk in the park. It would be hard work. To illustrate it, he'd chosen an example he couldn't possibly have realised would resonate so much with me.

'You are now going to bring your inner child into the light of day. Imagine being locked up in a cellar and ignored for years. And then one day the person who put you there comes by and says: "Oh, right, *you*'re here! Sorry for ignoring you so long. Let's be friends!" How would you react?'

'I think I'd be happy to see daylight again. But I'd have very little trust in the person who got me out of there,' I answered honestly.

Breitner nodded. 'It is crucial for your inner child to know that you can be relied upon.'

'OK. And how do I do that?' I enquired.

'By being open and honest, providing true insight into your feelings.'

'Maybe I should first get some clarity about my own feelings towards my inner child.'

'Correct. That is exactly the point of the following exercise: formally apologising to your inner child. In black and white. In writing. You will take the time to put your feelings truly and earnestly into words. Putting it on paper ensures the apology will not be fleeting. Your counterpart, in this case your inner child, can then decide whether to accept your apology, set it aside or read it over and over again.'

'You want me to write a letter to my inner child?'

'Exactly. As a trust-building exercise. And as a way for you to fathom, organise and study your own feelings.'

'When should I finish it by?'

'Whenever you're ready.'

Standing in the shower, I was reminded of this letter. Now, more than three weeks after that coaching session, I still hadn't been able to write a passable apology. But I did have a handwritten fragment. This attempt was tucked into the back of Breitner's handbook. I turned off the shower, got dressed, walked into the living room, and pulled it out:

I'm so sorry about everything. I've ignored you for so long, I never knew what a marvel I've been sharing my life with all these years. Only now do I realise how we made life harder for each other. I would like to release you without hurting you. I'd like you to be able to live your own life. With me as your friend, not someone who constricts you — we've tried that long enough. That simply doesn't work, I now realise. I hope you find happiness in your new-found freedom. Perhaps the ballast of our past can become the foundation of a new partnership . . .

That's as far as I'd got.

27

Coincidences

Getting upset over 'stupid' coincidences does not serve you. Either everything that happens does so because of a higher power – which would hardly be stupid. Or everything actually happens by chance, in which case no one is responsible. But absolutely no one would agree that no one is stupid.

Joschka Breitner, *Slowing Down in the Fast Lane: Mindfulness for Managers*

I left the letter on my dining table and went to make myself an espresso. In doing so, however, I realised that I'd unfortunately wiped the contents of my last Nespresso capsule from the kitchen wall. As I didn't want to let anyone take away my morning espresso, I decided to meet this need of my inner child and mine at the café on the other side of the park. After putting on a jacket and shoes, I set off. A little walk would do me good.

A refreshing October sun had risen over the park. The leaves on the trees reminded me of the celebrity guests on Saturday-night talk shows. Their best days might be behind them, but as they slowly withered, they could tell sunny stories of summers past. Swaying back and forth, their reminiscing couldn't help but put viewers in a good mood. They clung to their branches, no matter how thin, until a moody wind finally carried them away and dropped them anywhere, forgotten. Next spring, new buds would sprout and grow to meet their own inevitable decay.

I crossed the playground, which no longer bore any traces of last night. Both the broken glass and the lowlifes responsible had been removed. Only the scorched wood of the playground equipment, the graffiti on the benches and the smashed window of the little free library revealed that some big blokes had felt too at home here for too long, protected by the inaction of the state. At least, more at home than the littler visitors, whose carefree play area should've been protected. And who instead were forced to leave the playground with burst tyres. But after last night, I assumed peace would now reign here, at least in the near future.

I'd just passed the playground when Walter called. *At least there's a little ray of light*, I thought. The made-up story about the threat of the Holgersson family had secured me a quiet night. And hopefully also secured a park newly free from drunks. The first problem that'd been completely resolved thanks to my partnership with my inner child.

Far from it.

'Hi, Björn. I wanted to debrief you about last night. Your suspicions were correct.'

'What suspicions?'

'Two of the guys from the park are connected to the Holgerssons. They're small fry, but definitely members of their crew.'

This really threw me. I stopped abruptly, flopping onto the nearest park bench. Considering how wild my claim had been, what was the probability that, out of four and a half thousand members of a criminal family scattered across Germany, a single one happened to be loitering on my doorstep? I now knew the answer: 200 per cent.

'What – two of them? How did you find that out?'

'After your call yesterday, we went to the park with four teams of two. There were eight blokes in the playground. Quite drunk, some stoned. Highly aggressive. We overpowered them, secured them with zip ties and gagged them with duct tape. It wasn't easy, but good practical training for my people.'

I let my gaze wander over the playground and imagined the drunks' surprised faces. Finding out that violating a rule could have consequences must've been an other-worldly experience.

'Very good. Then what happened?'

'Then my people checked everyone's papers. Six of them are random losers with too much testosterone. Probably all over eighteen.'

'How do you mean, "probably"?'

'I think the X-rays of their carpal bones will confirm that.'

'Why should they be X-rayed?'

'Because three of them may have accidentally broken their wrists.'

'Ouchy.' That was exactly the kind of violence I'd been trying to avoid.

'What was especially ouchy was the broken glass. We neatly lined up six of these eight dunces on the ground in two rows of three – they hadn't been this well sorted in a long time. What may have been somewhat unpleasant for the gentlemen is the fact that they'd previously littered the place with broken glass.'

In previous days, only toddlers had been close enough to the ground to learn that broken glass can really hurt you.

'In any case, now the gentlemen can use the opportunity to complain to the city council that environmental services aren't cleaning the playgrounds with sufficient assiduousness,' I said, trying to neutrally frame my inner conflict between compassion and satisfaction.

'I doubt these gentlemen could even spell the word "assiduousness". In any case, this morning at seven, the park's cleaning guys found six blokes bound and gagged and freezing in the playground. The cleaners were the ones who called the police.'

'And the other two?' I had a bad feeling about them.

'They were exactly who you suspected. Members of the Holgersson family, according to their papers. We took them with us.'

'Where to?' The question was unnecessary. In the basement of Walter's security company headquarters was an interrogation room I knew very well. Six months earlier, that's where I had first made someone talk. At the time, I'd been able to overcome my initial internal resistance to torture thanks to a surprisingly pertinent mindfulness exercise. I was realising that the Holgerssons story my inner child and I had made up to protect ourselves against potential violence was instigating actual violence wherever it encountered reality. Although it hadn't touched me yet, that didn't mean it was what I wanted.

'In my basement,' Walter answered, as I'd feared. 'They're acting like they have no idea why we picked them up. They claim not to have heard of either Boris, Dragan or you.'

'You asked about all three of us?' Of course he had. After my call, he had to assume that the blokes were in the park because of me, so they must know who I was. But they hadn't, until he asked. After that, they definitely did.

'Of course. That's why you wanted us to go to the park, innit? And you were right.'

No, I wasn't. And that's why we were now in a world of trouble. The two gentlemen inevitably shared Boris's fate: two more cellar dwellers I didn't know what to do with. If they ever left Walter's basement, they'd significantly reduce my quality of life.

Unlike my inner child, none of these three would want to spend a partnership week with me.

But I really only had this Holgerssons problem because I'd listened to my inner child.

On top of all my existing problems with my marriage, my private life and being blackmailed by some crazy stranger, I'd now also gotten into trouble with a thousands-strong crime family, which was the very last thing I needed.

I got the feeling that my number of problems hadn't exactly diminished since the beginning of this partnership week with my inner child. But maybe it was normal for things to get worse before the real healing could start.

'So what are you going to do with those two guys?' I asked, hoping he had a plan.

'If you give us an hour, the two of them will give us all the answers we need.'

No, they wouldn't. Because there weren't any answers. These two had just had the wrong names in the wrong place at the wrong time. Poor sods.

'Did they have anything on them?'

'Fifteen grams of coke, two pistols, three knives.'

All right, OK, I didn't need to feel sorry for anyone

loitering on my daughter's playground with fifteen grams of coke, two pistols and three knives and shouting words like 'Twaaaaat!' loudly enough to reach my top-floor balcony. Walter had picked them up because of their crew's name. And now they knew mine, they could never leave again. Plus, Walter could never know that this whole Holgerssons-Boris-golden-child connection didn't even exist. Especially not during a spontaneous bit of interrogative torture.

'Walter, do me a favour and hold off on interrogations for now. Leave the two of them locked up. Don't let anyone talk to them. I'll come by and we'll sort this on the spot.'

I needed a solution to this problem with the two Holgerssons in Walter's basement.

I needed a solution for Katharina's suspicions that I was cheating on her.

I needed a solution for the unknown extortionist who wanted us to cut Boris's head off.

Not to even mention the fact that I had to dissuade a pack of hand-grenade mums high on sustainability from ripping the oil heater out of the preschool's cellar and thereby exposing Boris's hiding place.

And on top of that, I had to have lunch with Laura's ludicrous brother.

My agenda was packed. With exactly the kind of problems that annoyed me immensely – every single horrible one of them. I should be able to reduce the stress they were causing through mindfulness. In the future, however, what I really wanted was to avoid them ever arising in the first place. Wasn't that why I had started this dialogue with my inner child?

28

Real and Unreal

When some anxiety starts to trouble you, however unreal it may be, focus all your senses on a real object instead. What is it shaped like? What colour is it? How much does it weigh? What is its texture? What does it sound like when you rap your knuckles against it? What does it smell like? How does it taste? Once you have answered all these very real questions, your unreal anxiety will feel much less dramatic.

Joschka Breitner, *Slowing Down in the Fast Lane: Mindfulness for Managers*

At the other side of the park was Café Meier-Dennhard. Over their almost one hundred years in existence, they'd allegedly only changed their interior fittings (and that includes staff) three times. That was a good thing. Their last renovation had taken place in the early 1980s, and the staff had decades of service experience. Here, I felt at home both visually and spiritually. Although I'd only been living in the neighbourhood for six months, the waitresses knew me by name and sensed what I wanted to order before I did.

'Good morning, Mr Diemel. Double espresso and a glass of water?' they greeted me as I stepped through the door. Words that Nils from the Allgäu hut should perhaps have had embroidered on his sequinned T-shirt instead. I gave them a friendly nod in affirmation and sat down at a small table for two in the back. My espresso came right away, and after two small sips I felt invigorated enough to call Sasha. I wanted to tell him about the lippy monster and the Holgerssons in Walter's basement, but he had some news of his own.

'Good that you called. The blackmailer just got in touch.'

'Another letter on our doorstep?'

'No, an email. And before you ask – the name and address are made up. IP address in the Philippines. I already checked.'

'And what does he say?'

'I'll forward the email. Read it and then call me back, OK?'

'OK.'

For mindfulness reasons, I hadn't set up an email app on my smartphone. I didn't want to be able to check it every twenty minutes – and then get upset over either not getting any new messages or having to deal with new trivialities. Thirty years ago, no one would've thought to walk to their letterbox every twenty minutes to see if they had any new mail. The postman came once a day. That was quite enough. After that, the 'You've got mail' issue was resolved for the next twenty-four hours. I now handled my inbox exactly the same way. In mindfulness circles, this was called a 'digital detox'. On my computer at home, I'd even put my professional inbox on a separate desktop. I switched to it at set times exactly twice a day to check my email. I had finally gotten off that permanent availability merry-go-round I'd been stuck on.

But this was an emergency. So, to read Sasha's email, I opened the browser on my smartphone and typed in the URL of my email provider. I got the password wrong several times. Why they now had to include so many numbers and special characters was beyond me. In the past, the postman sometimes handed people their mail directly because he knew the recipients personally. Not because they knew to whisper 'C@t!p1xi3' in his ear. At least my computer at home now considered me senile enough that it always offered me the passwords before I could even type what it was asking for.

My phone didn't do this. Like in the board game Master-mind, I had to use a process of elimination to find out whether my email password was 'emily', 'EMI!Y', '3mily' or '3MI!Y'. After five minutes, I had it. The password was 'kathar1n@'.

Sasha had forwarded the blackmailer's email.

Nice that the preschool is open again. One head by Friday. One ear by tomorrow. Or the friendly preschool father in the attached pictures will find out who's been living under the Flipper group's room. Tomorrow morning, at 7.00 a.m., I expect the ear to be on the wall opposite the preschool, wrapped in the front page of that day's Bild newspaper. Before doing so, you will photograph the sliced-off ear from all sides. Along with the front page. And send the photos to this email address.

Two pictures were attached. Both featured a friendly preschool papa I knew only too well: Peter Egmann. The detective chief inspector.

This meant we needed to cut off one of Boris's ears in less than twenty-four hours. How sick and twisted. It felt unreal, and I tried to suppress the panic that came over me.

There was a mindfulness exercise that normally worked wonders. I wanted to focus on something real that I could take in and describe with all my senses. While my brain was busy perceiving something real, it had no capacity left to deal with a completely unreal notion like cutting off someone's ear. I tried concentrating on the attached pictures of Peter. As I found out, a JPEG was not an ideal object to take in with all one's senses. The file had no weight, no smell, no taste. But the image did have shape, colour, content. So, I mindfully focused on the latter aspects instead.

The first picture seemed to show Peter dropping off his son this morning. At least, that's what the date printed on the picture suggested. Like many parents' cars, Peter's was double-parked. He was carrying his son to protect him from the traffic.

The second picture showed Peter returning to his car without his son five minutes later and tearing up the ticket that had been stuck under his windscreen wiper.

Instead of calming me, however, the exercise immediately started to upset me. Not because of Peter. The blackmailer couldn't have realised just how much this image would make my blood boil. It was about the parking in front of the preschool.

During the peak times of drop-off and pick-up, the lack of designated zones meant that parents had no choice but to park illegally. Whereas any phone shop was given a designated delivery zone, preschools sadly were not. This meant that traffic wardens would regularly come by to give out tickets. And that's exactly what upset me when I looked at that picture of Peter. When I called the community safety office late at night to inform them that the playground was being misappropriated by adults, the authorities didn't give a toss. When residents called the community safety office early in the morning to inform them that parents were dropping off three-year-old preschoolers from double-parked cars, however, the authorities were immediately on the case.

If the authorities cared as much about public park offences as public parking offences, I wouldn't have two offenders in Walter's basement.

But when it came to illegal parking, us parents were to blame. Why didn't we just take our little ones to preschool on one of those e-scooters that are solving all our traffic issues? In fact, from time to time there would be an electric scooter parked on the pavement outside the preschool. Probably left by some idiot who took his kid into traffic with it.

Perhaps it'd help everyone involved if a wedding convoy blocked the street during drop-off and pick-up. Once parents were stuck in such a traffic jam, they could get out of their car and drop off their children without facing any penalties. But I hadn't yet discovered a start-up that disrupted the wedding-convoy market through a sharing platform.

At least getting upset about the parking situation had achieved one thing: I had gone minutes without thinking about Boris's ears. Or about the Holgerssons.

Unlike my inner child. It spoke up.

'*Sorry to bother you, but that letter isn't about illegal parking. It's about ears.*'

'*It's about one ear, to be exact,*' I corrected my inner child.

'*Even if it were about only half an earlobe – we're not cutting off even the tiniest slice of Boris's ear. We don't want to. We owe Tapsi as much. Can we agree on that?*'

'*I also don't want to. But right now I can't think of any alternative. You?*'

And sure enough: my inner child *had*. And given the undeniable circumstances, it wasn't even that bad.

29

Doubts

Doubting your own solutions is perfectly normal. There are at least two alternatives to any proposed solution: a better one and a worse one. Use that. If someone expresses any doubts about a solution you proposed, gently request they propose a better one. If they are unable to, share a worse one. This will not only rid you of the doubter, but also any remaining doubts of your own.

Joschka Breitner, *Slowing Down in the Fast Lane: Mindfulness for Managers*

Double-parking was the least of my problems. I called Sasha back to discuss the single biggest problem facing us: the blackmailer.

'We should meet.'

'Shall I come up?'

'I'm not at my office. I'm at the café across the street.'

'I'll pick you up and we'll go for a walk. You've seen it – obviously this idiot is freely and openly watching us. With a bit of luck, Walter's people will spot whoever's following us.'

'A shot in the dark?'

'Do you have a better idea?'

'Yes, but we should discuss it in person. Come over and we'll go for a walk.'

'With or without security?'

'With. Certainly can't hurt.'

I paid for my double espresso and was waiting outside when Sasha arrived. We decided to take a walk through the neighbourhood, which was deserted in the morning. There was enough to talk about. First, I told Sasha what had happened in the park overnight.

'In other words,' Sasha summed up my summary with a frown, 'this made-up story about the Holgerssons is gaining momentum.'

'Do you see an issue with that?'

'When it came to protecting us from an escaped Boris, I thought the story worked really well. Luckily, Boris didn't actually escape. So, building on the story only to have a quiet night was perhaps a bit . . . what's the word? Childish.'

'Childlike,' I corrected him.

'I know this isn't my native language, but what is *so* important about this difference that you've already corrected me on it twice since yesterday?'

'Childish means an adult behaving immaturely. Childlike means a child behaving age-appropriately.'

Sasha looked at me.

'Sorry, but if I'm not mistaken, you're a forty-three-year-old lawyer.'

'And inside every adult is the child they once were.'

Sasha didn't question the psychological concept behind this. And I had no intention of explaining it to him now.

'If you say so. But please tell that child in you that it's naive not to believe every action has consequences.'

I soothingly patted the parrot in my pocket.

'Didn't the boys in the park learn that exact lesson?' I responded, defending my inner child's wish from the day before. But Sasha didn't immediately follow my logic.

'Don't get me wrong – all that noise at night gets on my nerves too. Several times I've even been on the verge of going down and knocking those idiots around a bit myself. But didn't we want to renounce violence? Plus, what has Walter's violence brought us? Now we have two more massive problems on our hands. We already have one Boris, and personally

I find the idea of putting two Holgerssons in a basement at the other end of town rather alarming. Two more blokes we don't have even the slightest idea what to do with.'

'Maybe that just changed, maybe there's something we can do with them after all . . .'

I explained to Sasha the idea about Boris's ear that my inner child had shared with me. It took Sasha a beat to understand what I was suggesting.

'You want us to cut off their ears?' Sasha was stunned.

'Not *theirs* and not *ears*. This is only about one ear,' I said, keeping our facts straight.

'I don't think we should let this Holgersson story escalate any further. Cutting off ears is no joke.'

Funny that. When my inner child told me this idea, it'd sounded very coherent. I probably needed to explain to Sasha what I really liked about the idea. Namely, that it met my inner child's need to leave our cellar guest unharmed. And that meeting such needs could overwrite negative experiences from my childhood. Yet I had the feeling that might overwhelm Sasha, so my explanation had better dispense with lingo like 'partnership week', 'negative core beliefs', 'strengthening basic trust', 'armour' and, above all, 'Tapsi'.

'*One* ear,' I corrected Sasha again. 'And we wouldn't cut it off as punishment for sitting around in a park at night yelling "twat". We would cut off one ear of one random arsehole who, armed with guns and knives and carrying fifteen grams of coke, decided to shower a children's play-ground with broken glass.'

Sasha still wasn't convinced.

'Do you have a better suggestion?' I asked. He didn't. 'Listen, Sasha, what do you prefer: cut off one of Boris's ears tonight yourself, or have Walter's people discreetly deliver a carefully packed ear from one of those idiots this afternoon?'

'I mean, I don't know . . .'

'To put it like a simple formula: there are six ears on offer, four unknown and two known ones. We need to part with one of them. How would you decide?'

'*Good reasoning,*' my inner child commended me. '*For the first time, I feel safe without any armour.*'

'If you put it like that . . .'

'There you go.'

'And how do you imagine this happening practically? I mean – with one ear missing, we can never let them out of Walter's basement.'

'Would it be any different if they each had two intact ears? These guys know our names, they know who pulled them out of the park, they just don't know why – so they and the rest of the Holgerssons will want to find out by any means necessary.'

'So what should we do with those two and their three ears after? I thought we didn't want to kill anyone any more.'

My inner child spoke up again. '*Let's not worry about that for now. We've decided to live in the moment, with love and without judgement. If we need an ear, we need an ear. If we have another problem, we have another problem,*' my inner child noted, sounding somewhere between wise and precocious. Even when I had no idea my inner child existed, it had apparently been listening carefully and internalised my entire mindfulness course. But it was absolutely right. Now, in this moment, our one and only problem was that we needed to deliver an ear in the short term. Not what we should do about those guys in Walter's basement in the long term.

'I'm not worrying about that right now,' I answered. 'I live in the moment.'

'Right now, I'm wondering what exactly to tell Walter. On what grounds could we need one of the Holgerssons' ears cut off?'

'Pfft . . . Why do criminals ever cut other criminals' ears off?' I said, posing a counter-question.

'*As a message,*' my inner child answered spontaneously. '*With this ear, Dragan quite clearly tells the Holgerssons: no matter what Boris has done to your golden child – stay away from my crew! That threat might protect us.*'

That was surprisingly quick, and surprisingly convincing. What's more, it could be the first step in an ongoing strategy to de-escalate the Holgersson threat we'd made up for Walter.

'On instruction from Dragan. As a little message to the Holgerssons about what happens if they get too close to you or me.'

'But the Holgerssons aren't—' Sasha wanted to object.

I didn't let him finish. 'You, me and the Holgerssons know that. For Walter, we should stick with the story he still believes.'

'OK – sounds plausible. But it'll be an unpleasant affair for whoever ends up having to actually do it.'

'Not necessarily. When it comes to that, I have a pretty good idea . . .' Which was a lie insofar as this idea was another one of my inner child's. 'What we have are two petty criminals, fifteen grams of coke, two pistols and three knives. What we need is one ear. The solution consists of three simple steps. First, we give each of the boys one gram of coke back. Second, once the two of them have hopped themselves back up with it, we return one of their knives each. Third, we give the boys a mildly fictitious task: whoever cuts off one of the other's ears first gets to leave the basement with both ears intact.'

'And what happens if the two of them don't want to do any coke?'

'I'm sure Walter's people will adroitly address that particular problem if it should come to that. Make it clear to them that I appreciate their creative input.' I'd had enough of this annoying discussion. Dragan would never have had to face so many follow-up questions and quibbles. 'How hard could it be to convince two dealers to get high on their own supply?'

For my part, I found my inner child's plan utterly ingenious. At least, at this point I still did. When it wasn't yet clear to me that Sasha's concerns did indicate a not-insignificant problem.

30

Irritations

Your inner child's creativity may be disturbing to others – so was the invention of the wheel.

Joschka Breitner, *Parenting Your Inner Child*

'Wow.' Sasha was obviously impressed. 'Do they teach this kind of stuff in law school?'

'No, in handbooks. It's a long story. Could you please brief Walter accordingly?'

'Why don't we drive straight to Walter?'

'I have to meet a potential client for lunch.'

'Who?'

'Laura's brother.'

'Laura?'

'Laura Frieling, Max's mum. My deputy on the Nemo group's parents' committee.'

'That attractive doctor? Are you cosying up to the brother to get to the sister?'

I didn't want Sasha to have any part in my marriage crisis. 'It's purely professional,' I dodged. 'New client.'

'I thought you no longer wanted any new clients?' Sasha exclaimed. 'And then you pick an idiot like that?' Obviously, my inner child was not alone in doubting the wisdom of agreeing to see this new client.

'You know this Kurt bloke?'

'Of course, he picks up Max once a week. Often too late. And sometimes on one of those silly electric scooters. The week before last, he arrived more than an hour after closing.

Annoyingly, no one had noticed Max was still there. He must've hidden before the educators left. Max had the run of the place until that Kurt rang my doorbell. Good thing I live here too.'

Since the week before last, Max had been talking about this lippy monster that – what with our ears-based discussion – hadn't even entered my mind for the past thirty minutes. The week before last. That was when Boris had heard the kid whistling in the cellar. I told Sasha that Boris's first visitor must've been Laura's son, Max.

'Would Max have had a chance to get down there in that one hour?' I asked.

Sasha considered this. 'No idea. But . . . we can't rule it out. The preschool door wasn't locked. Nor was the door to the cellar. After all, no one lives here but us. When Kurt rang my doorbell, we found Max playing in the Nemo room by himself. Where he went in the meantime – no idea.'

'Does this Kurt know?'

'Again, no idea.' Sasha shrugged. 'But I don't think the bloke can be trusted. It might not be a bad idea to find out what he knows about this lippy monster story. Don't get me wrong, his sister is hot, but hot enough you'd take on the brother as a client? Well, you do you.'

I would appreciate it if Katharina had this tolerant attitude. In any case, I now knew there were a few more issues I should critically assess Kurt on.

We'd already reached our street when we quickly went through the results of our search for connections between Boris and the preschool.

I had made a list and so had Sasha.

On the side of Dragan's crew, two officers had a personal relationship to Little Fish: Walter's sister had placed her son at the preschool, and Stanislav, Dragan's human trafficking officer, had a girlfriend whose daughter was in the Flipper group. Both of them, however, had zero motive for wanting to take revenge on Boris, Sasha or me. They had neither any knowledge of Boris staying in the cellar nor any interest in harming Sasha or me.

Out of the preschool's more 'civilian' parents, only Peter Egmann, the detective chief inspector, and Mr Breuer, the head of the building control department, explicitly knew that Sasha and I were closely associated with a criminal organisation. Based on the aforementioned 'best interests' principle, we'd given three other parents a spot for their child. Although these parents had an idea of the operation behind the preschool, they had no idea of Boris's existence.

'These lists won't get us anywhere,' I summed up.

'Unfortunately not. The blackmailer must have *some* connection to Boris and to the preschool. We just can't see it yet. I tried something else – with equally little success.'

Sasha handed me another list of names.

'I also spent some time on which parents might have access to the prescription medication Boris was sedated with.'

'Good idea. Does that get us anywhere?'

'Not really, no. Two parents run a pharmacy. Four are doctors and could have issued a prescription.'

I looked over the list. As a doctor, Laura was also listed. But she had no connection to Boris. She'd only moved to the city six months ago. By then, Boris was already in our cellar. None of the other names seemed to have any connection to Boris either.

In the meantime, we'd arrived outside our building. We hadn't even had time to talk about the agenda for the parents' committee meeting. I'd have to bring that up that later. We said goodbye in the hallway, and I got to my apartment in time to expect Kurt's call. Back on the street, we'd briefly checked with the security team – no one had been following us.

31

Working Through

Not everything in life feels good. Not even everything in a single good day. But it is up to us how we divide our time between what feels good and what does not. Do not keep postponing duties just because they might not feel good. Make room for the good by working through and moving on from what is not.

Joschka Breitner, *Slowing Down in the Fast Lane: Mindfulness for Managers*

Kurt's promised call to say he was waiting outside didn't come at twelve thirty, however, but almost an hour later. And when I stepped out of the front door downstairs, I also noticed that Kurt hadn't arrived on foot – as Laura's characterisation had suggested – but in a Mercedes S-Class from a local limo service. With a driver. His window half down, Kurt sat in the back sucking on a vape, one of those gadgets that looks like it was born from the drunken coupling of an insulin syringe and a gas lighter.

On Kurt, however, it looked fitting. Visually, he also seemed the opposite of his sister. Late forties, badly proportioned and pallid. Flabby, at least three stone overweight, and going thin on top. As I approached, Kurt didn't get out of the car. He was waiting for me to sit down on the back seat next to him.

The rest of the man's appearance didn't require me to revise my initial impression. He wore expensive sneakers, designer jeans, and a far-too-tight T-shirt with a very expensive suit jacket over it. The greatest gap between money and taste. The exact kind of overpriced sporty outfit that embarrassingly underscores the wearer's utter lack of athleticism.

Out of nowhere, I suddenly found myself wondering whether I wanted to father a child with someone who shared 50 per cent of Kurt's genes. But fortunately, that's not what this was about; my thoughts often overshot their immediate target.

I was meeting Laura's brother for much more realistic reasons:

Because I couldn't say no to Laura when she'd looked so vulnerable on my sofa.

Because I still couldn't say no even after I'd suffered the consequences of her mirror message.

Because I wanted to wrap up the problem I'd saddled myself with.

And because I was still very interested in this guy's sister – despite her note on my mirror. Or perhaps because of it.

At least, these had been all the reasons until my conversation with Sasha. Now I was also interested in whether Kurt had any hitherto unknown connection to Boris, as that would make him a possible blackmailer. After all, so far his nephew Max's lippy story was our only solid indication that someone had discovered Boris was being kept in the cellar. Maybe on that very day Kurt was late picking up his nephew. But all of it was so elusive that, regardless of Laura, I now did want to meet Kurt in person.

'What's up, Björn!' Kurt grinned at me. 'Great that we could meet so soon.'

'Yeah, Laura said it was urgent.'

'Isn't it great to have a little sister who thinks of everything?'

I didn't have a little sister and primarily considered Laura an independent, adult woman. The car's melange of new leather, vape smoke and a rather repellent aftershave was nauseating. I glossed over that too. One lunch with this guy, then I'd never have to see him again.

'Laura is wonderful. But to be honest, I'm a little surprised you're picking me up in a car. I thought you didn't drive.'

'I'm not, am I? Mehmet's driving. Aren't you, Mehmet?' Kurt jovially patted the driver's shoulder.

'My name is Murat,' the man replied matter-of-factly.

'Lost my driving licence, didn't I? It happens.'

Right. If you drive too fast. Or drunk. Or too fast *and* drunk – and you have a bad lawyer to boot. The fact that he'd sold it to his own sister as a voluntary act of renunciation to save the planet said a lot about Kurt.

'But don't tell Laura – anything I say is subject to client confidentiality, right?'

'You could say that.' But you didn't have to. 'What happened?'

'Got clocked driving twenty-five kilometres too fast twice in one year.'

That kind of trifling offence would've gotten him a one-month driving ban at most. If Kurt had to do without his car for several months, then there'd been either quite a few more km/h or a higher alcohol percentage. So, he wasn't just lying to his sister, but to me too.

'What else did my sister tell you about me?'

I decided to play dumb.

'Not much. I'm curious to see what I can do for you.'

'I'll tell you over lunch. I've gotten us a table at Gaucháo-Rodizio.'

273

Gaucháo-Rodizio was a Brazilian steakhouse. The best in town. Meat so tender it melted in your mouth. This, even though – or perhaps precisely *because* – the meat had been airlifted from the deforested pastures of Brazil's former rainforests almost 10,000 kilometres away. It was a top-tier restaurant, but its offerings were neither regional nor organic.

Our table was in a quiet back corner of the restaurant, which was decorated with lots of tropical hardwood. You had to hand Kurt one thing: he was a dab hand at small talk. Throughout our lunch, he led the conversation.

It started with our starter. Small, easily digestible bites that made a great impression, as long as you didn't worry about their ethical provenance. Yet I did, with regards to both the starter – it starred foie gras – and what Kurt was telling me.

He presented himself as the green saviour Laura had described to me. At least, by what he said. Not in the slightest by his actions.

Kurt knew exactly how much less CO_2 would be emitted if Germany imposed a speed limit of 130 km/h and was outraged that it hadn't already been introduced ages ago. Irresponsible, he called it. An interesting position to take, considering he was a state-certified speed demon without a driving licence who'd always been free to voluntarily drive at 130 km/h.

Kurt could get upset about animal transports and piglets' castration without anaesthesia while he enjoyed big bites of foie gras from forcibly fattened five-month-old geese.

Neither Kurt nor the German proprietors of Gaucháo-Rodizio seemed to be interested in the fact that, for animal welfare reasons, the sale of foie gras was prohibited in Brazil.

Kurt was against the simplification of politics and the brutalisation of political culture. With the same bite still in his mouth, however, he also claimed that this was exactly why populists deserved to get smacked in the face whenever possible.

He was in favour of state subsidies for all train tickets. Railways being not only climate-neutral, but also a means of transport untouched by status anxiety. He never took the train himself, however, because he couldn't make or take any phone calls in peace, unlike in the car.

He was all for an equal, open, colourful, free society. Yet for his own company, I later learned, he'd hired exactly 0 per cent people with a disability, 10 per cent women and 5 per cent migrants.

I was firmly convinced that the narcissistic Kurt did not see this discrepancy in his own world-view because he was too busy admiring his ethical reflection. As I noticed with growing amusement, this was because he was simply unable to look another person in the eye.

Our main course he spent raving about his company. We were served one perfectly medium-grilled 400-gram fillet steak each. Kurt's came with chips. I too would've loved some chips, but I wasn't keen on having anything in common with Kurt, even just a side dish. I'd therefore ordered grilled corn on the cob instead. I drank tap water, Kurt a white wine.

As Kurt launched into his steak, he launched into this next topic: 'I own CN-Mobility.'

'Never heard of it.'

'We're the biggest electric scooter rental agency in town.'

'How many do you have?'

'About seven hundred and fifty of them.'

Or rather, as Laura had said: five hundred. But then rounding errors of 50 per cent can even happen when you're discussing world-saving transport innovations.

'My one scooter was taken away from me, but this total loser is allowed to have seven hundred and fifty of them?' my inner child balked.

'He only has five hundred. The rest is just showing off.'

'Fantastic. Two hundred and fifty pinpricks fewer. Please, tear this guy apart.'

All right then, I tried to take Kurt's argumentation apart a little. I owed my inner child as much.

'What does CN-Mobility stand for?'

'For a sustainable, colourful, liberal-minded society.'

'Ah. And here I thought you only rented out scooters.'

As Kurt didn't understand my sarcasm any more than he had my earlier question, I rephrased it.

'I meant, what do the letters C and N in CN-Mobility stand for?'

'For "carbon neutral", so carbon-neutral mobility.'

'Carbon-neutral? E-scooters?'

'Exactly.'

'Now help me out: if someone walks from A to B, that's carbon-neutral mobility. When someone uses an electric scooter instead, they're using a device that's made of a whole lot of plastic, some metal and a pretty toxic battery. Doesn't all that have to be produced first? What's carbon-neutral about that?'

'Well, the mobility part. After all, we're not called CN-Production. The batteries are charged with green electricity.'

'Ah. Does the city have its own green grid then?'

'No . . . but we have a green electricity provider. They feed that power into the grid.'

'And you have a coal filter on your outlets that prevents scooters from accidentally being charged with coal-fired electricity?'

'Perhaps you should read up on how a power grid works.'

There we were, at the turning point of every discussion nowadays: if you dare ask even one critical question, you're accused of lacking the necessary expertise.

Still, I'd promised my inner child I'd be its protective armour in this conversation. But I wasn't sure if I was meant to be on the defence or offence. I threw the facts back at Kurt.

'Well, if I understand correctly, a power grid works like a sewer. Whatever everyone wees in at one end comes out all mixed together at the other. So, I wouldn't drink a champagne flute of sewage just because one person was in a festive mood and poured a bottle of bubbly down their toilet.'

In Kurt's power grid, this was obviously different. Once even one solar panel or wind turbine is connected, green electricity arrives on the consumer's end untouched. Even at night. And if there's no wind.

Kurt opened his mouth – only to quickly stuff in a large piece of meat, concealing the fact that he apparently couldn't think of a counter-argument. As he chewed, he gestured as though wanting to say something. Smiling on the inside, I waited him out for a while, ultimately relieving Kurt from his embarrassment out of politeness.

'OK, so you rent out these . . . as you say . . . carbon-neutral electric scooters. How does that work logistically?'

Grateful to be back on solid ground, Kurt immediately got carried away again.

'Super easy. You sign in through an app. It shows you where the nearest scooter is and then you can zip off. When you get to where you're going, you just leave the scooter.'

'Where the next person can pick it up, through the app.'

'Right. It's called scooter sharing.'

For several centuries, 'sharing' very specifically meant 'possessing in common'. This apparently didn't prevent Kurt from rather freely interpreting it as a vague kind of 'taking' – as in 'shareholder value'. He didn't care one bit that his scooters were strewn all over the place and that he was filling up public space with his private business model.

'And if no one needs a scooter where the last customer left it?' I carefully asked.

'Then we pick it up – we have to anyway, to charge them.'

'That would be my next question: who makes sure the scooters are charged?'

'Well, we do. And the app tells us where all the scooters are.'

'Does that mean that someone carbon-neutrally walks over and carries back every single empty scooter to a wall socket at the end of every day?'

'No, our return service does that every night.'

'And how does that work?'

'Our trucks drive to the individual scooters, take them to our depot and plug them in.'

'With what kind of truck? One of those electric ones, like the mail delivery vans?'

'We've got fifteen Mercedes Sprinters.'

'With diesel engines?'

'Nothing cheaper!'

'So every night, fifteen diesel vans bring your roughly seven hundred and fifty electric scooters back to your depot for charging?'

'Yes. In two shifts. Around seven p.m., the first trucks swarm out, returning the scooters that have been charged during the day and collecting the first batch of empty ones. They're back at the chargers by no later than ten p.m. At four a.m., the next shift then returns the scooters charged overnight to the collection stations and collects the rest of the empty scooters, which are then charged again during the day. So, our depot gets crazy busy around ten p.m. and four a.m. A logistical bloodbath, I tell you. But that's how there are always enough fully charged carbon-neutral scooters distributed throughout the city at any time of the day.'

'Because your fifteen diesel trucks drive them there twice a night?'

Kurt jovially slapped me on the shoulder. 'Now you understand. You're practically one of us already!' This flattered neither me nor the child inside me. My inner child did have a follow-up question, which I was happy to pass on.

'Hmm . . . wouldn't it be easier for your customers to order one of those fifteen trucks via the app to be driven straight to their destination?'

I didn't know if Kurt's face looked confused or just stupid, so I clarified.

'I mean, if these fifteen trucks are driving after the scooters twice a day anyway, couldn't they take the customers along instead?'

'Huh? What would that do?'

'You would save yourself the cost of all the scooters, and your customers would get to their destinations much more safely – at the same price too. And it wouldn't take as much CO_2, because the scooters wouldn't need to be built first.'

'But that's not our business model. We rent out scooters.'

'Because of sustainability. I see.'

We were silent for a moment while Kurt took another bite from a steak sliced off a Brazilian bovine who, mere days earlier, had grazed where a sustainable rainforest had been cut down a few months earlier to make room for more torture breeding.

'So you make your money trying to prevent a climate catastrophe,' I said, trying to end our conversation on a conciliatory note.

'No, I earn my money *from* the climate catastrophe,' he said, toasting me.

Luckily, my glass was empty. Climate change as a business model, at least he was honest about that.

Despite his sporty outfit, the food and wine seemed to be affecting Kurt's own thermal balance. He took off his jacket and hung it over the back of his chair. His expensive designer T-shirt was not only too tight on his stomach, but also too short in the arms. This revealed some artwork. On his flabby right upper arm there was the kind of tattoo a person gets after they lose a drunken bet in Mallorca. A bright-red heart with a black border. With a band around the heart. Kurt's said 'ANNA'. If Anna was a younger Kurt's consensual 'indiscretion', then she'd certainly made the far greater mistake.

Though Kurt had been talking the whole time, his legal issue hadn't come up yet. Over dessert, I steered the conversation to the reason I was there.

'Laura told me you have a legal problem?'

'Right. I have a problem with my landlord.'

From his jacket's inner pocket, Kurt pulled out a plastic sleeve of documents.

'What kind of problem?' I asked.

'Naturally, we need quite a bit of power to charge our batteries. The wiring at our headquarters has already been modernised at my expense. But it still isn't enough. We need to get the electricians in again to basically rewire the entire building. Fire hazards and such. According to my contract, I'm free to do that at my own expense.'

'So, where's the problem?'

'I can't get to the main power line. It's in the cellar,

behind a thick steel door. And only the landlord has the key.'

I was a little irritated. I was a lawyer, not a locksmith.

'Then your landlord should unlock the door,' I concluded, my free piece of advice for this initial consultation.

'That's the issue. I haven't been able to reach him for months.'

'Is there no property management you could reach out to?'

'There is – but they can't reach him either.'

'And who is this landlord?'

Kurt handed me a copy of the lease. The landlord's name was printed in bold on the first page.

'I don't know him personally. Some Russian businessman who, for the past six months, seems to have just . . .'

I didn't have to hear any more. I knew this landlord. He lived downstairs from me. It was Boris.

32

Dialogue

The ability to communicate with your inner child is a gift. Once you have mastered it, you no longer need self-doubt, self-blame or self-talk. You can arrange anything through a friendly dialogue with your inner child.

Joschka Breitner, *Parenting Your Inner Child*

Kurt knew Boris. I needed to let that sink in for a bit. Although – he didn't know Boris at all. Supposedly, he'd never even seen him before. But at the same time, his god-child, Max, did happen to have an unobserved opportunity to overhear Boris in the cellar. And had been talking about a lippy monster ever since. No, this couldn't be a coincidence.

'*This can't be a coincidence,*' my inner child promptly affirmed. '*This scooter jerk is playing with us.*'

'*But why? How does that make sense?*' I asked us. '*Why would this climate catastrophe incarnate blackmail us? And then have the gall to meet with me?*'

'*For the same reason he can turn the climate crisis into a business model without a shred of shame,*' my inner child said. '*Because he's shameless and simply thinks he can.*'

Or because he had an inner child who he knew nothing about, but who *convinced* him he could. However, I was not a psychologist, but a lawyer. Consequently, I tried to approach the issue in legal terms.

'And how can I be of assistance in this as a lawyer?' I asked Kurt. 'After all, I don't know where your landlord is either.'

'You think I should call the police because my landlord disappeared?' Kurt volleyed back with a hint of feigned innocence.

'Depends on what you want to achieve,' I replied, my face studiously blank.

Were we talking about that blocked access to his power line or about the blackmail?

'I thought you could give the landlord some kind of legal deadline to open the door, or . . . just sue him. No idea. Whatever lawyers do.'

'OK. Suppose we sue him, then it'd still be at least nine months before you'd get a judgement that entitles you to have the door opened by a locksmith. Would that help solve your problem?'

'Let me put it like this: if the whole thing burns down within nine months because of some blown fuse, then I'll no longer have any financial worries.'

I looked irritated, and Kurt blurted out an arrogant explanation.

'I'm so well insured that a burning business would be even more lucrative than a thriving one. Still, we shouldn't spend nine months trying to force my landlord's hand, should we? What else can I do?'

'If you can prove that it's urgent, we can get a ruling more quickly through an interim order. That shouldn't take more than a few weeks.'

'There's no faster way?'

'Get a crowbar and break the door open. It's called DIY.'

'Do you have any idea how hard it is to break open an iron door?' Kurt asked me in a tone that was almost naive.

'No, you?' I asked, almost provocatively.

Kurt ignored my question. 'If that's your legal advice,

I'd be happy to give it a try.'

Were we dodging the issue, or was it all a stupid coincidence? Maybe I was just looking for suspects. Kurt happened to have a professional connection to Boris, and Max had come up with the lippy monster. That was really all I had.

Ah, yes – Kurt also could've gotten the sedative used on Boris through his sister.

However, many more important things were still far too unclear: why would Kurt want Boris's head? And why would he seek me out as well?

Sasha and I still had a full three days to find out.

In any case, I knew one thing: Kurt was deeply unlikeable. I tried to conclude our lunch meeting.

'Then have a think about whether you want to sue your landlord and get back to me. This lunch was certainly delicious. So, thank you very much.'

'*You want to see this guy again?*' My inner child was outraged.

'*Keep your friends close, but your enemies closer,*' I replied.

'*Ah, yes –*The Godfather Part II.'

I could play pretend to the whole world, but obviously not to my inner child.

Kurt and I each had an espresso, and Kurt paid the bill. I politely declined his offer to let his driver take me back to the preschool. Eager to get rid of this guy as soon as possible, I took public transport home.

On the way, I tried to reach Sasha to tell him about Kurt. No answer.

I tried Katharina again. She'd be picking up Emily right after preschool. And sometimes Emily wanted to stop by my apartment or the office for a bit before going home with Katharina. Neither of us would argue in front of Emily, but I also wanted to make sure there wouldn't be any non-verbal tension in the air either.

To my surprise, Katharina answered after three rings.

'Katharina,' I started cautiously, 'I would like to explain to you what you read on the mirror this morning.'

'You don't have to explain anything to me,' she replied.

I had no idea if she meant that positively or negatively.

'We should at least talk about it,' I said, trying to keep our communication going. 'Not in passing or on the doorstep.'

If you looked at it without judgement, the subsequent silence was at least more positive than if she had hung up on me or not even picked up.

'Katharina?'

'Yes, you're right. Let's talk.'

'Maybe later, when you pick up Emily?'

'I . . . feel a little worn out from my first day back at work. I was planning to pick up Emily and take her home. But tomorrow I could come and meet you half an hour before pick-up. Would four thirty be OK with you?'

'Great, yes. So – how was your first day at work?'

'Actually, really nice. It's good to feel like a full human again, not just a mum.'

'What's the difference?'

'Aren't you on a committee with five mums?'

'Touché.'

Seconds after I'd hung up, my phone rang again. It wasn't Katharina, but an unknown number.

'Björn Diemel speaking.'

'So, was it bad?' Laura asked.

'*It's hard to say which was worse,*' whined my inner child. '*Her mirror message or her brother.*'

'What do you mean? Your lipstick message or lunch with your brother?'

'What's wrong with what I wrote? I felt guilty for saddling you with my brother, so I wanted to make it clear that I would've stayed behind after the meeting even if it wasn't for my brother.'

That made me feel good.

'I would've been *very* pleased with the message – if I'd had a chance to see it before my wife did.'

There was a brief, honest, concerned silence at the other end of the line. It was interesting how differently women could use silence to communicate. Then:

'I'm so sorry. I didn't even think anyone other than you . . . That must have gone down a treat. Sorry, really. I hope you didn't get into too much trouble?'

'Well, I can afford a new mirror. The seven years of bad luck is what I'm worried about.'

'Is there any way I can make it up to you?'

Since I'd already caught flak for an affair I hadn't even had, maybe I shouldn't entirely rule out any future possibility of pleasure.

'*Kill your brother and move back to Bavaria,*' my inner child chirped in obvious disagreement.

'Maybe we can talk about it some time, just the two of us.' Luckily, Laura wasn't party to my internal dispute.

'That'd be wonderful. How about tomorrow? I have the night off. Kurt will be watching Max.'

Maybe I should clear up this issue with Katharina before I went on another date.

'I don't know if I'll be able to make that work yet. Would it be OK if I called you tomorrow afternoon to confirm?'

'That sounds good. And honestly – I'm really sorry about the mirror. That was childish of me.'

Childlike, I wanted to correct her. But suddenly I wasn't so sure.

33

Confidentiality

Discovering and liberating your inner child is the most personal thing you will ever do. The resulting positive changes to your life will make other people take notice and ask questions. When they do, keep your answers vague and do not bother people too much with the details. Conveying the nuances of inner-child work to the uninitiated can be an uphill task.

Joschka Breitner, *Parenting Your Inner Child*

I got back home around three in the afternoon. Outside the preschool stood Peter Egmann, his son on his arm and once again double-parked.

'Hi Peter,' I greeted him, 'was the parking ticket from this morning not enough?'

'How do you know about that?' he replied.

From the guy blackmailing me. If I don't cut off Boris's ear, he said he'd tell you that I'm holding Boris prisoner, would have been the factual but tactically unwise answer.

'I live here, you pick up on things,' I back-pedalled, wriggling out of my hasty remark.

Peter didn't notice. 'It's nice that there are still people with enough spare time to lean out the window and play block warden.'

'Instagram, only analogue,' I said, with a smile. 'Any news about the burglary?'

'Not exactly. Only that, last night, some council cleaners found six of those playground loiterers you suspected handcuffed in the park. Funny story that.'

'What's funny about it?'

'Well, apart from the fact that they were lined up like in a pencil case, the gentlemen claim that there were originally eight of them.'

'Why would anyone steal two pieces of shit from the park?'

'Perhaps for the same reason they'd tie up six of them in the park.' Peter studied me.

I returned the gaze, looking rather innocent. 'And?'

'Oh, never mind.' Peter waved it off. 'But now that I have you . . . Would you have half an hour to spare for me tomorrow morning? It's a work thing.'

'Because of those guys?'

'No, I'll explain it all to you tomorrow. Now I should really get . . .'

'Of course. Why don't you come up tomorrow after you've dropped off your little Lukas?'

'Will do. It's probably just a formality anyway . . .'

I got an uneasy feeling. A formality – like divorces, colon-cancer checks and executions.

When I got back upstairs, I took out Boris's files – as his lawyer, I'd taken most of them – to look for further connections between him and Kurt. But I found none. In fact, Kurt only appeared in that one rental agreement for the commercial property where he had his e-scooter depot.

In any case, I had to tell Sasha about the connection. By now, the preschool was closed. I called him.

'Lend me your ear for a minute?'

'To be honest, I've got four for you.'

'How do you mean?'

'Well . . . Walter called. The mutual cutting-off plan has backfired a little.'

'How so?'

'Maybe we should go see for ourselves.'

294

Walter's headquarters were in a featureless commercial building on the outskirts of the city, about twenty minutes from the preschool. Sasha and I drove over in my Defender, followed by one of Walter's security teams. On the way, I told Sasha about my lunch with Kurt. Sasha also couldn't figure out what motive Kurt might have to make us brutalise Boris. At least, we couldn't imagine where this apparently urgent hatred for us or Boris came from.

In the underground car park, Walter met us in person. He looked a little contrite.

'Guys, I don't know why you really made us rough up these blokes in the park. I don't care either – my crew enjoyed themselves, properly tidying up over there. I also don't know whether the fact that two of those playground losers are members of the Holgersson family is a coincidence. And I don't care either, because those two idiots in my conference room are pretty vile. I understand even less why one of them needed to have an ear cut off. Yet I also don't care about that, as I found the proposed solution very creative. It's a refreshing idea to make blokes who hang around playgrounds carrying drugs take the stuff themselves for a change.'

My inner child was pleased to hear about this appreciation for its proposed solution. And about Walter's attitude to drugs in playgrounds.

'That is, as long as it concerns outside drug dealers working a playground on our turf,' Walter continued, rather more enterprise-oriented, undermining the sympathy he'd just earned from my inner child.

'Unfortunately . . .' Walter concluded, 'and this is why I wanted you to come by in person – unfortunately, them taking their own drugs didn't have quite the desired effect.'

Whatever the effect *had* been, that speech already made one thing clear to me: Walter was clever. Like all of Dragan's officers – at least, the ones who were still alive. I quickly realised that we should cut back on his security team's protection. Before Walter's employees could answer his legitimate critical questions and use their own observations to figure out why they'd been asked to step in.

I didn't think this was the best time, however, to recap for Walter in a minute or two all I'd learned from my profound engagement with my inner child over the past several weeks.

Instead, I mindfully tried to put myself in Walter's place and address these issues accordingly.

'Walter, I want to thank you and your people for their great efforts over the last two days. I'm as surprised by these events as you are. If Dragan hadn't sent such detailed instructions, I'd also question every single part of this. But Dragan happens to see the Holgerssons as a threat. And he wants to respond to this threat in kind, by cutting off an ear. To put the Holgerssons in their place. You know Dragan, how cruel he can be. The sooner the Holgerssons understand they need to back off, the sooner this whole thing will be over. The ear thing is meant to de-escalate matters. According to Dragan.'

Only six months earlier, Dragan, with his irrational behaviour and tendency for escalation, had ignored what my inner child needed most. As I understood by now, this was one of the reasons he was then murdered. By me. Now, his changed behaviour already served as both excuse and justification for the actions of my inner child. A person's character can change quite a bit after they die. Which in this case worked in my favour.

'But,' I continued, 'surely we're not here to discuss the point of Dragan's instructions. We all know that'd be pointless. So then, which part of the plan didn't work?'

'Follow me.'

Walter led us through a fire door into the basement. Our security team stayed in the car park. The soundproof interrogation room was at the end of a corridor. Directly adjoining it was an observation room with a one-way mirror. Inside were two more of Walter's operators. We joined them in front of the 2 x 3-metre window into the so-called conference room.

In the middle of the room was a rectangular table that would've comfortably seated four for dinner. But there were only two people sitting at the table. On opposite sides. Yet 'sitting at the table' wasn't an entirely fair description of the scene. Yes, their bums were on chairs, and they'd clearly consumed something, but not through their mouths. Their upper bodies lay on the tabletop, their forearms fixed to the table with duct tape. Their upper bodies too. Even their heads were taped to the table, ensuring one of their cheeks touched the table and their noses were only a few centimetres above it.

Their mouths were also taped shut. Next to each nose lay a plastic clothes peg.

Clear traces of a white powdery substance could be seen on the duct tape over their upper lips. There were also little piles of the stuff on the table under their noses. Neither man was moving. But the one on the left had a noticeably swollen eye. And under the tape, the one on the right seemed to have a split lower lip.

The other thing they had in common was hard to miss: they were obviously dead.

Two more dead bodies?

Because I'd given in to one of my inner child's ideas.

My mind briefly disconnected from my heart. As my heart sped up from a steady throb to a frenzied clip, my mind grew completely calm. I tried to not let the panic over two more corpses affect me, and to see the positive side of this situation instead.

The two Holgerssons wouldn't be able to tell anyone anything any more. And I'd no longer have to worry about what to do with them in the future.

Neither Holgersson would fight back when it came to retrieving an ear.

And neither gentleman would be able to tell Walter they were only coincidentally sitting in the park outside my apartment.

Those were rather a lot of positives. My heartbeat slowed to a normal pace. As I considered all this, I'd been silent, blankly looking at the scene in front of us. Sasha was the first to speak.

'Quite the picture,' he said to Walter and his two employees.

'Now, I'm no art historian,' I added, 'but maybe one of you can explain this tableau?'

What neither Sasha nor I knew was that even Walter's company employed people with academic degrees rather unrelated to their employment in security. As one of the two employees had actually studied art history, he was only too happy to interpret the composition.

'Let me first provide some historical context. Ten minutes before the installation snapshot you see here, we handed the two protagonists two little cellophane bags – as you requested – with one gram of cocaine each. When we requested they consume the cocaine, nothing happened at first.'

'*Shit, I really thought they'd dig right in,*' my inner child lamented.

'We waited five minutes. A polite query on our part did not result in an increase in drug consumption. Only in a swollen eye for one and a split lip for the other.'

I didn't really need to hear about the problems they'd run into; I wanted to know how these two gentlemen came to be taped to the table.

Slightly annoyed, I asked the erstwhile art historian, 'And then?'

'Since Sasha had pointed out to us that you'd appreciate our creative involvement, especially when it came to their cocaine consumption, we decided on a little artistic intervention.'

I looked back at their disturbing creation. After that prefatory commentary, the interpretation quickly followed.

'In the right and left halves of the image, you can see the mirrored but identical results of our work. Focusing on the left half will suffice as an example. Since we didn't want to use any further force to promote their drug use, we fixed the gentlemen's noses in such proximity to the table that they would inevitably inhale the cocaine we'd deposited there. To make sure this strategy would be effective, we put out three grams each.'

'And why the duct tape over their mouths?' I enquired.

'It turned out to be more harmonious for the overall picture if the gentlemen's air supply was completely cut off first. Their mouths were taped shut, clothes pegs stuck on their noses. When you remove the plastic peg again after a minute, the nose automatically suctions the surrounding area. More powerful than a hand-held Dyson.'

'I don't think that's cool,' Sasha said, looking at the clothes pegs.

'What do you mean?' the art-minded employee protested, clearly expecting praise for his droll explanation.

'That you used plastic pegs. That litters up the ocean. Just get wooden ones.'

'Why would these two clothes pegs end up in the ocean?' I asked.

'I don't know, but the Nemo group is talking a lot about the environment right now, so I can't help but absorb it.'

'Ah, I wanted to talk to you about that anyway—' I started saying, only to be cut off by Walter.

'Excuse me, please,' Walter intervened. 'The real problem isn't what the pegs are made of. The real problem is that our plan worked. At least the first part. Each of the two sucked in two nostrils full of coke. Unfortunately, both fell into a short-lived coma afterwards.'

'I realise that much,' Sasha replied, 'but the problem is too complex for me. That's why I'd prefer to have a diversionary discussion about plastic pegs.'

'And what does a "short-lived coma" mean?' I asked.

'It means that shortly after inhaling the cocaine, the two passed out but still showed vital signs. Not any more. Hence: a short-lived coma. It was short lived. Like the both of them.'

'Was the issue quality or quantity?' I asked, also as a diversion.

'No idea,' Walter said. 'But I think there must've been a reason the Holgerssons didn't want to sniff their own coke. They must've known it was shite. It's not as dangerous in smaller quantities. But three grams were probably lethal.'

'*Crap. That means we have to cut off one of their ears ourselves,*' my inner child grumbled.

'*What it means is that, because of your hilarious idea, we're now saddled with two corpses we need to get rid of,*' I grumbled.

'*If it's about getting rid of the bodies, I think I've thought of something.*'

'*Please, no,*' I muttered.

But the idea my inner child conveyed to me through a flash of inspiration wasn't even that silly. It certainly made me curious enough to ask Walter about its practical implementation.

'What's the security like on their phones?' I asked, breaking the brief silence. The answer was entirely satisfactory.

34

Energy

Do not waste your own energy fighting a problem, use the *problem's* energy. Instead of barricading yourself, open your door, and let the problem take a running leap into the wall all by itself.

Joschka Breitner, *Slowing Down in the Fast Lane: Mindfulness for Managers*

On our way home from Walter's, I finally had time to talk to Sasha about the upcoming parents' committee meeting. I was driving, Sasha was in the passenger seat.

I'd cancelled our security team. Walter's people would already have enough to do for us that night. Even in Walter's eyes, the Holgerssons no longer posed any real danger.

Sasha was holding a Tupperware container. There was a unicorn on the lid. Inside was an ear. Aseptically stored.

Whoever the blackmailer was, we'd be able to meet the ultimatum. If not with Boris's ear.

'Did you get that plastic container from the preschool?' I asked, looking over.

'No, I just really like unicorns. Why do you ask?'

'Because I had this conversation yesterday with the ladies from the committee.'

'Ah, right, tell me everything! Any hand-grenade parents?'

'None of them, really. They're all pretty nice. It wasn't so much about the kids either. More about the climate crisis.'

'You're not saying the climate crisis doesn't have anything to do with our children, are you?'

No, I wasn't. I only wanted to report what we could expect at the meeting on Thursday.

'Well, it all started with a discussion about squeezy

pouches being banned in the Nemo group to prevent the planet from dying. For which the children would be to blame. Do you know anything about that?'

'Nothing specific. They've got this rather passionate placement student there this year. If it bothers you, have a chat with her.'

A very practical solution, and one I'd wanted to pursue anyway. Although the current ban on squeezy pouches bothered me more right now than the end of the world in four billion years. I moved on to the trickier topics.

'Among the parents, there's also a growing need for the preschool to do away with plastic altogether.'

Sasha took this calmly.

'Good idea. But I don't know if all the parents really want their kids to play starkers in the woods every day.'

'Why would they do that?'

'There's no other way to realise a fully plastic-free preschool environment.'

That made sense. 'Though at least that would also solve the parents' next proposal – for the preschool to become carbon-neutral.'

Sasha nodded. 'We would only be truly carbon-neutral if we didn't even go into the forest – because we didn't exist.'

Another helpful approach. 'Great, because if we didn't exist, the third issue would also be off the table, and that's the one worrying me the most. The parents' committee would like to take a look at the heating system so they can meet the carbon spewer that's heating the preschool.'

'The heating system in front of Boris's bunker?'

'The very one.'

'Well, before a gaggle of mums discovers that the heating system's carbon footprint is the least of our cellar's problems, we'd better tear the whole thing out ourselves and present it to them as a gift.'

Something clicked inside me. During my mindfulness training, Breitner had told me that it was sometimes better to embrace a problem than to try and fight it. Let the problem work itself out using its own energy. What if we just fulfilled every single wish of the mums on the committee – going carbon-neutral, banning all plastic and ensuring that the group photos didn't violate anybody's privacy rights – to the point that the actual implementation became *their* problem? That way, trying to avert them wouldn't become a problem for us.

My inner child was inspired, and I shared its inspired ideas with Sasha.

Sasha was thrilled, to say the least. During the remainder of our drive, we roughly sketched out the dramaturgy for the committee meeting two days later. Sasha promised he would work up our ideas so they'd be presentable by Thursday's meeting.

My inner child's ideas were becoming more and more mature. This time, they seemed not only promising, but also solution-oriented – and not reliant on violence.

35

Authority

Your inner child has a deeply childlike claim on you. It craves a protective authority it can trust.

Joschka Breitner, *Parenting Your Inner Child*

The next morning, I got up at six. There was a lot to do. Not only had DCI Peter Egmann asked to speak with me, Sasha and I also had to appease the blackmailer. He needed us to photograph the ear from all sides, wrap it in the front page of today's tabloid, and leave it on a wall in the park.

Sasha and I had agreed that he'd pick up the newspaper and some fresh bread rolls after his run. As someone dedicated to maintaining a healthy work–life balance, I had suggested that we do the ear thing as a working breakfast. All I needed to do was set the table.

So I cleared the dining table first. I took the handbook to my inner child, put it back in the newsprint tote with the article about the golden child and brought it to my bedroom. I didn't notice that my apology letter to my inner child was no longer where I'd left it the previous morning, nor did I see it anywhere when I set the table afterwards.

It takes practice and a strong stomach to photograph a severed ear from all sides over breakfast. We'd never had any such practice. I kept involuntarily comparing the ear to the mortadella and hard cheese on the plate of sandwich meats and cheeses I'd put out. Somehow the ear resembled both. It was wrinkled, shiny, bacony.

Holding one of those ears in front of a camera with one hand while holding a bun with some honey in the other was simply impossible. Doing bad things doesn't get any nicer if you're eating a nice bread roll while you're doing them. So we soon stopped trying to have breakfast and concentrated on the work at hand instead.

Once we'd photographed the ear from all sides, Sasha loaded the images onto his computer and sent them to the blackmailer's email address without further comment. It seemed our working breakfast had satisfied neither our hunger for breakfast nor our thirst for knowledge. To the contrary.

'What's the point of sending photos of an ear to someone who's going to pick up the ear anyway?' Sasha asked.

'It only doesn't make any sense if the guy actually picks up the ear.'

'You mean the blackmailer doesn't even want the ear?'

'The blackmailer would be pretty stupid to pick it up. That's way too risky. All he wants is for us to cut Boris's ear off. Making us put it on the wall is pure humiliation.'

'You mean we're just this clown's puppets? That doesn't feel great . . . Still, we should keep an eye on the ear.'

As Walter's people had been pulled out yesterday, at least they wouldn't be watching our blackmailer lead us by the nose. Our lives were in no immediate danger. And to observe our anonymous extortionist, we could rely on modern consumer tech. I stuck a GoPro action camera to my balcony window and pointed it at the wall in the park.

Sasha wrapped the ear in the front page, put on his jogging shoes and went downstairs. It was only twenty to seven.

In crystal-clear HD, my camera registered how Sasha put the small newspaper-wrapped package on top of the wall. How nothing happened for thirty minutes. And how, at a quarter past seven, a cat came by, unwrapped the ear and stole it away.

Thus concluding the matter of the ear. Or so I thought.

Like every morning, Peter Egmann dropped his son off at preschool at a quarter past eight. At twenty past eight he rang the bell outside my apartment door.

'Come on in. Coffee?' I greeted him. Peter and I knew each other from our student days. Since then, however, our paths had gone in very different directions. His had led to the police, mine to the private sector. He battled the criminals, I represented them. He was happily married, I was unhappily separated.

'An espresso, please.' Peter followed me into the kitchen and noticed the stain on the wall. 'Did you have a Nespresso explosion?'

'An explosion, yes, but not my Nespresso. What you see there on the wall is Katharina's superfluous contribution to an unnecessary argument.'

'At least machines have their emotions under control.'

'Artificial intelligence, yes. After all, coffee machines can vent before bursting.' I handed Peter his espresso and slid another capsule out of a newly purchased bulk pack for myself.

'Cheers to the invention of pressure-relief valves.' Peter raised his cup and waited until I had one too.

I didn't beat around the bush. 'You said you wanted to talk to me about something unrelated to either the pre-school or the blokes from the park?'

'Yes. Just a formality, I think. Since yesterday, however, a few more questions have come up about the events in the park.'

My ears perked up. 'What about?'

'Well, it doesn't make a lot of sense for someone to assault eight young men, leave six of them tied up on the ground and kidnap the other two. Unless . . .' Peter faltered.

'Unless what?'

'Unless there's something personal at play.'

'And how can I be of any help in this?'

Peter shrugged. 'Over the past six months, it looks like you've made twelve logged calls to the police and eighteen to the community safety office complaining about noise.'

'Those were the only times someone picked up the phone. The number of calls that the community safety office didn't answer is considerably higher.'

Peter nodded. 'The number of calls does suggest you might have some kind of connection to the guys in the park.'

'I beg to differ. To me, the number of calls proves that I have absolutely zero interest in establishing *any* kind of connection with these people. The reason I repeatedly contacted the authorities was to prevent exactly that from happening.' I camouflaged a brief breathing exercise by taking a sip of espresso at my own mindful pace. 'Yet the fact that all my calls were logged but those idiots could still have their fun every night is quite revealing about the authorities.'

Somehow this made me feel like the ignored inner child of the justice system. No matter how loudly I screamed for help, I wasn't heard.

'How so?' Peter asked.

'If they'd adequately responded to my first call, I could've saved myself the other ones.'

'But your calls were logged.'

'Right. And if, instead of the caller's personal details, the personal details of those that *prompted* the calls had been recorded even once, the system would've had to log far fewer calls from me.'

'According to police statistics, the number of regulatory offences in this district hasn't increased significantly,' Peter responded, clearly protective of other public servants.

'The police prioritising clean statistics might explain why every second call goes unanswered. Unfortunately, the guys loitering in the park are not very likely to have a maths background, which might explain why they're not sticking to the statistics. But just like you, I hope you find whoever tied up these lowlifes very soon . . .'

'Great to hear we're in agreement here.'

'. . . so that I can thank them with a bottle of sparkling wine. Since two nights ago, the park has enjoyed a heavenly tranquillity.'

'*A big thanks from me too!*' exclaimed the little blond boy who'd been able to sleep in peace the past two nights. Both of us utterly disregarding the fact that this was all our idea.

'Now, as for the disturbances, I can see where you're coming from for sure. Since last night, however, there's been a small catch,' Peter dithered. I raised my eyebrows. 'As I already told you yesterday, six men were found in the park. But they all claim there were originally eight of them.'

'What's the problem?'

'On the basis of descriptions by the other six, we were finally able to establish the identities of the missing men yesterday. They were both members of the so-called Holgersson family. Little fish, to be sure. But still.'

'Holgersson? Ah, from that golden Baby Jesus that disappeared, right?'

'Right. The main difference being that, last night, unlike the Baby Jesus statue, these two Holgerssons reappeared.'

This didn't surprise me. It was exactly as my inner child had planned, but I acted like I had no idea. 'Oh – where?'

'It's a little bizarre . . . But the two of them were run over by a van on an arterial road just after four o'clock this morning, riding an electric scooter hand in hand.'

'*I knew my plan would work!*' my inner child cheered. I had to be careful Peter didn't hear its jubilations. It was already hard enough to keep my inner grin under control.

'I'm sorry. What's bizarre about that?' I asked, feigning ignorance.

'Well, the two were tied together with a red sash around their hips.'

'We live in a free country. These days, anyone can tie the knot.'

Peter took a deep breath. 'In some cultures' wedding

ceremonies, sashes like that are considered a symbol of virginity.'

'Then maybe the two boys got married. Surely by now gay weddings should be considered normal, not bizarre.'

'OK. But it *is* bizarre that the driver of the van claims that, shortly before the accident, he was distracted by some fireworks on the side of the road. Apparently, some flares went off. The road in front of him was clear, he claims, except for a van fifty metres in front of him. He briefly looked off to the side to see what was going on with the fireworks – and the next moment he'd run over two guys on their scooter. Who apparently popped up out of nowhere.'

'Goes to show, drivers should always keep their eyes peeled.'

'What I'm wondering is: what were those two doing in the middle of the street at night?'

'Now, Peter – the police are usually quite tolerant when it comes to wedding convoys. Or are homosexuals in love not allowed to block roads at night?'

'OK. Let's *assume* that two missing members of the Holgersson crime family held a gay wedding convoy on an electric scooter at four a.m. . . . One thing still puzzles me.'

'Which is?

'According to the coroner, the two had been dead for at least six hours at the time of the accident. This was evidenced by the corpses' body temperature. A blood test also showed that both were completely strung out. And on very poorly cut coke at that.'

'How disturbing.'

'It's especially disturbing that one was also missing an ear.'

'This really is getting absurd.'

'So you agree? That's reassuring.' Peter honestly sounded relieved not to get any further push-back.

But I had to disappoint him once again. 'What's bizarre is you telling me this story. Just because I asked the police a few times to intervene before those boys from the park caused some real bollocks, I'm somehow responsible when they *do* cause some bollocks?'

'Björn, someone broke into the preschool on Monday. You suspected the guys from the park.'

'I didn't suspect those boys. I was only asking you to look at them.'

'That same evening, the boys from the park were incapacitated, and two of them kidnapped.'

'Apparently not. They even got married.'

'The two of them died some time on Tuesday, and that evening their corpses were run over by a van. The corpses of guys you called the authorities about several dozen times over six months.'

'Minus one ear.'

'What?'

'Well, obviously it wasn't their complete corpses that were run over. One ear appears to be missing.'

'But this is about *your* ears now. You complained about the noise these guys were making. Now they're dead.'

I shook my head in genuine indignation. 'How stupid would I be if I called the police and then committed vigilante justice over a noise disturbance? What is it you want from me?'

'*I'm not stupid, I'm a child!*' my inner child complained.

'*Right,*' I reassured it, '*but the police probably don't understand the difference.*'

'All right, I just wanted to ask, for the record, if you noticed anything the night before last,' said Peter, his tone making it clear he wanted to wrap this up.

'Apart from the fact that it was wonderfully quiet? Apart from that, I didn't notice anything.'

I felt good. This was the first of my inner child's ideas that had come off as planned. There was no connection between me and the Holgersson family. I had left no traces, because I'd not been involved in the actual act at all. And my inner child's plan, in its both excessive and naive unpredictability, deviated so completely from any sense of logic that Peter couldn't draw any logical conclusions from it.

My inner child's plan had been a success.

The previous night, we'd been able to use the two Holgerssons' fingerprints to easily unlock their phones. One of the two already even had the CN-Mobility app on his phone. It was one thing to book them an electric scooter, but it was altogether more challenging to convey both them and the scooter into the back of a delivery van. Thanks to Kurt's boasting, I knew that many of his vans would hit the road from four a.m. onwards. So, Walter's people drove one of their own vans up and down the main road around Kurt's company's depot until they spotted one of his vans and sped out in front of it. Another member of Walter's crew stood on the side of the road and was given a signal to distract the CN-Mobility driver with some flares. The guys in Walter's delivery van then opened the back doors and gave the scooter with the two dead Holgerssons a little push. Whereafter they were tragically run over by one of Kurt's vans. Ultimately, the whole plan was a small salute from my inner child to Kurt's immense arrogance. Somebody had to deal with the dead Holgerssons, why not Kurt?

'How's the driver?' I asked, because he hadn't been mentioned yet.

'What driver?'

'Well, the guy who ran over the Holgerssons. Is he OK?'

'Oh, that one. He's a student. He was relieved when we told him that at least the guys he ran over were already dead.'

'Was it his own van?'

'No. Another coincidence. He drives one of these vans all over the city at night to distribute the exact kind of e-scooter the two victims had rented. The company is called CN-Mobile or something.'

That was no coincidence. I was proud of my inner child.

'I'm familiar. The biggest e-scooter rental company in town, right?'

'Its boss certainly seems to be the biggest moron in town. Lives in the same building where his company is located. This way, we were able to inform him about the accident immediately. It seemed to leave him completely cold that one of his employees had run over two people. Only when he learned that one corpse was missing an ear did he even ask a question.'

'What did he ask?'

'Which of his ears was missing, as if that had any bearing on the accident.'

Fuck! Maybe my inner child's plan hadn't worked as well as I'd hoped. I followed up.

'Were you able to answer his question?'

'Yeah, it was the right ear.'

If Kurt was the blackmailer, he now knew that a right ear was circulating. Exactly the kind of ear we'd sent him pictures of. In order to figure out that we hadn't delivered Boris's ear but a Holgersson one, Kurt would have to be the blackmailer *and* establish a connection between me and the Holgerssons.

'By the way,' Peter added, 'the guy's godchild goes to this preschool.'

'How did that come up?'

'He mentioned it after I told him that the last time the two dead men had been seen was twenty-four hours earlier, in the park opposite the preschool.'

So there – Kurt had found the connection between me and the Holgerssons. How nice that cops always got chattiest at the least appropriate times.

'And did he say anything else?'

'No, he said if we had any questions for him, he'd give us the number of his lawyer. He was going to contact him about this today.'

This could cause some problems. But not necessarily. At this moment, all was well. The blackmailer had an ear. The Holgersson bodies had been disposed of. Peter had no concrete way to connect me to them, and Kurt was in a bit of trouble over the accident. Whether Kurt was the blackmailer, whether he would connect the Holgersson's ear to Boris and whether there would be trouble because of it – all that was pure speculation. Living mindfully in the moment, I decided not to worry about Peter's visit for now.

At least for about fifty-seven seconds. Because then Peter got to the *real* reason he wanted to talk to me.

36

The Past

If you consistently live in the moment, you never have to be afraid that the past will catch up with you. The only time you live in is the present. And only a very small part at that: in the moment. Not a single moment should be spent worrying about not being able to change the past. Just be pleased that every moment is another opportunity to shape the present.

Joschka Breitner, *Slowing Down in the Fast Lane: Mindfulness for Managers*

Peter's espresso cup was empty. Mine too.

'Can I make you another coffee?'

'No, thanks, I have to leave in a bit.'

'But you weren't only stopping by to talk about those guys from the park. There was something else, right?'

'Yeah, it's only a formality. Colleagues from the Allgäu have requested our assistance in questioning you as a witness on some case, a fatal accident.'

An icy chill ran up my entire upper body. That could only be Nils's fatal accident. How on earth did the police get to me so fast? And why?

Through the work I'd done with my inner child, I'd only just managed to bring down my guilt about the accident to a realistic level. I didn't want it to all come back up now.

Instinctively, I did what for the past ten years I'd advised each of my criminal clients: nothing. I waited. And stayed silent.

'*Tell him what an arsehole that waiter was! He poked my bruises!*' cried my inner child. I stuck my hand in my pocket and soothingly stroked the parrot. Mindfully, I focused on its various textures. I could feel the individual fibres of its feathers, the smooth surface of its eyes, its small pointy plastic beak. That calmed me down a little too.

When Peter noticed I wasn't about to say anything of my own accord, he continued.

'You did go to the Allgäu last month, didn't you?'

I put my empty espresso cup on the table and looked him straight in the eyes. 'Peter. We went to law school together. We both took the same criminal justice courses. For over a decade, we've been working on different sides of the same field. You know I don't have to answer such trivial questions, nor will I, until you tell me what this is all about.'

Though I'd managed to cover up my panic quite professionally, Peter's discomfort was definitely showing.

'Right. So, last month a waiter working at a hut up there fell to his death under somewhat questionable circumstances. And a few patrons present testified that, at some point before his accident, the waiter had an altercation with you.'

I'd gone to the Alps to finally be among people I neither knew nor ever would have to – only for some of them to invite me back for a police-facilitated reunion a month later!

'I don't remember seeing a waiter falling anywhere. Help me out here?'

'Patrons at the hut say you lashed out at him because he didn't serve you first.'

'Even if that were the case – did the waiter fall during this alleged "altercation"?'

'No, afterwards, but . . .'

'Then I wouldn't qualify as a witness.'

'But if you argued with the waiter, you might've had a motive to arrange the accident.'

'Peter, I'll ask again – do you want to speak to me as a witness or as a suspect?'

'I don't know yet. It's just a routine thing. It's two lines on a form.'

'To cut a long story short: if there's even the slightest possibility that one of my clients will be questioned as a suspect, I always demand access to the relevant files beforehand. So, here's what I suggest: please tell me how your colleagues arrived at my name in the first place, then I'll consider whether there's anything I remember pertaining to this incident.'

'OK, during his break, the waiter probably went to sit down on a few empty Almdudler crates. The crates then toppled against the gate of the loading dock to the hut's freight cable car. The gate wasn't properly bolted. The waiter and the crates both plunged into the ravine below the terrace. The waiter broke his neck.'

'A tragic case, to be sure, but not one for the police.'

'The owner of the hut has testified that he'd placed the boxes *next to* the gate that morning. Now they were in front of it. The owner also testified that he'd bolted the gate himself. When the waiter fell, the gate was unbolted. Patrons have testified that, shortly before his accident, the waiter had an altercation with a guest who then went in the direction of the loading dock.'

'And where do I come into this story?'

'The closest public cable car is twenty minutes from the hut. They have CCTV of all passengers passing through their turnstile. The hut's patrons were shown images of all the people who used the cable car that day. One of those images showed you with Katharina and Emily. The witnesses identified you as the quarrelsome guest.'

'One question about data protection in the Alps: how did your colleagues get personal details from this CCTV picture?'

'As passengers pass the turnstile, each passenger's ticket number is assigned to the corresponding images. Though you paid for your ticket in cash, you took advantage of the guest-card discount. And the tourist office's system registered your name.'

At the preschool, mums worried over whether their children's privacy rights would be endangered if they were in a group photo, while in the Alps they obviously collected mountains of data without any consultation. What could I say to that?

'I see.'

'Do you have anything to add to that?'

To be honest, I did. *I'm sorry.* Or: *I wish I could undo what happened.* Or: *There's this thing with my inner child* . . . Yet none of those would improve my situation. Rather than say nothing at all, I decided to share a comment from my inner child.

'Maybe making helmets mandatory across the Alps wouldn't be a bad idea.'

'What?'

'Well, in the city, every kid riding a bike wears a helmet. If that waiter had worn one, he might not have sustained the type of injury that now requires an investigation.'

'Come off it, were you at that hut or not?'

'By when do your Allgäu colleagues need you to fill out this form?'

'If it's on my desk for a few more days, I guess it won't be the end of the world. Just let me know by the weekend.'

So for the moment, I could postpone the problem of Nils's death. As long as I lived in the moment, that was quite enough. But the future would have more moments in store for me. And I hadn't entirely conquered my fear of those quite yet.

In addition to the questions of whether I needed to cut Boris's head off by Friday, whether I could pacify my baselessly jealous wife this afternoon and whether I could keep a pack of climate-warrior preschool mums away from my boiler room's hidey-hole tomorrow, now I also needed to deal with the question of how to pull my head out of the Nils noose by the weekend.

I hated deadlines. They never respect the moment.

37

Wisdom

What you know about your inner child grants you wisdom. But wisdom is like light: it illuminates the darkness, but it also attracts the most bizarre creatures.

Joschka Breitner, *Parenting Your Inner Child*

I needed to get out of here. Out of my apartment. Out of the building. Out of the city even.

I was being mindful. I had established a good relationship with my inner child. And yet, since Monday, I had more problems than ever. Too many things could blow up in my face. The fact that Boris had been discovered could still be very dangerous for me. If I couldn't get the better of this blackmailer – who was probably Kurt – the whole big web of lies I'd created around Boris and Dragan would collapse. With the exact same results as if Boris *had* escaped.

Katharina's accusation of infidelity might be unfounded, but her delusion was still very real. One parent's *idée fixe* could demolish the foundation of both parents' co-parenting.

And then there were the people who'd died.

Well, sure – Nils and the two Holgerssons could ultimately be chalked up to my parents. After all, they'd been the ones who had moulded my inner child so badly. But that wouldn't be of any interest to the approximately 4,498 Holgerssons still alive, nor to the police.

And Nils somehow re-emerging from the ravine would be the icing on the cake.

What I needed was a clear head. I decided to drive my Defender to the woods and go running for an hour.

By now, I'd gotten in pretty good shape. Not in as peak physical shape as Sasha and his daily 10K, but enough to be able to clear my head. I put on my running gear and left the apartment.

I made it to the building's entryway. There was Kurt.

It was Wednesday. Had I paid attention to Laura's words and not only her lips, I'd have realised that Wednesday was Max's day with his favourite uncle.

Kurt had his godchild the entire day, including preschool shuttle service. Apparently, he'd just dropped Max off. Now he was standing in the hallway, holding an almost empty glass travel mug of coffee.

If it really had been Kurt to whom we'd sent an email with pictures of a severed ear two hours earlier, he didn't show a trace of triumph. And if he knew that it wasn't actually Boris's ear, he didn't let that show either. Kurt looked neither arrogant nor angry. He looked devastated.

'Björn, hi, I was coming to see you.'

'This isn't the best time. I've got an appointment . . .' With myself.

'I'll walk with you a bit. I . . . need your help.'

Kurt hastily finished the last sip of coffee in his mug. His walking with me was the last thing I needed right now. But I also couldn't leave him standing there. I was too curious how he was really feeling. Contrary to our conversation the day before, he was no longer interested in toying with me; it looked like he really needed my advice. I decided to treat him like a moth: wave it away if it gets too close.

'OK. My car is parked just down the road. Come along. I should have a minute or two.'

I opened the front door for Kurt. He scanned the hallway for a moment and then put his empty travel mug on top of the mailboxes. Even reusable mugs must have a negative ecological footprint if you only use them once. But coming from Kurt, this behaviour honestly didn't surprise me. It fitted him.

Kurt walked past me out of the door. There were deep circles under his eyes. Which made sense, because the police had kept him up after one of his vans crashed into a 'happy couple'.

'There was an accident last night . . .' he started.

I widened my eyes. 'What happened?'

'One of my vans ran over two people, under somewhat strange circumstances.'

'Was anyone hurt?'

'That's one of the things that's so strange . . . It looks like the men that were run over were already dead.'

We walked around an awkwardly parked electric scooter with a cup holder for lattes.

'Then I'm sorry, but I can't help you. I am not well versed in traffic law, only criminal law. Grievous bodily harm resulting in death would be my thing, death by dangerous driving not so much.'

If Kurt wasn't a damn good actor then the staged accident was really getting to this idiot, and I enjoyed the satisfaction.

'The two guys who were run over were members of a very close-knit family—'

I didn't let him finish. 'Maybe send them some flowers.' By now we'd reached my car. I reached into my pocket for the keys.

'They've already sent *me* something. This was stuck under my windscreen wiper earlier.'

Kurt pulled a piece of paper out of his jacket pocket and handed it to me. Hesitating at first, I took the note and looked at it sceptically. I knew this piece of paper. This was due to the fact that I myself had torn it out of Sasha's notebook the day before. Now crumpled, it was covered in what looked to be the innovative handwriting of a pre-literate calligrapher. In short, chicken scratch a brainless illiterate would be proud of. This effect is quite easily achieved if a right-handed person like Sasha writes with his left, with a few letters randomly sized or absent.

In any case, the note read:

'Stoln honour cant be forgivn.'

I knew that line. From my work as a criminal defence lawyer. Albeit spelled correctly. It was a quote from *The Code of Lekë Dukagjini*, an ancient Albanian book of traditional laws on blood vengeance not necessarily compatible with the German criminal code. Apparently, the Holgerssons hadn't found the deaths of their two underlings all that funny. At least, that was the impression this piece of paper intended to convey. My inner child had come up with it.

Personally, I didn't think any Holgersson would worry too much about the deaths of their two smallest-time drug dealers. As long as their death was assumed to have been accidental. What's more, they probably wouldn't care whose van had run over their corpses. But it was nice Kurt thought the opposite.

I read the line out loud.

'"Stoln honour canot be forgivn" . . . Do you only rent out e-scooters or also individual Es? There are two missing here.'

Kurt didn't feel that the spelling errors committed by the person who'd slipped this threat under his windscreen wiper were the most important issue at hand.

'I googled it. This is an announcement of blood vengeance! The two guys that my van ran over were members of the Holgersson family.'

Very good. Kurt had swallowed the bait. If this was why he was so desolate, my inner child had done everything right.

'The Holgerssons? Aren't they the ones who stole that shiny Baby Jesus? That sounds bad. I've heard those guys have no sense of humour. But how can I help?' I asked, almost too innocently.

'Don't you have . . . I mean, I heard that you . . . As a lawyer, you must have contacts in that world. Can't you arrange something? Communicate something?'

I distanced myself, literally as well as figuratively.

'First of all, I don't know what you're talking about. Secondly, even if I had contacts "in that world" – I don't have any with the Holgerssons. And thirdly, this is what the police are for. You should take this note to them.'

At this point, Kurt rather unpleasantly closed the gap between us, suddenly centimetres away. I could smell his disgusting aftershave. As if comforting me rather than being comforted, he grabbed me by the shoulders, drew me close, and whispered in my ear.

'If my life is at stake and I need to bring the police into this, then I'll have to tell them a lot. A *lot*. For instance, why one Holgersson is missing an ear. And the police will certainly relay that to the Holgerssons.'

Kurt had no intention of dying like a man. Before being swallowed by the waves, he wanted to take everything down with him. That's why you should never help a drowning person if you don't have a strong chance of getting back on the rescue boat yourself.

Fuck. Perhaps I should've pointed out this potential danger to my inner child. Then again, I hadn't expected Kurt to react so self-destructively. Kurt mistakenly interpreted the disappointment in my eyes as the intended reaction to his threat. He grew more conciliatory.

'It doesn't have to go that way though. You keep the Holgerssons off of me, let other people lose their heads. Then I might be very grateful to you.'

He gave me a hug, stepped back and smiled. 'And if you don't want to do *me* the favour – do it for my sister. She seems to find you quite attractive.'

So even his sister was only a means to an end for him. What an arsehole.

'I'll . . . think about it. Maybe there's one or two things I can do. But I'd need a little time. Would it be OK if I got back to you by tomorrow?' I eventually managed to stammer in his general direction. Not because Kurt scared me, but because, after the hug, his disgusting smell was clinging to me as well.

338

'OK, fine. Tomorrow it is. Tomorrow I want to hear your plan to keep the Holgerssons off my back. Otherwise, it's your neck.' Kurt got on his electric scooter and scuttled off.

I found the whole situation utterly absurd. To me, unjustified hugs were just as suspicious as justified threats.

There was no longer any doubt: Kurt was the blackmailer. But I still didn't have the slightest idea why. I also didn't like the fact that, instead of me illegitimately threatening him, he was now legitimately threatening me with the Holgerssons. I was not alone in this.

'*I don't think we'll be able to manage this without some mindful murder,*' my inner child opined.

'*What?*'

'*Well, the bloke is obviously running amok. Before Kurt destroys everything that means anything to us, we should maybe destroy Kurt instead.*'

I was reminded that Breitner had explained to me that children live in extremes. They want all or nothing. This also seemed to be very true of Kurt's inner child: it either wanted to achieve everything or destroy everything. *My* inner child, on the other hand, seemed quite mature in this regard: it wanted to murder mindfully. It was me who wanted to stop murdering altogether.

But I had no idea how to get around murdering Kurt.

Yet what I needed most, and soon, was a plan to quash Kurt's threat of letting the police set the Holgerssons on me. To do that, I first had to find out why Kurt hated Boris so much that he wanted us to maim and kill him.

To figure out the former, I wanted to pick up my plan of heading out to the woods, so I could think in peace as I jogged. To figure out the latter, however, I'd need to head down first. To the cellar.

38

Understanding

Knowing about your own inner child will also make it easier for you to understand other people. Some people you meet might be arseholes, but even arseholes have their own arsehole inner children.

Joschka Breitner, *Parenting Your Inner Child*

Sasha dropped everything to join me on my visit to Boris. The fact that Kurt was pressuring us because of the Holgerssons didn't please him any more than it did me. But at least it was also exactly why we could be so sure Kurt was our blackmailer. We just didn't know why. Only Boris could tell us what connected him and Kurt beyond their rental agreement.

I opened the padlock and pulled open the prison door. It was shortly after nine, and Boris was still asleep. Sasha turned on the light. I leaned over our prisoner to wake him.

'Hey, Boris. Wake up!'

'Go away. I'm dreaming.'

'If you want to keep your head and keep dreaming, wake up.' Sasha kicked the bed, and Boris scrambled up.

'You . . .' He fell silent and started to sniff. 'What's that awful smell? Hey . . . That's the disgusting aftershave of the guy who drugged me.' Boris looked at me and sniffed my neck. 'And you're telling me you're not behind this?'

'That proves it then,' I noted. 'Now we know who was behind your short-lived escape. The guy who hugged me earlier.'

'Does this guy have a name?' asked Boris.

'Kurt Frieling,' I informed him.

Boris considered this. 'Never heard of him. Who's he supposed to be?'

'He rents an office building from you,' Sasha said.

'If I could remember the names of all my tenants, I'd sign myself up for *Mastermind*.'

'Even if that show was still on in Germany, the new lock on your cellar door would prevent you from taking part,' I couldn't help but note.

Sasha pulled out his phone. He'd saved a photo of Kurt from his company website and now showed it to Boris.

'Maybe this'll jog your memory. This is a picture of the guy whose aftershave you don't like. He dragged you out of the cellar, sedated you and put you in the princess playhouse.'

My patience was wearing thin. 'And he wants us to cut your head off by Friday. So, do you know him or not?'

Irritated, Boris studied the photo. 'What's his name again?'

'KURT. FRIELING,' Sasha and I shouted, almost at the same time. Suddenly, something clicked for Boris.

'I can't believe it. That's Little Thirty-Second Kurt! Twenty years older and almost five stone heavier, but sure: I know this guy. I can't believe it though. *That* idiot is the one who's behind all this?'

'Why's he called Little Thirty-Second Kurt?' Sasha wanted to know.

'How do you know him?' I wanted to know.

Boris enlightened us both.

'He was a regular at our first brothel, oh, twenty years ago.'

'Just knowing who banged who at your brothels over the last twenty years could earn you a lot more money than you'd ever win on *Mastermind*,' Sasha remarked, clearly impressed.

'Go on,' I urged Boris. 'What do you remember about this guy?'

'Twenty years ago, Dragan and I opened our first proper brothel. Super discreet. Great location. Great girls. Great service at great prices. Really more of a theatre than a knocking shop. The girls could act like they were head over heels for every single customer to such an extent that most of their johns quickly became regulars. But one stood out. That guy, Little Thirty-Second Kurt.'

'What was so special about him?' I asked.

'He was there at least once a week. Sometimes even more. Always with the same girl. Completely besotted. At some point, he even brought flowers – roses, for a whore!'

'And why that nickname? Little Thirty-Second Kurt?' Sasha now insisted.

'Because he not only came several times a week, but also after just thirty seconds.' The memory made Boris laugh. 'But he brought in decent money, unbelievable. And his lady love really only had to show him her breasts, then his spontaneous emission meant that the main part of the job was already done. The rest of the time, Little Kurt only wanted to talk. He even made plans for the future with that whore. All things considered, it was almost a pity she hung up her boots.'

'Why'd she leave the game?'

'Cos a woman doesn't fuck other men when she's married to me. Not even for easy money.'

'Kurt's favourite tart was . . .' I inferred.

'Annastasia, the one I married. Correct,' Boris confirmed.

Suddenly, it all made sense. Even the ludicrous tattoo on Kurt's flabby upper arm. The one that read 'ANNA'. Kurt had fallen in love with Annastasia. *That* was the unhappy romance Laura had told me about. Annastasia had quit the trade because she married her boss, Boris. Kurt, however, clearly hadn't been able to get over her.

And then, Boris had cut off Annastasia's head. Because he'd caught her cheating on him with Dragan. No one had ever been able to pin it on Boris. But the press had considered him a suspect for weeks.

Kurt had not only lost the supposed love of his life to another man. That same man had also ensured the love of his life lost her head.

There was no clearer way Boris could have shown he didn't give a single toss about what Kurt wanted than by sawing off Annastasia's head.

The fact that, when her head was still attached, Annastasia was stringing him along had obviously never even popped into Kurt's own head. Poor sod.

Kurt, who'd distrusted everyone since losing his great love and who apparently never really saw anyone except for his sister and his godchild, Max, had found out from Max that there was a lippy monster living underneath his preschool. Unafraid of cellars and bored of himself, Kurt broke into the cellar one night to see what his godchild might have discovered. He found the prison door in the boiler room and shone his torch inside only to find, lying there, the very man who had ruined his dream of a happy ever after.

It took Kurt a few days to plan his revenge. Not just on Boris, on the whole world. To do the dirty work, he roped in Joe Bloggs and his mate – in this case, Sasha and me. In Kurt's revenge-addled mind, there was probably even a meaning behind the day of the week we were supposed to behead Boris.

'Do you remember what day of the week you sawed Annastasia's head off?' I asked Boris.

'Sure, it was a Friday. Fittingly, the thirteenth.' Hence Kurt's fixation on Friday.

I could understand why Kurt wanted revenge. At least, since I knew that Kurt must have an inner child of his own. A child whose parents had shaped him with the belief that 'you can suffer for our mistakes'. Kurt's parents had let him pay for Laura's entirely unexpected birth. They didn't care about him enjoying a carefree childhood. And Boris had poked exactly this bruise on Kurt's inner child.

Kurt suffered because of Annastasia's mistake of marrying Boris. Neither had considered his feelings.

Kurt suffered because of Annastasia's mistake of cheating on Boris with Dragan. She hadn't even considered his desire to be her secret lover.

And Kurt had suffered because of Boris's decision to cut off Annastasia's head. The Russian hadn't cared that Kurt wanted the heart of his great love to go on beating.

As Kurt saw it, for the past two decades, he'd been made to suffer by people who'd never even considered him, costing him the ability to form relationships at all. And that called for a bloody revenge. It all made sense.

As I understood it, Kurt was not at all to blame for the situation Sasha and I found ourselves in. Boris wasn't really to blame either. He had been the trigger, but the real culprits were Kurt's parents. After all, they were the ones who shaped his inner child. But Kurt's parents were on the Canary Islands, so they weren't much help. Boris was under the protection of my inner child, so he couldn't be held liable either. Which only left Kurt to bear the consequences of his blackmail. And with all due respect: I wasn't Kurt's therapist. In this case, I was just a guy who didn't want to saw Boris's head off. In any case, my inner child didn't want to be told whose corpse it'd be confronted with. Not even by someone else's inner child. And when the needs of two inner children were pitted against each other, my own won out.

Either way: Friday was only two days away.

39

Monotony

You can anchor yourself in the present especially well while doing monotonous things. When running, dancing or swimming, pay attention to your running, dancing or swimming. You will find your thoughts are only on what you are doing at that very moment.

First, draw your mind into the monotony of whatever you are doing. Stay in this relaxing state as long as your soul requires. When your mind senses it is thus anchored, it will eventually let go quite naturally. Your body will move by itself, as if hypnotised. Freeing your mind for new things.

Joschka Breitner, *Slowing Down in the Fast Lane: Mindfulness for Managers*

It was only ten o'clock. I still had plenty of time before my appointment with Katharina in the afternoon. Now it was finally time for the woods.

I parked my Defender outside the deer park. I needed to be immersed in nature. I needed to move. Luckily, I didn't have to push my inner child in a running buggy like other jogging parents. Through my eyes, it could look at the deer on its own. Or it could help me.

The running route around the deer park that I'd discovered a few weeks earlier felt perfect for a few liberatory laps. One lap was almost exactly two kilometres.

I left my phone in the glovebox and got out of the car. I was a very conservative runner. I didn't bring a watch. No heart-rate monitor. No bracelet tracking my vital signs. I didn't need more input while I was running; I had no shortage of data. Quite the opposite. I'd brought my head, which contained plenty of information.

I also didn't run in odourless microfibre athleisure. Which, although it admittedly wouldn't reek of sweat, would smell all the more pungently of athleisure. I wore cotton sweatpants, a T-shirt, a hoodie, and a woollen beanie. I ran like Rocky in the original *Rocky*. Only with fewer muscles. But with the same goal. I had no idea how I was going to get out of the mess I'd gotten myself into and emerge victorious. But I wanted to give it my absolute all. Instead of beating up sides of pork in a meat locker, however, I'd run past the sounder of fully functional and intact wild hogs on the other side of the fence.

I locked my car, threaded the key onto a leather cord and hung it around my neck. I started with a light trot. After two months of training, my body was already conditioned to this. I didn't need to think about putting one foot in front of the other. I just did it. Again and again. The automatic nature of running calmed me down. After half a lap around the park, I started to sweat. That did me good. After the first full lap, my head started to perceive the environment separately from my body. I felt as if my brain was effortlessly perched atop my torso, being transported comfortably through the landscape. A little like travelling first class on the train. Only without having to worry about delays.

After a lap and a half, without needing to be prompted, my mind started playing Tetris with my various problems. One problem after another slowly dropped out of my thoughts into my imaginary playing field. The problems all had names. They were called Kurt, Holgersson, Peter, Boris and Katharina. Each was a different shape. As they fell, I could turn and drop each wherever and however I wanted. As in Tetris, some problems fitted together and merged, whereas others got in each other's way. And I cherished the hope that some problems might also clear each other up. The nice thing about running was that I had time. If something got stuck in one game of problem-Tetris, I'd simply rotate it differently next time.

The biggest problem was Kurt. He had Sasha and me in his grip. Even if he didn't go rampaging straight to the police, he could still tip them off about Boris anonymously. Then we would go to jail. He could tell Boris's or Dragan's people about Boris. Then Sasha and I would be dead. Or he could tell the Holgerssons why their deceased family member was missing an ear. But he didn't really want any of that: he wanted to take his revenge on Boris. And he could only do that if he kept what he knew about Boris to himself.

The Holgerssons would only become a problem if they knew I was behind the death of their two family members. But they could only find out through Kurt. This was how these two problems connected.

Of course, Kurt could also tell the police about the ear. However, probably unlike the Holgerssons, the police would require evidence. Kurt only had *photos* of the ear. After all, a cat had devoured the sole physical evidence.

The next-biggest problem was called Peter. However, Peter was a double problem: firstly because of the dead waiter investigation, and secondly because of a potential confession from Kurt. Fortunately, Peter thought Kurt was an idiot. That could be useful.

Boris would always be a problem. As long as he was alive.

Katharina was a problem as long as she was thinking. At least, as long as she was thinking I'd cheated on her. But she had sounded quite reasonable on the phone yesterday. I wouldn't know more until we met later in the afternoon. In short, I could take the Katharina problem out of the running.

I could kill Kurt and Boris. That would solve two problems.

However, this solution would miss the mark due to a completely different issue:

I didn't want to kill any more.

'*Maybe* you *don't. But what about me?*' my inner child said. Apparently, it'd had enough of watching the deer. My steps started to falter.

Breitner had taught me that the interests of an inner child weren't always congruent with those of its adult. In this case, they were diametrically opposed. I wanted a non-violent solution; my inner child preferred one involving dead people. Which presented another issue.

'*And what about Boris?*' I pressed it. '*You want to kill him as well now?*'

'*We're not killing Boris!*' was the unequivocal answer.

The challenge now became to balance our interests. The inner child should feel safe, yet the adult's free will shouldn't be restricted either.

I fell back into my relaxed run and put a hundred metres of deer fence behind me.

I didn't want to kill anyone.

But Kurt and Boris's deaths would solve both problems.

My inner child wanted corpses.

But it didn't want to kill Boris.

Were the two really irreconcilable?

As long as I didn't have to kill anyone myself, or order

someone else to, I shouldn't care about other people dying if it was to the benefit of my inner child. And though my inner child didn't want us to kill Boris, if someone else killed him of their own free will, the situation would be rather different. Being killed was one of the professional risks of being a mob boss. Even if my father hadn't taken Tapsi away from me, I still wouldn't have had any guarantee that the cat wouldn't be run over by a car two days later. Perhaps it even had been. But who'd kill Kurt and Boris of their own accord? Aside from each other . . .

I stopped short. That could be it!

But how?

I put that aside for now. Back to Tetris-ing.

So far, the Holgerssons problem had been the smallest. They still seemed to have no idea I even existed. And nothing suggested this would change in the foreseeable future. Once Kurt and Boris were neutralised, there wouldn't be anything left to connect me to the Holgerssons anyway. Except for the entirely made-up story of Boris and the golden child. But only Walter knew that one. What if Kurt, Boris and the golden child all just did a disappearing act? Maybe to a farm somewhere? Then my problems with Kurt, Boris and the Holgerssons would be solved in one fell swoop.

Only the Peter and Katharina problems would remain. Katharina I would meet later in the afternoon. Peter could wait until the weekend.

So I could use my next lap around the park to get creative with my inner child.

'*Fancy a fresh round of problem-solving?*' I asked my inner child.

'*Yes, but can we please change the rules a bit?*' was the answer.

I grew curious.

'*Unlike usual, let's not play with objects from within a two-metre radius, but only with information from within a two-day radius.*'

I was truly surprised. '*Why?*'

'*Because within a two-metre radius there's only the deer park. And, sure, Boris could kill Kurt with a fence post. And Kurt could've made a wild boar so angry beforehand that it immediately charges and gores Boris after Kurt's murder. To do so, however, both would first have to be brought here, and then we'd have to deal with their bodies afterwards. I think both of those things would be rather impractical.*'

First and foremost, I was baffled that my inner child was even able to plan two murders using only what was at hand within a two-metre radius.

'*And what good is information from within a two-day radius? How does that help us get Kurt and Boris in one place, away from prying eyes?*'

'*Well,*' the child in me began, '*let's see. The police think Kurt is an idiot. He has a poorly running but well-insured company. He believes that he and his company are being watched by a vengeful crime family. His only social contact other than his sister and Max is his new best frenemy: his lawyer.*'

And so, through the eyes of my inner child, I could see countless puzzle pieces fit together just so, piece by piece, creating one wonderfully cohesive plan. Out of bits of information from the past two days that were irrelevant in and of themselves, the overall picture of a solution still emerged. There was indeed a viable way in which Kurt and Boris could eliminate each other, one that would go unnoticed, yet still produce a definitive result.

However, it would only work if Kurt wasn't at home or at work tonight. Which was why I needed to call Laura right after my run. To ask her out, against my will. At least, against my will insofar as I wouldn't be able to settle matters with Katharina first.

40

Morality

Morality is something we acquire in our earliest childhood. This makes your inner child a moral authority. Overwriting your inner child's core beliefs will also change their sense of morality. And that in turn impacts your own morality. This may be irritating, but it is worth taking on.

Joschka Breitner, *Parenting Your Inner Child*

'Since we no longer want to kill anyone ourselves, it makes sense to have Kurt and Boris kill each other . . .' Sasha had always been able to grasp things quickly. 'But why do I need to torch Kurt's company headquarters beforehand?'

I took my time before I answered. I stood across from Sasha in his office and took a sip of excellent espresso from a rather expensive portafilter machine that had come with the preschool when we took it over.

'Because I want Kurt to be so desperate that he'll blindly trust me when I present him with a course of action. A course that leads him straight to Boris,' I explained.

'Arson as a trust-building exercise?'

'Yes. Kurt thinks he's being threatened by the Holgerssons. That's why he came to see me earlier. So, if his company is suddenly on fire, he'll think the Holgerssons are behind it.'

'Why wouldn't Kurt go to the police after the fire and tell them everything? About Boris, the ear *and* the Holgerssons.'

'Firstly – because revenge on Boris is his be-all and end-all. He won't give that up so easily. As soon as he spills about Boris, the Russian will slip from his grip. Secondly – because after his first shock, Kurt will realise that the police wouldn't believe him anyway. Kurt is underfunded but overinsured. The police will therefore immediately assume he torched his struggling business himself. On that topic, I have a purely technical question: is it possible to make a Molotov cocktail from a glass travel mug?'

'I can mix you a Molotov cocktail out of anything that can contain petrol and burst on impact. Why do you ask?'

I took out a paper bag with the travel mug Kurt had left on the mailboxes and placed it on Sasha's desk.

'Because then, one of the Molotov cocktails will unfortunately have Kurt's fingerprints on it. This ensures the police won't believe a word Kurt says about the Holgerssons. The link between Kurt and the Holgerssons is just a single ear. An ear that was supposed to be Boris's but was actually cut off one of the Holgerssons, and was ultimately eaten by a cat. If that's what Kurt wants to tell the police . . . let him! It wouldn't change anything about his situation, only deprive him of his chance for revenge.'

'Which leaves you, of all people, as the only person he can trust?'

'Kurt is completely sociophobic. He doesn't have any friends. This means that the only person who can help him is me. He has verbally already hired me as his lawyer. And at least I'm in his grip – or so he thinks. He will assume I'll help him out for fear of going under myself. You'll see: when his business and his apartment have burned down, he'll come crying to me for protection. There's simply nowhere else he could go.'

'He could go to a hotel.'

'He wouldn't be safe from the Holgerssons there.'

'He has a sister.'

'Her apartment is too small. Besides, he may be OK with putting his sister in danger, but certainly not Max.'

'And why should the attack take place at exactly eleven at night?'

'That's when CN-Mobility's late shift is over, but the night shift hasn't started yet. All the vans will be in the yard. All the scooters will be charging. No one will be on the premises, and Kurt will still be with his godchild. Maximal damage with minimal risk.'

'Why would Kurt be at his godchild's that late?'

'Because his sister will be with me.'

Laura had immediately said yes when I'd invited her over for dinner at eight o'clock. What with cooking, eating, talking and everything, we'd be busy for at least three hours. Although I didn't know what else might be included in that 'and everything'. In any case, her brother would be with Max at the time of the attack, not in his apartment above his offices. Moreover, the police wouldn't consider a sleeping five-year-old a very credible alibi.

A grin appeared on Sasha's face. 'You just want me out of the house for selfish reasons, so you can feel up our blackmailer's sister. I cannot support that.' His grin disappeared. 'Besides, you're married. Give it a rest.'

Sasha had summed up all my *actual* moral conundrums. I primarily wanted to see Laura tonight because she was Kurt's sister. In that respect, I'd be taking advantage of her for selfish reasons. Not sexual ones. I didn't have the headspace for an entirely normal date. This was also the only reason I was able to somewhat suppress my existing guilt towards Katharina – who'd already baselessly accused me of what I'd only do later this evening. If for a good reason: planning a date with Laura was part of my job. It was the only way to ensure that Kurt wouldn't be in his building. And that I wouldn't accidentally kill again. Kurt, for example. In addition, Laura would provide me with an alibi should anyone – Kurt, for example – think that I had burned down his business. In this respect, I'd be a little at Laura's mercy tonight. She could take advantage of me if she wanted to.

The moral issues of my date with Laura could thus be explained very objectively.

Interestingly, neither Sasha nor I considered burning down Kurt's company a moral problem. Only a logistical one.

41

Mistakes

Your parents may have made mistakes in your childhood. They probably made these mistakes with the best of intentions. But your parents also gave you a gift that you should enjoy until the day you die: they gave you your life. Forgive your parents.

Joschka Breitner, *Parenting Your Inner Child*

That afternoon's conversation with Katharina was coming at me from two angles: it was hanging over my head and gnawing at my gut. I certainly had more pertinent things to do than defend myself against my estranged wife's entirely unfounded accusations – defend myself against actual blackmail, for instance, against actual police investigations and actual changes that wouldn't only be life-altering but might actually be life-ending. And all that while being a true ally to my inner child.

But I not only had an inner child, but also an outer one. Together with Katharina. And every outer child is the root of their own future inner child.

I was willing to do everything I could to make sure my relationship woes with Katharina didn't affect Emily. To avoid any future problems our real child might have with *her* inner child.

Despite all our differences, I wanted Katharina and me to at least be good parents.

While I was waiting for Katharina at my apartment, I kept thinking of a coaching session with Breitner. It had started with a question of mine:

'My inner child's emotional state is the reason behind my problems as an adult. And my parents' shaping of me is the reason behind my inner child's emotional state – did I get that right so far?'

Breitner nodded.

'If I now patch things up with my inner child, that's all well and good. But since realising all this, I've developed a huge grudge against my parents. How do I deal with that?'

'With forgiveness.'

'So my parents screwed up years of my life, and I'm supposed to just forgive them?'

'Imagine if I gave you a Ferrari and then keyed a deep scratch all along its left side. Would you be angry at me?'

'Because of the Ferrari or because of the scratch?'

'See? You couldn't have the one without the other.'

'What does that have to do with my parents?'

'Your parents gave you your life – and then left a scratch or two on your soul while raising you. Scratches we have been repairing here. These coaching sessions are the virtual counterpart to a Ferrari body shop. When we are done here, you will get back the Ferrari that is your life. Only scratch-less.'

That comparison to the Ferrari body shop at least explained Breitner's hourly rates.

'OK. The question remains why my parents didn't prevent these scratches in the first place.'

'The exact question your daughter will ask you in about thirty years.'

'And is the answer to both questions also the same?'

'Life leaves its marks on us all. Only people who never live never make mistakes. Your daughter will most definitely come to ask herself why you made mistakes raising her. It is simply unavoidable. What would be stupid is if you recognised the mistakes your parents made and still make the same mistakes raising your own daughter. You should pass on the experiences you gained from the past, not the same mistakes. In this respect, you can be grateful for your parents' mistakes. These are mistakes you can spare your daughter.'

Breitner's words aroused my guilty conscience towards my daughter over my evidently failed relationship with my wife.

'We're already burdening the little one enough with our separation,' I muttered feebly.

'But maybe that is already one thing you are doing better than your parents.'

'How do you mean?'

'Why don't we go through the facts you gave me.'

Breitner pulled out a questionnaire from a folder on the side table. It listed facts about my family. I had completed it before my second session. So far, we'd never discussed it.

'Your parents got married in August of 1975?'

'Yes.'

'You were born in December 1975, and you do not have any siblings.'

'Indeed.' I had no idea what Breitner was getting at.

'So you either moved straight from your mother's womb into an incubator, or you were conceived five months before your parents' wedding.'

'What does that matter?'

'When did you get married? And when was Emily born?'

'Married in 2011. She was born in 2016.'

'So you had five years to look forward to the child you were dreaming of. Your mother had only four months to avoid an illegitimate child. And any further children she may have dreamed of never appeared. You and Katharina obviously married for love. Whereas your unplanned arrival may have played a significant role in your parents getting married. If that is not a difference, I do not know what is.'

'But my parents never separated.'

'It can be preferable for a child if their parents separate with love, rather than stay together in hate . . .'

This coaching session had given me a great deal of insight into the guilt I was feeling about Emily. But it still didn't help me answer the now rather central question:

How do I separate with love from a woman who hatefully assumes I'm having an affair?

Minutes before Katharina's arrival, the problem of my marriage still utterly perplexed my inner child and me. Neither of us suspected that, thanks to my inner child, the solution was already at hand.

42

Gift

If fate presents you with a gift, do not question it. It does not matter why something is good. Just enjoy the fact that it is.

Joschka Breitner, *Slowing Down in the Fast Lane: Mindfulness for Managers*

At half past four in the afternoon, the problem of my marriage appeared in the form of Katharina. There had been a time, early in our relationship, over ten years ago, that I'd get nervous with love and desire before seeing her on my doorstep. Nervous with joy too – I couldn't believe she fancied me.

Now, I was nervous with fear. And because I was tired of these unnecessary quarrels and accusations. I couldn't believe she was accusing me in the first place. Funny how marriage could have such a negative impact on the feelings of the two people in question.

Katharina rang the bell. I opened the door. Katharina kissed me on the mouth – for the first time in months – and then proceeded to quietly, lovingly embrace me.

I was speechless, stunned with surprise. I readily returned the embrace, however. Katharina drew back and finished her unusual greeting.

'I have to apologise to you too,' was how she opened the conversation.

'*Why "too"?*' my inner child wondered, right as I was wondering the same.

'I . . . I . . .' was all I was able to stammer, entirely at a loss.

'Please don't say anything yet. Let me get something out first, OK?'

Katharina went ahead into the living room and sat down on the oversized sofa. I sat next to her and waited.

'For one, I should apologise because I came back here yesterday.'

OK, that wasn't a big deal. I had nothing to hide from Katharina. After all, we were married. So, why this apology 'for one'? And what about 'for another'? But I'd promised to let Katharina speak first, so I didn't ask any questions.

'Yesterday after preschool, Emily wanted to see you, and I was so distracted that I forgot to ring the bell and just let myself into your apartment. And while Emily ran around looking for you, I . . . found your letter.'

What letter?

'That apology you wrote was the most loving thing I've heard from you in years.'

I hadn't written Katharina any apology letter. I hadn't written an actual letter to anyone in a long, long time. Except . . . to my inner child. I looked over at the dining table. Yesterday, the letter I'd drafted to my inner child had still been sitting there. I'd not taken it to my bedroom along with Breitner's handbook when I was setting the breakfast table for Sasha and myself. Yet it was no longer there. The question marks in my eyes slowly turned into exclamation marks. Katharina's eyes, on the other hand, were filling with tears.

'I have no idea what you and Mr Breitner talk about in your coaching sessions. But you've changed a lot over the last few weeks. And your letter perfectly put into words the same things I've been feeling but haven't been able to tell you. So, I'd like to read out your letter to me. And I want you to know that I also mean every single word of it, when it comes to you.'

Katharina took the letter out of her bag and began to read aloud in a tear-choked voice:

'I'm so sorry about everything. I've ignored you for so long, I never knew what a marvel I've been sharing my life with all these years. Only now do I realise how we made life harder for each other. I would like to release you without hurting you. I'd like you to be able to live your own life. With me as your friend, not someone who constricts you — we've tried that long enough. That simply doesn't work, I now realise. I hope you find happiness in your new-found freedom. Perhaps the ballast of our past can become the foundation of a new partnership . . .'

Katharina started sobbing freely now. I took her in my arms. We were both crying. The letter, which wasn't addressed to her at all, seemed to unite us. Breitner had been right: reconciling with your inner child can also heal your external relationships.

It just wasn't quite clear to me how Katharina interpreted that 'release'. Because I didn't want any more freedom. After all, I'd been suffering from a lack of intimacy for months. But Katharina wasn't done yet.

'And I have no right to make any kind of accusations about you having an affair . . .'

I'm not even having an affair — at least not yet, I was about to dissent, when Katharina told me what she meant by both that 'release' and the other thing she wanted to apologise for.

'. . . because for the past three months I've been having an affair myself. Phew, I've finally said it.'

The buzz of voices in my head was deafening. And to this day, I still couldn't say which of these competing voices was my inner voice and which that of my inner child. It didn't matter in the end. Both voices were shouting the same thing.

'*Excuse me? You've been ignoring my desire for intimacy for months because of some other man? And all the while you've been telling me it was my fault? Because of my mood swings? You sent me to a mindfulness coach because you couldn't handle your guilt about fucking some other bloke? I'm absolutely furious. Fucking furious!*'

But my fury was like a firework: burning brightly, crackling fiercely, and then suddenly over. With one big 'whoosh', my fury burned up all the unspoken accusations that had been piling up for months. And instead, there was suddenly . . . room. Room for fresh new thoughts. There was nothing wrong with me; it was Katharina. That was liberating. Once my fury had turned to smoke, I could feel that there was one thing I wasn't: hurt. And neither was my inner child. I wasn't jealous either. Why *shouldn't* she have an affair? I still found my wife attractive and desirable, but I no longer felt any claims of ownership over her. At that moment, I realised I was no longer in love with her. Hadn't been for a long time.

And I didn't even have to forgive my wife for what she had confessed to me. I'd already done that in the letter. Which I hadn't written to her at all.

I could simply take her confession as what she had mistakenly interpreted the letter to my inner child to be:

376

a selfless gift. A gift that could form the foundation of a new relationship between us. Without reproaches. Without claims. But intimately familiar.

At this moment, I could accept all this with the right reaction.

Or undo it with a wrong one.

I looked at Katharina. I kissed her forehead. I took her in my arms.

'Thank you,' was all I said to her.

I thanked Katharina for all the things that had enraged me seconds earlier. For opening up to me emotionally after rebuffing me for months. For acknowledging her part in our troubles after refusing to for so long. And, above all, for sending me back to Breitner. Without that, I would probably never have found out I even had an inner child. To whom I had written a letter. Which Katharina had taken to be about her. Which was why we were now reconciling. We'd come full circle.

'Don't you want to know who it is?' Katharina asked.

I honestly didn't care.

'You don't owe me anything. You are a free woman. But if you want to talk to me about it as a friend, you're welcome to tell me.'

Katharina was as surprised by my answer's largesse as I was.

'It's . . . Oliver. The colleague who stepped in for me while I was on maternity leave. The one . . . I went to lunch with two days ago. We always got along well even before Emily was born, but there was never more to it, and . . .'

The guy she'd gone to lunch with was called Oliver? At some point, Katharina must've told me about her maternity cover at the insurance company. Like anything pertaining to her work, however, I'd simply disregarded it as uninteresting. Exactly like I did now. Katharina was pouring her heart out about her affair. And I just didn't care. But no one can look more understanding than someone who couldn't care less about the issue at hand. Such as the fact that Katharina's colleague was called Oliver. I think I too would've started an affair with some Oliver if Katharina showed as little interest in my work as I did in hers. Then again . . . Katharina *hadn't* shown any interest in my work. But that no longer mattered in the slightest. We'd forgiven each other. Katharina had even forgiven my affair with Laura. Which I hadn't even had yet. But I could. Now without a guilty conscience too. I suddenly found myself looking forward to tonight.

'No more reproaches?' Katharina asked.

'No more reproaches. Let's just stay who we are – good parents.'

'And become who we should be – good friends.'

We had set each other free.

And I hoped I'd be able to enjoy this freedom beyond that rapidly approaching Friday.

43

Distraction

After reconciling, your inner child is naive in the best sense of the word. It is entirely trusting of you and easily distracted. Use that. If your inner child starts up about any situation, distract it with a story.

Joschka Breitner, *Parenting Your Inner Child*

Laura and Sasha could've almost run into each other in the hallway. Which wouldn't have changed anything. Though both were part of the same plan, each had a completely different evening ahead of them.

Sasha would implement my inner child's plan, properly and professionally sending Kurt's headquarters up in flames. Lovingly planned, sensibly executed.

Whereas I'd have to improvise. In any case, I needed to keep Laura busy until I'd ensured that her brother, Kurt, wouldn't leave his babysitting post until his business was ablaze.

As attractive as I found Laura, I'd have happily changed places with Sasha. He knew what he needed to do. Whereas I . . . My last real date had been over ten years earlier. And with the woman who was now my wife. Meanwhile, Katharina and I had 'released' each other. Which left me free to enjoy my new-found freedom with Laura – only I couldn't.

Only when you don't have to do what you don't want to do – only then are you truly free. And this evening, what I *had* to do was distract Laura, whether I wanted to or not. I wasn't free. Personally, I would've preferred to spend the first evening after harmoniously separating from my wife by myself. Just me and my inner child, quietly commemorating a future that once was and would never be.

But I couldn't. Because my immediate future was still obstructed by a moron who needed to be eliminated. And because his sister was now ringing the doorbell – shortly after Sasha had gone down the stairs and I'd heard the front door shut behind him.

I buzzed Laura in and heard her coming up the stairs.

I'd prepared everything the way I always imagined a romantic affair back when I was a married husband. A record with ballads from the 1980s was spinning on the turntable. I'd lit the large candelabra in the living room. In the kitchen, all the ingredients were set out to cook a three-course meal together. I was freshly showered, wearing jeans, a T-shirt and a fairly new sweater.

My apartment door was ajar. Laura knocked. I opened the door. She looked stunning. Unfussily attractive. Her ripped jeans underlined she could wear anything, or nothing, and look fantastic either way. She had tied her hair back into a plait. Which hung down over a faded bomber jacket. Which she had pulled on over a plain white shirt. Which, loosely unbuttoned, revealed the edge of her lacy white bra. Her bare feet were tucked into a pair of Nikes. In one hand, Laura carried a large pizza box. In the other, a bottle of her favourite Rioja. I gave her a kiss on the cheek and eyed the box with some irritation.

'Do you doubt my kitchen skills that much?' I asked, nodding at the box.

'I had nothing else to transport my present in.'

She handed me the box and the wine. I looked back and forth between my hands, because I'd actually wanted to help her out of her jacket. But she'd already dropped it behind her, kicked it up and then nonchalantly hung it on the coat rack.

The contents of the box were heavier than a gastronomically procured pizza. And smaller.

'Just open it already,' Laura urged me. I put the box down on the dining table and opened it. Inside was a Fullen mirror from Ikea. I laughed.

'I thought your cloakroom could probably use one.'

I gave Laura a hug. She returned my hug for exactly that extra second distinguishing it from mere courtesy.

We went into the kitchen, and after I opened the Rioja, we started cooking.

Sasha had also prepared for his evening. For the absent Kurt, he hadn't brought a hospitality gift. Instead, five Molotov cocktails, a crowbar, a large screwdriver and a can of car spray paint. For *his* rendezvous, he'd put on black jeans, a military-grade black sweater and a balaclava that left only his eyes, nose and mouth exposed. Plus black SAS boots.

Earlier that afternoon, Sasha had bought all the items necessary to carry out our full plan at the home improvement store, using my Defender for easy transport. To torch the e-scooter company, he'd more carbon-consciously take his own compact car.

While Sasha had bought his evening's ingredients at the home improvement store, I'd found what I needed in my supermarket's Asian aisle. I'd planned to have Laura join me in cooking our dinner. Vietnamese summer rolls as a starter. And a chicken-veggie stir fry as our main course. With lovingly store-bought individual chocolate mousses for pudding. To prepare those, we'd only need to remove the foil. But the two more time-consuming previous courses we could prepare together.

Only we wouldn't get a chance to.

It happened as I was about to wash the lettuce leaves for the summer rolls and Laura wanted to move the unsoaked rice-paper wrappers out of the way. We bumped into each other. The salad slipped out of my hands. Laura dropped the rice paper too. We kissed.

'*Stop that!*' my inner child protested. '*This isn't about you canoodling with Laura. This is about me having my revenge on Laura's brother. Keep it professional.*'

Breitner had prepared me for the fact that an inner child would never completely lose its stubborn and selfish aspects. This was precisely why this first week of partnership, when I should seriously engage with each of my inner child's concerns, was so important. This was the only way I could slowly but steadily learn how to manage my inner child's moods in real life.

One tool for coping with the stubbornness of your inner child was to use your imagination. Like real children, inner children were easily distracted by a great story. I don't know how many times I was able to jolt Emily out of a tantrum by exclaiming, 'Look, a unicorn's flying by!' OK, fine, I know. Probably no more than a handful of times, Emily wasn't that gullible. But the imaginative distraction did work.

As an adult, I could escape my stressful thoughts by practising mindfulness. The best way to get my inner child out of this apparently stressful situation was by whisking it away on a narrative voyage.

Breitner had developed a very easy-to-understand guiding principle:

'*If your inner child starts up about any situation, distract it with a story.*'

If I mentally entered a world that appealed to my inner child, I'd be able to distract its emotions from the world I was actually in.

So while I physically stayed with Laura that evening, I started thinking about the attack on her brother's business.

I only peripherally and mechanically noticed that Laura and I were already kissing on my comfy sofa. My hands slipping under her shirt.

My thoughts, however, focused on what my inner child wanted: to witness the action at CN-Mobility's yard. So, I mentally left my apartment and immersed myself in what was happening at the depot.

Back in reality, Laura's hand slipped inside my jeans through my opened zip, and I briefly feared for my sanity.

In my imagination, Sasha's hand slipped through the opened zip of his gym bag, reaching for the spray can so he could leave a message on the wall.

The hand pushed past the bag's other contents until its cool, gloved fingertips tenderly brushed the white cap of the can. Now, the hand confidently grabbed hold of the can's elongated body. It seemed almost as if the can, which only moments ago had been casually lying in the gym bag and had gone untouched for untold months on a store shelf, was standing up on its own out of sheer joy. Yes, it wanted to live. The hand gently drew the can out of its fabric enclosure. A pair of knowing eyes took in the desired object. Until the hand started shaking the can rhythmically. At first slowly, quietly. Then faster and faster. With each movement, the can seemed to be more ready to achieve its long-awaited purpose. Inside, weeks-old encrustations loosened. Until the whole can was one single body filled to the brim with liquid. So pressurised that it could exclaim absolutely any message into the world with total conviction.

And then it happened: the hand, which had been shaking the can to the point of unconsciousness, targeted it precisely at a smooth, clean, virginal wall mere centimetres away and squeezed the nozzle with sensual determination. The can discharged its message:

REVENGE!

Perfect. During that story, my inner child had never once complained about what Laura had just done to me in real life.

Laura and I were stretched out on the sofa, giggling like teenagers.

'Now it's my turn,' Laura murmured in my ear.

'*Not again . . .*' my inner child started whining.

As I kissed Laura, my hand slipped into her jeans. As my fingers wandered, my thoughts also wandered back to her brother's depot. My inner child lost interest in Laura and eagerly awaited to learn how Sasha would penetrate the building.

It didn't take a crowbar to open the door. It was ready and willing to be opened tenderly. The tip of the screwdriver drifted inquisitively along the door frame to the crack in between. After pausing for a moment, it tenderly brushed the cleft. Then the small screwdriver slipped no more than two centimetres inside the narrow slit. With a few susceptive movements, the tip of the screwdriver widened the gap until its full length could enter the dark opening. It was hunting for the lock. Rhythmically moving back and forth, the screwdriver confidently overcame the hesitant last doubts of the lock, which finally yielded to the pressure of the hard shaft and, with a satisfying sound, surrendered all resistance . . .

I was no longer worried Laura wouldn't stay long enough. Because I was no longer worried about anything. And I completely lost track of time. It was all so uncomplicated. It had only taken us two glasses of Rioja to be no longer next to but all over each other. Kissing wildly.

But whatever we were doing – we interrupted it. Not because my inner child intervened, but because we needed to take our jeans off.

There are two moments at which every act of mating, however fluid, comes to a logistical halt. The first is when trousers need to come off. The second is when a condom needs to go on. If someone ever invented trousers that, at the push of a button or at a specifically elevated heart rate or hormone level, automatically turn into a condom that's secured in place, they'd be able to tap into an enormous growth market.

During the first of these two moments, my inner child reached out.

'*Don't forget why we staged all this.*'

So I shifted my focus back to what my inner child wanted to see. In my mind's eye, I visualised a glass vessel, filled to the brim with highly flammable petrol, that until this morning had led a misunderstood life as a reusable travel mug. It almost spilled when a rag was pulled over it. Practised fingers placed the rag at its tip, where it started to soak up the flammable liquid. I felt the rag being fixed to the rim of the mug with a rubber band so it wouldn't slip off until the explosion. Once lit, the rag was immediately in flames. I noticed a hand grasping the mug to guide it to its destination. I sensed the burning cocktail briefly move backwards in a delicate arc, only to be loosed with great gusto. How the mug slipped from any control and weightlessly travelled through a dark room towards its destination, relishing the flight. The blaze of the flaming rag lit up the room, briefly illuminating countless electric scooters below. The flames were flying towards the fuse box where all the power lines converged. The mug made contact, bursting into hundreds of pieces. Discharging all its pent-up energy. Half a litre of petrol poured in all directions, only to be caught by the rag's flames a fraction of a second later, setting fire to at least four square metres of wall. The plastic cladding of the fuse box reared up briefly and then willingly melted in the heat.

Sasha used all five Molotov cocktails that evening. To distract my inner child, two would've sufficed. But I was pleased with the result. Kurt's company burned right to the ground, including half of his scooters and ten of his fifteen vans. Nobody was injured. The word 'revenge' was emblazoned in smoky red letters on the wall of his still-smouldering yard.

And Laura was in my arms, tired and happy. Until exactly twenty-eight minutes past eleven, when her moronic brother called.

44

Roundabouts

If the journey is your goal, every roundabout is also part of your journey to yourself.

Joschka Breitner, *Slowing Down in the Fast Lane: Mindfulness for Managers*

Laura had come by bike. I drove her back to hers in my Defender. Astonishingly, she didn't seem at all concerned when Kurt phoned her to say his business was on fire. Instead, she seemed angry that our beautiful evening was broken off prematurely.

'Typical, pfft. Kurt has always been unreliable. I can't even rely on him long enough to escape for a cosy shag with a fellow parent rep.'

That made me laugh again.

'Well, maybe a fire at his company is an acceptable excuse.'

'As an isolated incident, any disaster would be an excuse. But if disasters are the rule, like they are with Kurt, at some point they lose their argumentative power.'

'How do you mean?'

'Well, Kurt's whole career has been a failure. In his mid-twenties, he borrowed fifty thousand Deutschmarks from my parents. Allegedly for some unbeatable business idea. And then he burned right through it. To this day, no one knows what he spent it on.'

Not no one. Boris, Sasha and I knew. On lots of roses and a prozzy. But I needn't burden Laura with any of that.

'And ever since then he's been running one business

idea after another into the ground. He calls it the "clever roundabout": always adding one more turn or twist than everyone else – that's supposed to be the trick.'

For example, not killing the person he hates most in the world the moment he finds them in someone else's cellar but forcing other people to do it instead.

'What other clever roundabouts has Kurt come up with?'

'A regional organic produce subscription, e-cigarette rentals, a dating portal for married people . . . All utter insanity. Do you know why he was so eager to start an e-scooter company?'

'Enlighten me.'

'Because he happened across some great property, which he then desperately needed. And he couldn't think of anything else to use it for. The bloke found the site first and *then* looked for the right business idea – no wonder his company is arse over tit in debt.'

So, it wasn't a coincidence Boris was Kurt's landlord. The one thing Kurt had doggedly stuck to for years was almost masochistically trying to get close to Boris. Even as a tenant. What a gift it must've been for Kurt to unexpectedly chance upon Boris in our cellar. And what did this idiot do? Take a 'clever roundabout'. Well, if everything went according to plan, Kurt would soon get very close to Boris indeed.

'But you still trust his babysitting skills?'

'He's good with kids. Though I do always lock away any valuables when he's going to be there alone. One of my prescription pads went missing a week ago – but of course Kurt had nothing to do with that. So he says.'

So that's how Kurt got the prescription sedative. 'Does he have addiction issues?'

'No idea. Maybe he wanted to play doctor. He certainly has the handwriting for it. Anything over four words, he types on a computer. Even *he* can't read his own handwriting.'

Interesting that.

'It sounds like you have quite a bit of resentment towards your brother. And I thought you two were so close. Him being the best godfather in the world and all.'

'My parents gave me twenty-five thousand euros to move back here from Bavaria. That was the remaining balance on my student loans. As I said, twenty years ago, they just handed Kurt fifty thousand Deutschmarks. My parents didn't move to Spain of their own free will – they were fleeing Kurt. They finally wanted a rest after decades of parenting their adult son. They no longer speak to him; they only communicate via snail mail. In exchange for paying off my loans, he's my problem now. Him taking care of Max from time to time is probably the least he can do.'

So some children also left their *parents* with psychological injuries. I made a note to ask Breitner about the possibility of 'inner parents' next time. In any case, those letters from his parents explained the Spanish stamp on Kurt's first blackmail envelope.

'But let's not end this lovely night talking about my dumb brother. Why do you have all that masonry stuff in the back of your car?'

I glanced over my shoulder. In the back, Sasha had left a few aerated blocks, bags of cement and masonry plaster, plus eye plates, chains and padlocks, as well as a couple of palette knives, trowels and buckets.

'I need to do some renovations in the cellar. The old oil heater needs to come out soon, then I can fix some damage behind it while I'm at it.'

'You seem skilled at working with your hands,' Laura said, with a suggestive smile.

Then she pointed out her building. A limousine from the rental service that had taken Kurt and me to lunch was already waiting outside.

I kissed Laura passionately before she got out. This time, my inner child didn't mind. With her animosity against her own brother, Laura must've suddenly become much more appealing. I watched her disappear through the front door and then drove back home. Running into Kurt would be counterproductive, as he might've asked me to accompany him to the crime scene as 'his' lawyer. Better he face his fear of the Holgerssons there alone – and reach out to me after.

When I got home, I saw a light in Sasha's apartment. I entered the building and rang his bell.

He greeted me with a mischievous grin.

'Well, did you have a good night?' he asked.

'One could say that. How was yours?'

'Zero complications. I left the message on the wall. Broke down the door. Threw two Mollies inside and three under the vans. In and out like a flash.'

'*You described it much more beautifully,*' my inner child kindly chimed in.

'I have to say, after six months of building up the pre-school as the managing director, it was great fun to just destroy something again. And now?'

'Now we wait for Kurt to reach out. I don't think he will before some time tomorrow morning. Once the police are through with him.'

'So, by the committee meeting tomorrow afternoon, we'll know if the first part of your plan worked.'

'And then we'll find out whether everybody involved will also stick to the second part.'

After Sasha and I moved the rest of the stuff from his shopping trip out of my car into the cellar, I cleaned up my apartment. I put the uncooked food back in the fridge and went to bed satisfied. Today had proven that a partnership with my inner child could work for both of us. Together, we'd solved my problems with Katharina. And despite my inner child's initial reluctance, it had accepted my nascent affair. Tomorrow would prove whether I could appease its indignation regarding Gaia and the committee's plans. And above all: whether we, despite our conflicting interests, could pull off our joint solution for the problems of Boris and Kurt.

Each of us was looking forward to what lay ahead.

45

Surprises

Children love surprises. But they have a different definition of them than adults. Children also consider it a happy surprise when everything happens exactly as expected: Santa comes, the Easter Bunny drops by, the sun comes up day after day. Make the most of this. Enjoy how your inner child enjoys even everyday surprises.

Joschka Breitner, *Parenting Your Inner Child*

Kurt was at my door by 7 a.m. Expecting his visit, I was already awake, showered and caffeinated. Although I hadn't slept very long, I felt in great shape. Entirely unlike the man at my door.

Kurt obviously hadn't slept a wink. This time, he didn't smell of his disgusting perfume and vape smoke, but of his disgusting perfume and the toxic smoke of a torched e-scooter depot.

'Kurt!' I exclaimed, beaming. 'What brings you here so early? Come in, come in.'

'We need to talk,' he said in a mixture of desperation and pig-headedness.

I led him to the dining table where I'd almost had dinner with his sister the night before – I didn't want Kurt sitting on the sofa where I also hadn't had dinner with his sister.

Kurt looked numb. I made him an espresso and put the cup in front of him. He drank it in one. I waited for him to start.

'Last night, the Holgerssons burned down my company.'

'*What a pity!*' my inner child sneered. A great start.

So, Kurt believed that part of the story.

'But the police think *I* did it. They think I set fire to my own company to collect the insurance.'

'*Yay!*' a sweet child's voice cheered inside me. This kept getting better. Then that part of the plan had worked too.

'So, I'm being threatened from one side and not being protected from the other.'

'*Bingo!*' What a happy surprise that everything went to plan.

'Whoa. That's a surprise. Listen . . . as promised, I wanted to figure out the best way to get in touch with the Holgerssons. But, of course, this changes things . . . Maybe just tell me – what can I do for you?' I asked, probably a touch too kindly.

Kurt slammed the empty espresso cup onto the table and looked me in the eye.

'It's time we both drop this pretence. You know I found Boris in your cellar. I know that's why you cut an ear off one of the Holgerssons, of all people, and then tossed two of them in front of one of my vans! That's the only reason I'm in all this shite!'

No, you're in this because you started toying with Boris and provoked my inner child.

For now, I went along with Kurt's version: 'OK, then let's be frank. What do you want from me?'

'I have no idea why you're keeping Boris captive. And I don't care – as long as you kill him! But if the Holgerssons want my head, I'd rather serve them yours on a platter. I already tried to make that plain to you yesterday. You have two options: either you tell the Holgerssons point-blank that you're responsible for the death of their people, or I'll tell the police that Boris lives in your cellar.'

I took small sips of my espresso and pretended to mull this over.

'Hmm. The downside of both those scenarios is that they don't lead to Boris's death.'

Kurt's ears pricked up.

I continued. 'I have no idea what you want Boris's head for. For whatever reason, it seems to be important to you that it's someone else who kills Boris, not you.'

It was none of Kurt's business that I knew about his obsession with clever roundabouts. I continued casually: 'Unfortunately, in both your solutions, Boris's head would still be attached – and Boris very likely a free man afterwards. If the Holgerssons kill me, the police would search my building top to bottom and thus find Boris. And if you tell the police that he's in my cellar, he'll be freed within the hour.'

Kurt seemed to realise this only now. 'Fuck.'

I sighed. 'But maybe there's a third option.'

Now Kurt was all ears. 'Which is?'

'I'll see to it that Boris dies, and you go into hiding and start all over again somewhere else. No more Holgerssons. No more suspicion of arson. No more vital signs for Boris.'

Kurt seemed equal parts surprised and interested. Of course, innovative businessmen like him were always open to fresh ideas.

'I'll guarantee you that Boris will die. You'll even be able to see it for yourself. When that's done, I'll help you go into hiding.'

'How's that supposed to work?'

'Killing Boris?'

'No, going into hiding.'

'How far are you willing to go?'

'If Boris is dead and the Holgerssons are entirely off my back? Then I'll gladly pack up and go anywhere. I've got nothing keeping me here.'

Not a word about his godchild. Or his sister. Who had moved here especially for him. And 25,000 euros.

'Then that's what I suggest: Boris dies, you disappear. If I scatter a few clues hinting at suicide, no one will ask any questions. Especially not the police. The investigation against you will be closed soon after. They'd just half-heartedly look for your body. And once the police assume you're dead, the Holgerssons will swallow it too. Do you speak any French?'

'I . . . A little. Why do you ask?'

'Because I can get you papers for a new start on a small farm in France.'

'And what would I live on?'

I was starting to enjoy this performance. When I was small, I'd enthusiastically participated in school plays. Apparently remembering this, my inner child went a little overboard with its melodramatic ad libs.

'I will only be able to live in peace if you can live in peace. I'll support you financially as long as you remain in France and stay silent about my crimes.'

Kurt seemed to see a light at the end of the tunnel.

'Right. After all, I essentially have the upper hand in this negotiation,' he mused.

'*Essentially, you're a complete idiot,*' my inner child mused.

'Exactly,' I said aloud. 'So, are we doing this? Boris dies, you disappear?'

'It certainly sounds good. But I need to think about it first. I haven't had a bit of kip the last two nights. Before I make a decision like that, I should at least get a few hours of sleep.'

'Take all the time in the world. Or as much as the police give you,' I said with deliberately implausible ease, surreptitiously pressing send on a text I'd pre-written to Sasha.

'What if the police want to talk to me *today*?'

'They'll definitely have questions. Does anyone know you're here?'

'No.'

'Did you call your sister?'

'My phone battery is dead. And I lost my charger in the fire.'

Very good. The idiot had completely dropped off the network grid.

'Then no one will find you here either. Everything we discuss is subject to lawyer–client privilege. As long as you haven't officially committed suicide, I can officially be your lawyer. You'd have to sign a power of attorney first though . . .'

'Give it here.'

I looked around, as if searching for one.

'Hmm. I don't have one right here . . . one second.'

My phone rang. Unknown caller. I picked up.

'Oh, hello, Peter . . .' I said, knowing that it was really Sasha. 'No, of course I can't tell you where Kurt Frieling is. Why would I? . . . No, if he were my client, I wouldn't be allowed to share his whereabouts . . . And if he's not my client, why would I know where he is? . . . Yes, you too.' I hung up.

'Sorry, that was the detective chief inspector, Peter Egmann. You are already wanted by the police. It was a bit of a shot in the dark for them to ask me, since I'm not officially your lawyer yet. Don't worry about it too much. Once I am your lawyer, no one will be allowed to question you without me being present anyway.'

Hearing the phrase 'don't worry about it' is the biggest indication you should've started worrying a long time ago.

'So let me sign this power of attorney already!' Kurt almost begged.

'The power of attorney, yes . . . One second. I'll get a piece of paper. You can just sign at the bottom, then I'll go print the power of attorney on it at my office right away.'

I got up, went to the kitchen, made Kurt another espresso and fetched a sheet of paper from the shelf in the living room.

'Sign it right there. Then I can officially keep the police off your back. You're welcome to take a nap here and decide whether you want to go into hiding once you feel refreshed.'

Kurt wanted to take the piece of paper. But I drew it back.

'But you'll have to promise that you won't contact anyone until you've made your final decision. Not even your sister. We need to be able to trust each other – as business partners.'

Kurt nodded, obviously flattered not to be seen as the obvious failure he was.

I gave him the blank sheet. As my new 'business partner', he studied it as though he was actually reading what he was supposed to sign first. He didn't seem to take any issue with the non-existent legal language and signed the blank sheet. He gave it back to me and drank his second espresso in one go too.

'Urgh. That one was bitter. Was it a different brand?'

'Same brand, only with a shot of midazolam.'

He gave me a bewildered look. By the time he realised this was the sedative that he'd acquired with his sister's stolen prescription pad, which he'd intravenously administered to Boris and which I still had a half-full bag of in my cupboard, his eyes were already shut. His head dropped onto the tabletop, next to the empty espresso cup.

46

Identity

People are more valuable than diamonds, but both have numerous facets. And depending on how the light hits it, each and every facet shines differently.

If someone thinks they can describe a diamond with a single word, it is usually not because the diamond is in any way simple, but because the person looking at it is.

Why would it be any different when it comes to people?

Joschka Breitner, *Parenting Your Inner Child*

From now on, it was imperative Kurt wouldn't be seen by anyone. Except for Sasha, me and Boris. Since this meant Kurt would only be able to leave my apartment after preschool closed for the day, I was forced to use a touch of violence. After I zip-tied his hands and feet to my bed frame, I gagged him with duct tape and a sock. As a precaution, I locked the bedroom door and took the key. It wouldn't do for Katharina to show up at the apartment unannounced again only to revise her positive opinion of me after making a more gruesome discovery.

After I swiftly informed Sasha that all was going to plan, I headed down to the cellar. I basically had nothing on my calendar until the committee meeting in the afternoon, and there were still a few preparations that needed to be made for afterwards. To celebrate, I even brought Boris a fresh espresso. He didn't ask why I'd broken with tradition, but simply swallowed the special beverage without batting an eyelash. The midazolam's taste didn't seem to bother him, or if it did, it was too late. Because the next instant he, too, was off to dreamland.

I made good progress and wrapped things up in the cellar shortly after 1 p.m. I'd just showered and changed back at my apartment when Laura called.

'I completely forgot to leave a thank-you message on your mirror for the nice evening,' she said.

I smiled to myself. Laura was wonderfully straightforward. I especially appreciated the fact that we hadn't talked about my relationship status but simply enjoyed our time together.

'That explains why I've had such a very peaceful morning,' I replied. 'How was yours?'

'Utterly peaceful. I dropped Max off at half past nine and went to work. I'm on my lunch break right now.'

At half past nine, I'd been zip-tying her brother's ankle. Still on the phone, I strolled down the hallway and opened the bedroom door a crack. Tied to the bed, Kurt looked dazed, but his eyes were open.

'Hear anything from your brother?'

'No, but that doesn't surprise me. Whenever he's in deep shite, he always gets really quiet. Often he doesn't reach out for months after he colossally cocks something up.'

That was reassuring. Laura wouldn't miss her brother any time soon. Kurt registered I was standing in the doorway and looked over at me, perplexed.

'Your sister says hi!' I stage-whispered to him, blocking the phone's microphone with my other hand. But the duct-taped sock prevented Kurt from saying hi back.

'See you at the meeting?' I asked Laura.

'Of course. I wouldn't want to miss our discussion about saving the planet by making the preschool carbon-neutral. Did you have a chance to talk to the placement student about Max and Emily's key role in the apocalypse?'

'Not yet, I'm just about to.'

We hung up. What an uncomplicated woman.

I went down to the preschool. I wanted to clear up the apocalypse issue – not only because Laura had suggested it, but above all to make my inner child happy. As a father. No matter what the other mums thought. I knocked on Sasha's office door and stepped inside. He was looking over the preschool's blueprints. When I entered, he looked at the clock in surprise.

'Björn? There's still plenty of time before the meeting . . .'

'I wanted to have a quick chat with Gaia about her ban on squeezy pouches.'

'Gaia?'

'My nickname for that placement student. What's her name again?'

'Oh, you mean Frauke.'

'Right. I want to talk to Frauke.'

'As Emily's dad or as a parent rep?'

'Are you asking me as a friend or as the managing director?'

'As the managing director, I need to point out that if parents have any issues with educators, they ought to follow proper channels: contacting me or a parent rep. The parent rep can then talk to the educator in question in the presence of preschool management.'

For a former gangster's driver, Sasha had certainly picked up the formalities of a properly run preschool very quickly. Then again, those same skills had also ensured he'd become managing director in the first place.

'I'm here as a father in the body of a parent rep. But what would you tell me as a friend?'

'As a friend, I'd cautiously suggest that a conversation in this particular constellation of parent rep, preschool director and placement student would be a little tricky, of course. Two old white men and one young woman – that's not really acceptable.'

'You're not an old white man,' I interjected. 'You're a Bulgarian in your mid-thirties.'

'If only it were that simple,' Sasha tried to explain. 'Two weeks ago, I did a training course for preschool directors on inclusive and gender-sensitive leadership. Turns out, the situation is a little more complex.'

'And what exactly did they teach you there?' I enquired.

'They basically taught us a politically correct version of rock-paper-scissors to determine who's right. It's actually quite fun.'

'Pray explain.'

'So, let's take you, me and Frauke as an example. A foreign-born man in his mid-thirties, a white German in his mid-forties and a full-figured woman in her mid-twenties. All three sit around a table for a discussion: who is in the right?'

'What's the discussion about?' I naively asked.

'That question already shows that you haven't understood the problem. With politically correct rock-paper-scissors, it doesn't matter what it's about, just who's right. What's key is acknowledging the participants' identities. The person who embodies the most protected minorities is always right.'

'How's that supposed to work?'

Sasha got up and moved to the whiteboard on his office wall. He wiped away a list of names, the results of the educators' committee election.

'Basically, like in rock-paper-scissors. So – rock beats scissors, scissors beat paper, paper beats rock.'

'Which practically means . . . what?'

Sasha started writing on the whiteboard. 'Minority beats majority. So, female beats male . . .' he began to explain.

'More than half the world's population is female,' I interrupted, 'how's that a minority?'

'Women are a minority when it comes to executives at publicly traded companies.'

'But the preschool isn't a publicly traded company. What's more, ninety-five per cent of the people who work here are women.'

'Don't get hung up on facts! I, a man, am running this preschool. This makes women a minority. Can I continue?'

'Go on. I'm excited to hear what's next.'

Sasha jotted the next sets of terms on the board. 'So, female beats male, foreign-born beats native-born, gay beats straight, young beats old, impaired beats unimpaired and left beats right. Clear so far?'

'Clear enough.'

'Perhaps you then also see why us two engaging in politically correct rock-paper-scissors with a young, full-figured woman would present certain difficulties?'

'Is "full-figured" the new word for "fat"?'

'If that question were acceptable, the word wouldn't have been changed.'

'OK.' I understood. 'Young, full-figured, female: she's right times three.'

Sasha nodded proudly at his pedagogical success.

I still had questions. 'But what about you? After all, you're still foreign-born.'

'If it was just us, I would be right.'

'Only because you're from Bulgaria?'

Sasha got right in my face. 'Are you questioning that, you Nazi?'

'No, no, no, it's fine.' I had no counter-argument – anything not to be called a Nazi. But it turned out I did have one more question. 'So, when Frauke as a woman, you as foreign-born and I as a white German man talk to each other – no matter what about – two-thirds of the participants at the table are always in the right because they're in the minority. The remaining third – i.e. me – is in the majority and is out . . . Why is that again?'

'Because you're an old white man.'

'So, I can be discriminated against on the basis of my age, race and sex in order for me not to discriminate against anyone on the basis of their age, origin or sex. Sounds logical. What if it was just you and Frauke at a table?'

'Sexism beats racism. Unfortunately, my male gender cancels out my migrant bonus in favour of Frauke. Unless Frauke is politically conservative. Then left trumps that.'

'OK. So, in terms of the three of us: if there's two older men with one fa— . . . one full-figured young woman talking about scaremongering among three-year-olds about the climate crisis, we're already in the wrong, even if you're foreign-born?'

'Exactly.'

'Then we should spare ourselves the conversation?' I asked, almost resignedly.

'Not at all!' Sasha grinned from ear to ear. 'I only wanted to officially explain to you why what's about to happen isn't politically correct. But it'll certainly be a lot of fun.'

After Sasha's explanation of politically correct rock-paper-scissors, I felt slightly guilty towards Frauke about the discussion I'd been planning. Unlike my inner child. That little blond kid in lederhosen was still suffering the consequences of its politically correct upbringing in the 1980s. It wanted to spare other children the experience. And since it was the express wish of my inner child to confront Frauke, and it was still our partnership week, I set my own concerns aside. The old white man should take a back seat. Inner child beats fat woman. And the child in me couldn't wait for our little chat.

47

Childhood

Children do not have a special right to the future. They have a special right to the present. There is even a special word for this right: childhood.

Joschka Breitner, *Parenting Your Inner Child*

The three of us – Sasha, my inner child and me – were eager to talk to Frauke.

Temperatures would increase. Poles would melt. Sea levels would rise. Species would go extinct. But one thing was absolutely certain: our planet would not die. Not within the next four billion years. And even then, not because of some three-year-olds enjoying a squeezy pouch.

I wanted my daughter's childhood to be unencumbered, innocent. And it wasn't our planet's eventual demise that stood in its way, but the claim that my daughter was somehow to blame.

That claim painfully prodded the bruise left by the 'your needs don't count' badge my parents had stuck in my inner child's soul.

However, I'd agreed with my inner child that we wouldn't respond to this prodding by prodding Frauke instead. We wanted to flood Frauke with so much love she'd stop prodding of her own accord. Or at least we wanted to pretend like we did. I planned to have the conversation in an atmosphere where both Frauke and my inner child felt comfortable.

Online, I'd found a New Year's message Frauke posted that had really moved me. A selfie of her in front of a buffet with a wide expanse of sea in the background, captioned: 'Happy New Year to you all! Even if the future of our planet worries me, on board the *Aida* I can feel far away from it all for a few days. Yay!'

What a sad woman. At least firefighters who commit arson so they can be hailed as heroes are recognised as pyromaniacs. For people like Frauke, there wasn't even a clinical diagnosis yet.

I didn't want to hurt Frauke. I wanted to help her.

That's why I asked Sasha to bring her to the preschool's outdoor play area. It'd be easier to talk about the end of the world next to the mud kitchen than in his office, which was set up to meet the needs of adults.

Frauke wanting to become an educator probably had a lot to do with her own inner child. Working at a preschool, Frauke could live out all that she'd been denied in her own childhood. For example, not to always be made fun of because of her old-fashioned first name. Whatever core beliefs her parents instilled in her, it was hard not to spot the defensive armour of Frauke's inner child, even with the best intentions: it largely consisted of food and make-up. This offensive armour seemed to be born of a great need to save the planet.

'Hi Frauke, glad you could find the time.'

Frauke shook my hand with irritation.

'It's not the end of the world, promise,' I reassured her. 'I just wanted to clarify an issue that came up among the parents.'

'Of course,' Frauke said, a little nervous. 'What's this about?'

We sat across from each other on the frame of the sandpit. Sasha and I on one beam. Frauke on another.

'You are very involved in environmental issues?' I asked. This seemed to be safe ground for Frauke. She visibly relaxed.

'Right. The future of our planet and its inhabitants is very important to me.'

'Very good. As a fellow inhabitant, I appreciate that,' I praised her. 'In the Nemo group, you were the one who explained the connection between squeezy pouches and the climate crisis to the two-to-five-year-olds, right?'

'Yes!' Frauke exclaimed, proud that her activism was being recognised. This was a pride we could build on. 'I think even our littlest ones should do their part to save the planet.'

'How admirable.' I patted her shoulder in appreciation. In Germany, the fact that children could also do their part in upholding a political ideology had already been a custom through two world wars, one empire and two dictatorships.

I tried to bolster Frauke's self-confidence even more.

'Due to your activism, the parents' committee has received a letter from the UN General Assembly. They have a proposition for you regarding your work on squeezy pouches in the Nemo group. Would you have some time to go see them next Friday?'

Sasha looked at me with disapproval, but didn't step in. For one, because he wanted to hear Frauke's response.

Frauke hesitated, but didn't seem at all surprised. 'Hmm . . . next Friday? Isn't that when we have our staff outing?'

Saving the planet was important, but please – keep it to regular working hours. I accepted this attitude.

'Crap. Those people at the UN didn't even consider that, selfish bastards. OK . . .' I pretended to think for a bit. Then I pointed to Sasha and me. 'So, instead of you going all the way to New York, maybe we should present the United Nations' proposition on their behalf right now.'

Clearly thrilled, Frauke didn't even notice Sasha silently mouthing to me if I'd lost my marbles.

But I was in full possession of all my marbles.

Together with my inner child, I'd decided on the same beautiful solution to avoid a squeezy-pouch ban as almost all cruise operators and airlines had concerning *their* carbon footprint: offsetting. By planting trees, for example.

Squeezy pouches, however, only required very small trees to be offset.

'What do you think about not banning squeezy pouches, but over-offsetting instead?'

'What does "over-offsetting" mean?'

'Well, planting a single tulip in Amsterdam would compensate for the carbon emissions of one squeezy pouch. The United Nations has proposed that we break new ground with regard to the squeezy pouches at this preschool and overcompensate instead: for every squeezy pouch consumed here, we'll have not just one, but *two* tulips planted in Amsterdam. This way, having a squeezy pouch even contributes to a better world. Would that be OK with you?'

'That would be . . . great!'

'From now on, our preschoolers are no longer to blame for the death of the planet – they're saving it with every squeeze of their pouches, deal?'

'Deal!'

I handed Frauke a pad and a pen.

'Then from now on, you will be Little Fish's official squeezy-pouch-offsetting officer. If you would please meticulously keep track of each pouch that is consumed, we will over-offset them at the end of every month with tulips in Amsterdam.'

Frauke was speechless. With joy. Sasha was speechless. At my inner child's audacity, which he ascribed to me. I was speechless that the whole issue had been so easy to resolve.

My inner child was not speechless. It was giggling with joy.

48

Support

The phrase 'Your family is behind you all the way' can be both reassuring and threatening. There are families who stand behind you so they can better stab you in the back. And there are families who stand behind you so they might catch you if you fall.

Joschka Breitner, *Parenting Your Inner Child*

As I left the preschool to head up to my apartment, I ran into Peter Egmann. Like Kurt that morning, he looked bleary-eyed. Like Kurt, he'd spent the whole night among the smoking wreckage of Kurt's former e-scooter company.

'Peter, hi! You all right?' I asked, suitably casual.

'Officially or unofficially?'

'Officially, you look like shite. Unofficially, can you say why?'

Peter took a step towards me and nodded me towards the cellar entrance to avoid being overheard by other parents picking up their children.

'Officially, I spent the whole night up to my ears with that e-scooter arsehole I was telling you about yesterday.'

'The bloke who ran over that ear-less guy?' I asked, incredulous. 'Why?'

'His company burned down last night. A lot of scooters, half his fleet. Damage in the seven figures.'

'Poor sod.'

'Well, if you're six figures in debt but insured up to seven, a fire like that can make you – quite unofficially speaking – quite a *rich* sod.'

'You mean it was him who . . .'

'Though to us he kept crying that it must've been an act

429

of retaliation by the Holgerssons. Showed us a note that was supposedly stuck under his windscreen wiper in the morning. Funnily enough, however, the incendiaries were targeted very specifically at the most expensive parts of his inventory. And as the forensic team has informed me, there's even a fingerprint of his on a shard of the Molotov cocktails that were used. If you ask me, I wouldn't be surprised if he never came back to pick up his godchild here again. But at the end of the day, I don't care. The main thing is that I'll get a solid night's sleep.'

'Case closed? That's quick.'

'Yeah, if only all cases could be solved so quickly. Which reminds me, what about your statement about the thing in the Alps?'

'What thing in the Alps?' Katharina's voice suddenly intoned. She'd come through the front door to pick up Emily. Like me, she knew Peter from law school. 'Hello, Peter.'

'Oh, nothing, just routine – hi, Katharina.'

'What kind of routine takes you up to the mountains?' Katharina asked sceptically.

As Katharina was not only my future ex-wife, but since yesterday also my best friend, I decided to go for it.

'Peter was asked for assistance by some of his colleagues in the Allgäu to determine whether I was to blame for the accident of that waiter at the hut.'

'That snooty git with the glittery T-shirt?' Huh, although Katharina had defended him at the time, she actually had a rather negative impression of the bloke. 'What about him?'

430

'He's dead,' Peter said, visibly intimidated by Katharina's brusqueness. 'He fell off the terrace and broke his neck.'

So far, Katharina had thought the waiter only broke a leg. Unlike me, she'd obviously not even googled the accident. She simply wasn't interested in how the waiter was doing – or, due to his lack of a pulse, *wasn't*. Presented with news of the death of a person in whose life she'd never been interested, she reacted without emotion.

'And what does that have to do with the father of my child?' That wording was a good sign. The father of her child was a good man.

'Well, a witness saw Björn walk behind the hut after an altercation with the waiter.'

'What witness might that be? Maybe one of those drunk Bundeswehr soldiers?'

Interesting how Katharina not only remembered details about that day, but also basic lessons from her law studies. If you want to invalidate a witness's testimony, portray them as unreliable and their testimony as untrustworthy.

'The witness indeed is a fixed-term enlistment soldier,' Peter admitted.

'As a witness myself, I can also tell you how quickly that soldier and his brothers-in-arms knocked back two dozen beers at our neighbouring table. Did those other police officers check the blood alcohol levels up there? No? That's a pity. The judge will certainly want to know in order to assess the validity of their statements.'

'This is merely about a short statement from Björn, whether he went behind . . .'

'No, he didn't. Björn was by my side the whole time we were up there. He didn't go behind the hut. Please just write that in *my* witness statement. My husband refuses to testify.'

Katharina stared at Peter like a lioness who was disturbed by a hyena while feeding her young at a watering hole. Like the hyena, Peter trudged away.

I was speechless. Katharina had honestly never stood up for me like that. Then again, she hadn't done it for me, but for the father of her child. I raised my eyebrows at her. She looked right back at me. I was the first to break the silence.

'Thank you for doing that for Emily.'

'I didn't do it for Emily. I did it for you.'

She gave me a hug and wordlessly communicated what I'd always hoped to hear as a child: *No matter what you did – you didn't do anything bad.*

For the first time in my life, an adult person who knew I'd done something wrong had chosen to protect me. Well, I never! I have no idea how many of my inner child's wounds this one gesture had just healed.

49

Destruction

The best way to destroy a beautiful plan is to expect to implement it exactly as is.

Joschka Breitner, *Slowing Down in the Fast Lane: Mindfulness for Managers*

The parents' committee meeting took place in the preschool's gym. To ensure open communication, we sat in a circle – the three group leaders and their deputies in one half of the circle, me and the two other parent reps and our deputies in the other. As the managing director, Sasha sat in the middle between the two groups. Behind him was a flip chart.

In front of the others, Laura had greeted me warmly but not noticeably more intimately than usual. She took the seat beside me.

I was curious to see the outcome of our plan to lovingly let the other mums' interest in our outdated heating system wane by itself. I could tell Sasha had enjoyed elaborating the plan in great detail.

He opened the meeting.

'As you know, this is the first full school year I've been managing director of Little Fish. And I would like to set an example *with* and *for* our preschool.' Sasha paused here to look into everyone's eyes in turn. Personally, I found it a bit much, but it went over well. Once Sasha had gone around the circle, he continued in equally dramatic fashion. 'I would like our preschool. To become the first. Plastic-free and carbon-neutral preschool. In the entire city!'

Among the uninitiated ladies there was astonishment and surprise.

I play-acted astonishment as I delivered the next line in my script: 'What a great idea! But won't that be too difficult?'

'Just because something is difficult is no excuse not to act. We're in a climate emergency. To secure our children's future, we must overcome those difficulties – and probably make some sacrifices.'

The astonishment turned to admiration once Sasha turned the first sheet of the flip chart, revealing the three key elements of his vision.

'With your assent, we can immediately reduce the preschool's use of plastic by a third, switch to green electricity and dispense with fossil fuels, starting today.'

A murmur of approval went through the gym.

'Wow, I'd like to say, on all the other parents' behalf, we're completely on board,' Tina exclaimed, immediately supportive of these goals, without even a clue as to how they should be achieved.

'I'm glad I can rely on your support. Then, it's decided.'

Sasha turned the flip chart to the next sheet, which listed how to achieve the goals to which the committee had now committed itself.

'We can reduce plastic usage by a third simply by having a third fewer children. In a bit, we'll draw lots to determine which kindergarten group will need to close.'

The speechlessness of Tina and Co. presented a slight contrast to the sacrifices they'd been willing to make only a minute earlier. Sasha pretended not to notice the vibe shift.

'One great advantage for the children who will be cared for at home from now on will certainly be the heating at home. This evening, we will switch off the preschool's old oil heater. I haven't determined which other type of heating makes most sense ecologically. But just because winter is around the corner, we shouldn't let that distract us from our goal of carbon-neutrality. What else are sweaters for?'

The parents were starting to get restless. Sasha ignored it and moved to the next sheet on the flip chart. It was a construction drawing of the preschool property. In the garden, however, now stood a hundred-metre-tall wind turbine.

'And as a proudly visible sign of our carbon-neutrality, we'll generate green electricity ourselves. In the outdoor play area, we'll build our own wind turbine – I mean, in the *former* outdoor play area. It may be difficult in terms of construction permits, but as the children of the head of the building control department also go here, a solution can surely be found. In any case, we will start preparatory excavations for the turbine's foundation before the winter. This means that, from next week on, the outdoor area will be closed. Proposal accepted?'

Sasha beamed at the ten shocked faces around him. Only Laura couldn't stifle a giggle. I tried to suppress my laughter.

Tina was the first to find her voice again. 'Maybe . . . we should first discuss the details . . .'

'Which details?' Sasha wanted to know.

'Well, the thing about closing one group, removing the heater and building a wind turbine.'

'Closing an entire group of the preschool is a detail?' I queried.

'No, of course closing a group is not a detail,' Tina defended herself. 'Maybe we should let the whole issue marinate a little and . . . discuss the other topics first.'

'What other topics?' Sasha feigned surprise.

Steffi, of perineal-tear fame, came to Tina's aid. 'We have a few questions about the group photos. How are you going to make sure no one violates our children's privacy rights?'

Sasha pulled a black woollen item out of his pocket.

'With this small accessory, we can meet all the GDPR requirements. If every child wears one, we can take group photos as usual, and they can even be shared online!'

'What *is* that?' Claudia wanted to know.

'A children's balaclava made of organic virgin wool.'

Another ten pairs of incredulous eyes.

'If every child in the group photo wears one of these, not a single privacy right is violated. And it even makes the group photos more sustainable. With these, any future discrimination based on age, gender or origin will simply be impossible. And if in a few years your child realises they were assigned the wrong gender at birth, they'll be able to look back painlessly at their old preschool photo and say proudly: "That's me!"'

Had we been able to harness the sheer energy with which Tina, Steffi, Claudia and Beate suddenly backtracked on their need for a plastic-free and carbon-neutral preschool and for GDPR-ready group photos, we could've heated the preschool for two full years. Though I was a little sorry to have taken the wind out of the sails of their more legitimate concerns by offering to meet their needs to the extreme, fortunately this had also ensured that the impending field trip to the boiler room was off the table.

My inner child was happy.

50

Traces

Everything is fleeting: childhood, love, life. What remains are the traces you leave behind, whether alive in your children or concrete like stones in a wall.

Joschka Breitner, *Parenting Your Inner Child*

On the bed in the narrow cellar room in front of us, two grown men sat a metre and a half apart. They looked disoriented. Which might've been due to the too-tight children's balaclavas made out of pure organic virgin wool that they were wearing back to front, covering their eyes. Neither of them could do anything about it, as their hands were shackled to an iron chain in front of them. In addition, each of the two men had their arms pinned to their upper body with the same chain. This iron chain also led through an eye plate freshly installed in the cellar wall behind each gentleman over to the eye plate behind the other one. There, it was attached to the eye plate with a padlock. The key was in both locks. Each shackled man's possible range of motion would just allow them to reach the lock at the end of the other's chain.

In short: each man could unlock the other's shackles. But not his own.

Simultaneously, Sasha and I pulled the masks off their eyes. Boris blinked as he spat out an old sock. As soon as he saw Sasha and me, he was about to complain about his treatment . . . when he noticed the other man out of the corner of his eye: Kurt.

'What's that wanker doing in my cellar?'

My cellar! It was nice to see Boris had come to embrace his unique living conditions.

Kurt also wasn't satisfied with what he saw. A few hours ago, he'd been expecting to get to witness Boris's death and then start a new life. To find himself shackled next to Boris in a cellar wasn't what he'd been expecting at all.

He, too, spat out a sock and started roaring. 'You promised me that pig would die! That arsehole doesn't deserve to live a single day more.'

In the same situation, less emotional people probably would've first complained about their shackles. Not Kurt. He probably considered it a minor misunderstanding that would surely be clarified soon.

Wanting to elucidate the discrepancy between Kurt's perception and his reality, I opened the conversation with a few preliminary remarks.

'Seeing as you two are already acquainted, we can dispense with introductions.'

'What the—' Boris started, only to be interrupted by a motivational smack to the back of his head from Sasha.

'Shut your gob and listen up.'

'We've all had some issues with each other this week. Kurt really wanted us to cut Boris's head off, otherwise he would report us to the police. But Sasha and I don't want to kill any more. However, we also didn't want the police on our backs. And as soon as Boris would be freed, our lives would be forfeit anyway . . . You understand our conundrum?'

Neither Kurt nor Boris responded to my rhetorical question.

Sasha took over. 'Somehow, however, Kurt's behaviour also made us realise that things were never going to work out between Boris and us in the long run. Neither inside nor outside this cellar.'

Before one of the men in question could comment, I pointed out our moral dilemma.

'We promised ourselves and Boris not to kill him. But I also promised Kurt that he could be there when Boris died. And on top of that, Sasha and I promised each other that we wouldn't kill anyone any more. I know what you're about to say: "We're all adults here, free to reassess our needs at any point . . ." And it might amaze you, but Sasha and I did just that. We conscientiously contemplated shooting both of you morons and being done with it. Yet we decided against it. We don't want to kill any more. But we also do not want to stand in the way of your needs and our promises.'

Neither Kurt nor Boris came up with the obvious solution on their own.

'So that is why what's going to happen now is . . .'

Sasha pulled out two butcher's knives and put them on the small bedside table. Both Kurt and Boris flinched.

'No need to panic,' I reassured them. 'Whether these knives get involved will be entirely up to you two. Each of you is shackled to an iron chain. The chain leads from your body through the eye plate on the wall behind you to that on the other wall. There, each iron chain is secured with a lock. The keys are in both locks. So, each of you can liberate the other at any time. The only issue will be that you yourself will still be shackled. The one who's been freed can do whatever he wants with the other – with one of these beautiful knives, for example.'

Sasha took over.

'Of course, you can also free each other at the same time and see what happens. Maybe together you'll manage to escape. Or kill each other on a more equal footing.'

'Or don't do anything. Then each of you simply kills the other by dereliction. As you wish, like I said, you're both adults. In any case, Sasha and I will now leave the room, shut the door behind us and brick up the entrance.'

'But you can't . . .' Boris shouted.

'But how are we going to . . .' Kurt interrupted.

'See?' I said to Sasha. 'After only three minutes together, the two of them have already become a *we*.'

'People will be looking for me,' Kurt bristled.

'Me too,' Boris concurred, knowing full well that no one had come looking for the past six months. The same went for Dragan. So, when it came to Boris, it really made no difference whether he was dead or alive.

But just in case, there would still be a slightly different justification for Boris's and Kurt's disappearances than there'd been for Dragan's.

'No one will come looking. Kurt, you killed yourself. And Boris, you've made off with the golden child.'

'Me? Killed myself?' Kurt was obviously lost.

'The golden what?' Boris was also dumbfounded.

I turned to Boris first. 'One year ago, you helped hide the golden statue of the Baby Jesus that the Holgerssons stole. Now, you've run off with it to start your gilded retirement.

Somewhere in the South Pacific. All bridges burned. One big "Toodle-oo!" to your long, fulfilling criminal career. Everyone will envy you. No one will come looking.'

'Who would believe that nonsense?'

'Walter already does. He'll convince the rest of Dragan's crew without us needing to step in. Your crew, Boris, will follow suit. If they stop hearing from you, that'll be proof the rumour is true. And the police will stick to the facts: you're gone, and the child is gone too.'

'But what about the Holgerssons?' Boris clearly thought he'd found a flaw in my logic.

'Since only the Holgerssons know you never had their statue in the first place,' I explained, 'they'll probably enjoy the unexpected gift of this utterly false lead and keep shtum.'

Now Kurt wanted to participate in the discussion. 'But when the Holgerssons find out you cut off one of their people's ears, they'll come after you.'

'Quite cheeky for someone claiming the exact opposite in his suicide note, Little Thirty-Second Kurt,' I replied.

'Why would I kill myself?'

'In your farewell letter you write it's because you killed the two Holgerssons on Boris's order. You've known Boris for over twenty years. First as a punter and now as a tenant. You're horrendously behind in your rent, but Boris forgave your debts after you killed the two Holgerssons and made it look like a traffic accident. At the expense of one of your drivers. Sadly, it didn't work.'

'What sense would that make?'

'What are you asking me for? According to your farewell letter, it was Boris's idea. Maybe the two of them got in the way of his plans to escape with the golden child. But your killing the Holgerssons was actually very convenient for you. After one of your trucks fatally collided with the two dealers, the Holgerssons got a motive for the arson you actually committed yourself. So you could collect the insurance money. Unfortunately, the police don't believe your story.'

'What a barmy idea,' Boris interjected.

'It's called the "clever roundabout",' Sasha informed him. 'Kurt came up with that.'

'Anyway,' I continued. 'Debt, murder, arson – and none of it worked. Cleverer people kill themselves over less stupid ideas without any roundabouts. It's all in the suicide note.'

'You'll never get me to write that.' Kurt looked at me mulishly.

I calmly raised the printout of a letter signed by him.

'You won't need to. You already did. Signed it blank this morning in my apartment. And considering your terrible handwriting, even your sister will confirm the typed letter is real. Not even Laura will miss you.'

Kurt was speechless.

Sasha broke the silence. 'With Boris, we had to pretend he was alive for at least a few more months. With you, it doesn't matter.'

I made to leave. 'Have a nice life. However brief.'

Boris and Kurt simultaneously found their voices again.

'Hey, wait! You—'

'Now don't be so childish—'

The click of the cell door ended any further attempts at conversation.

Childlike, not childish, I thought to myself.

Doing crafting projects with your children can be very soothing. My inner child and I built the wall blocking the cellar door brick by brick – I'd asked Sasha to wait for us upstairs. At some point, I happened to glance at the clock. It was after midnight. Friday was here, our partnership week was over.

My inner child was unreservedly happy about how it went.

And I was satisfied with the results too.

I had discovered my inner child, earned its trust and overwritten my core beliefs. I had helped my inner child lay down its armour and taken the lead myself. I had benefited from its creativity and come away with a reliable inner voice.

My problems with Katharina, with my job – they were all gone. The little blond boy with scratched-up knees below his lederhosen no longer had any reason to be afraid of the future. My inner child now had a partner by its side: the big boy who'd grown out of those lederhosen.

And now that we no longer needed the hidden bunker behind the boiler room, we'd really be able to update the heating system.

Was that the rattle of a chain behind the wall?

It didn't matter one bit.

My inner child had been freed from its cellar.

Acknowledgements

My Inner Child Wants to Murder Mindfully is a new sibling. It is from the same gene pool as *Murder Mindfully* but a character all its own.

After using mindfulness as a serious starting point for a humorous book, I wanted to tackle another holistic subject, which gave birth to the idea of dealing with the 'inner child'.

The theory behind the inner child is an explanatory model. As a concept, I believe it to be absolutely useful. In Björn Diemel's words: it's the ideal way to eliminate the causes of the problems whose consequences you mitigate by practising mindfulness every day.

As with mindfulness, my search for the inner child brought me to endless inspirations in books, blogs and videos. Many inspired me, several vitalised me and some made me laugh.

Yet I never laughed at the concept itself, only at how some self-help books portrayed it as a cure-all.

Self-help books are a great way to learn about a holistic subject. Personally, however, I consider talking to real people with in-depth psychological experience to be indispensable if you want to develop real insights into your own psyche.

No one would suture a serious cut themselves after only consulting a book. Why should it be any different with wounds to the soul?

That's why Björn Diemel goes to see Joschka Breitner.

And, because people always ask: I really did make Breitner up.

I would like to take this opportunity to sincerely thank all the people who accompanied this book from before its conception to after its birth.

I'd like to thank the people at Heyne Verlag for taking such wonderful care of us.

I thank all the booksellers who helped *Murder Mindfully* grow so big that it can now take its younger sibling by the hand.

I would like to thank Oskar Rauch at Heyne Verlag for maintaining the balance of freedom and security I need to write.

Thanks also to my editor, Heiko Arntz, for his wonderful work with and on my writing.

I'd like to thank my agent, Marcel Hartges, and his team. For everything.

And thank *you* for reading this book all the way to this final full stop.

Sincerely,

Your Karsten Dusse

and his inner child